S.V. LEONARD

THE
INFLUENCERS

First published in the United Kingdom in 2022 by

Canelo
Unit 9, 5th Floor
Cargo Works, 1–2 Hatfields
London, SE1 9PG
United Kingdom

A CIP catalogue record for this book is available from the British Library.

Print ISBN 978 1 80032 356 8
Ebook ISBN 978 1 80032 355 1

Look for more great books at www.canelo.co

Printed and bound in Great Britain by Clays Ltd, Elcograf S.p.A.

1

To my family for their support and enthusiasm

for everything I do.

The Influencers

S. V. Leonard grew up in the little coastal town of Formby, a suburb of Liverpool. She studied Classics at Oxford University and has been lucky enough to live in Australia, Poland, and Malaysia. She is now based in London. When not writing, she can be found breaking out of escape rooms; doing historical walking tours of London; or drinking wine.

Also by S. V. Leonard

The Islanders
The Influencers

Prologue

Wednesday

Extract from The Social Sleuth, *posted one minute ago*

If you're reading this then there's a chance I'm dead, and that my investigation into the murder of world-famous influencer Stella Knight has been cut short.

I know who killed her and why, but at the time of writing I lack the evidence to prove it, and without it the police will never believe me. My goal is to expose the truth, for Stella, regardless of how dangerous it might be. I write to you, my loyal followers, hoping that if I fail, you can finish what I've started and bring the killer to justice.

This case had everything: secrets, lies, money, sex. Stella Knight − beautiful, rich and loved by millions − was surrounded by a group of people all of whom had motives to make her disappear...

Click here to read on.

Chapter One

Extract from The Social Sleuth, *posted twenty minutes ago*

> Today is so important. The first day of the
> rest of my life. I can't believe I have such an
> opportunity. All I need to do is prove myself.

The atmosphere is electric. Ahead of me, there's a crowd
of people split in the middle by a long red carpet and
penned in by rope. They chatter with one another
excitedly and hold their mobile phones out in front of
them to snap pictures of the individuals standing on the
red carpet. The photographed smile, flashing their bright
white teeth, their hands on their hips.

Behind them is a yacht; its colossal size casts a broad
shadow, protecting them from the merciless heat of the
late morning sun. It's only just smaller than a cruise ship
but far much more luxurious. The angular body of it is a
dark, glossy grey and there are about six levels. I've never
seen anything like it in real life before, I thought yachts
of this size only existed in pictures taken in the south
of France where Russian billionaire playboys filled them
with bottles of Dom Pérignon and models. Not in central
London. The yacht, moored beside Tower Bridge with a

view of the ancient Tower of London in the background, cuts an impressive figure. The collision of modern and old should be jarring but it isn't – it's commonplace in this city.

I walk further along the street, closer to the crowd and the blood red carpet that lies between them. Their feverish babble makes my stomach fizz like the champagne that will be served on board. I can almost taste it. I can't believe this day has finally come.

A group of five teenage girls stuck right at the corner of the rope enclosure turn to me and stare. Then they bow their heads towards each other and whisper, glancing at me as they do so. Their stares take me back to my school days. The tallest of the group shakes her head, shrugs and points her mobile at me. I don't shrink from it – instead I throw my shoulders back and smile. Nothing can extinguish my flame today. There's a faint snap as she takes a picture and I feel almost dizzy with pleasure. They think I'm worthy of taking a photograph of. They don't want to have trekked all the way to the red carpet of the Influencer of the Year awards and not get a picture of me, Maggie Shaw. I could be a wildly successful influencer. I'm not, but I could be. I raise my hand and wave as another camera is pointed towards me. Maybe one day they won't be taking the photographs just in case.

My blog *The Social Sleuth* is only a year old, and my most popular post has had 1,220 views. I'm under no illusions that I've not got a lot to do, but I have huge ambitions for it. I will be the go-to girl when people need their true crime fix. Being invited to this event is a positive step towards that. The crème de la crème of the social media world will be here. If I can establish a connection with just one of them, it could change everything for me.

3

The end of the red carpet is guarded by a beefy man in a tight black T-shirt holding a clipboard in hands so large one of them alone could crush my skull. He eyes me with a mild look of suspicion, but like the teenage girls before him, hasn't been able to dismiss the idea that I could be important. That's the fascinating thing about internet fame. Some of the most followed, observed and idolised people on the planet exist in niche corners of the world wide web doing things that twenty years ago would have had no meaning, let alone be considered a talent. Fame in this arena isn't like Hollywood. Influencers are much harder to spot in the real world, and the forced neutral expression on the security guard's face makes me wonder if he's been burned already by dismissing someone too quickly.

'Name?' asks the security guard. A car door slams, cutting off my answer. The heads of the crowd, and my own, turn as footsteps pound against the cobblestones and a short, blonde, harassed-looking woman sprints towards me and the man with the clipboard. She wears the expression of someone not to be trifled with so I step back, allowing her to go before me. She whispers something urgently to the security guard and points to a narrow alleyway. He nods and talks into his radio. The crowd vibrates, everyone unified in their understanding that this will be someone big. Seconds later another security guard in an equally tight black T-shirt approaches and walks with the woman towards the alleyway. The crowd strain their necks now, desperate to see who is waiting to be escorted onto the boat. Every passing moment only serves to intensify our excitement. Whoever it is knows a thing or two about delayed gratification. When the atmosphere is so tense it seems about to explode, the second security guard exits the alleyway. His fingers are wrapped around a large silver suitcase, the type you'd take on a two-week holiday, not for a twelve-hour boat trip. The sound of the crowd stops abruptly and we all stare in silence to see who is walking behind him.

'Oh my God,' gasps a middle-aged woman several metres to my right. 'It's her, Graham. It's her,' she adds, slapping her hand against the bare arm of a man who couldn't look more out of place or disinterested if he tried. But Graham is alone in his disinterest, everyone else is focused on the woman, excitement shining in their faces. I edge around to get a better look, but I can't see *her* yet.

A pair of lime green stilettoed feet appear behind the bulky legs of the security guard and my eyes follow them until they plant themselves on the red carpet, which seems to pale in comparison. Smooth, shiny legs rise from the shoes. The woman is petite both in height and figure, and wears a thigh-skimming, strapless silky dress the colour of which matches her stilettos. Her hair frames her face in a poker-straight long bob and shines like molten chocolate in the afternoon sunlight.

'Who?' says Graham, pulling his arm away before the woman that I presume is his wife hits him again. She sighs and rolls her eyes.

'Stella,' she says. 'Stella Knight.' He blinks at her with a blank expression and then shrugs. 'Oh Graham, I talk about her all the time. She's my favourite.'

'And I tell you all the time, Kathy. I don't give a flying whatsit about influencers, or whatever it is they're called.'

'Stella Knight isn't an influencer,' replies Kathy, not taking her eyes off the woman making her way along the red carpet. 'Stella Knight is *the* influencer.'

Kathy is right, Stella is the pinnacle of this industry. Seeing her walking the red carpet is really something. She's magnetic, she radiates confidence and power, and the effect she has on people is incredible: they stick out their phones for photos, pens for autographs and arms for hugs. I survey her as she poses for pictures and gratefully accepts gifts thrust in her direction and wonder if it's tiring being so adored, being put on a pedestal by millions of fans who worship you, because no matter how much they seem it, nobody is perfect. I know I'm not. Behind her sparkling eyes, is Stella Knight a woman worn down by the pretence of keeping up appearances?

My phone trills from inside my handbag, breaking the spell that Stella has cast over me. I pull it out in time to see a message pop up.

> Where are you?

My chest tightens for a fraction of a second when I read it. My fingers are poised to respond but I stop myself and instead swipe the message away. I'm not dealing with that right now. I have an event to get to. I put my phone back in my handbag and push the message from my mind.

Stella Knight is now at the end of the red carpet and it's empty, ready for the next arrival. I shuffle towards the security guard holding the clipboard and he once again gives me his attention. His eyes take in my slightly scuffed ballet flats and the silk Karen Millen dress that put me into my overdraft last month. A dress that, despite the cost, hangs limply off my body, not quite sitting as it should. The light layer of make-up I put on for the first time in a long time feels like it's sliding off my face and my low bun is too tight. I've made an effort, but after seeing Stella, it suddenly doesn't feel like enough. I chastise myself – this type of thinking is unhelpful. I was invited. I am enough.

'Last name?' he asks when I reach him.

'Shaw. Maggie Shaw, I'm here as a guest,' I reply.

'Guest entrance is at the back.' He gives me a small smile, as if he can feel the nerves radiating from me. I nod and follow the line of his arm, walking to join the short queue of people leading into the belly of this beast.

The line moves slowly forward and my stomach flutters. What if I'm not on the list? What if my invitation was retracted somehow and I'm turned away? The shame of having to walk past the red carpet again and see those teenage girls looking at me and judging me. The one who took my picture would instantly delete it, and all five of them would laugh at my failed attempt to get into an event that I'm clearly not cut out to attend. The disappointment at my lost chance would engulf me, my one chance to make something of myself.

Stella Knight would never have to worry about being turned away, not with a follower count of 10 million. It's a number those of us at the beginning of our careers can only fantasise about. Her rise was quick and meteoric and nobody has ever understood quite how she did it. What I wouldn't give for her secret.

'Name?' says the bored-looking security guard manning the guest entrance, glaring up at me. I swallow and give it as before. The security woman doesn't seem to notice that I'm twisting my hands together. Her eyes run down the list in front of her. I hold my breath. Then she nods and ticks my name off. The nervous flutter in my stomach flips over and changes to hopefulness. It's real;

I'm a guest at the Influencer of the Year awards. I take another deep breath and step aboard.

The door leads me into the lobby of what could easily be mistaken for a five-star hotel. Green velvet chairs and mirrored coffee tables are dotted across a floor of pale gold tiles. A glass staircase spirals upwards from the centre of the lobby. I clench my jaw to stop myself from shouting with joy. *Look at this place*, I want to say, *can you believe I'm actually here?* But I push the words down, knowing that squealing like a child at Christmas would expose me as an outsider. The well-heeled couple standing at the mahogany reception desk in front of me are calm and nonchalant, as if these surroundings are a normal, everyday occurrence.

A petite woman with cropped hair dyed a deep electric blue stands behind the desk; a black lanyard on which the word *staff* has been repeatedly printed in white hangs around her neck. The couple give her a nod of thanks, collect the papers she has given to them and move away from the desk towards the spiral staircase. Then the blue-haired woman turns to me.

'Welcome,' she says, giving me a wide smile. The skin on her face pulls tightly as she does so and, despite the thick layer of foundation trowelled onto her face, she looks tired. I hope she's OK. I guess organising a huge event like this is stressful – there are probably hundreds of things that could go wrong, especially at sea. 'Welcome to destiny.'

My own smile falters, her words are jarring. I can see she's trying to be friendly, but I suddenly feel like I'm talking to a robot that's malfunctioning. Sensing my confusion, she adds, 'This is *Destiny*. The yacht is called *Destiny*.'

'Oh,' I say, wincing for not realising that sooner.

The woman places a leaflet in front of me and unfolds it, revealing a drawing of the yacht spread across the two paper folds. The side of the image is cut away to reveal its insides and I'm reminded of the drawings in the medical journals my sister Jessica has at home, where one half of a man's flesh has been pulled away to reveal the bones, muscles and organs. The thought makes me queasy.

'This is a map of the ship. The awards ceremony will be taking place here.' The woman points at the lowest open deck. 'But unless you're nominated for a prize or the selected guest of someone nominated for a prize, you'll have to watch the ceremony from any of these.' She points to three more open decks that concertina upwards, each one shorter than the one below it. 'All the facilities are marked on here: the toilets and smoking area. And this,' she says, handing me an A5 piece of card, 'is the order of events. The welcome party is taking place now on the top deck and the yacht will depart at one p.m., so in just under an hour. The awards ceremony will start at four, once we're out at sea. So lots of time to drink and mingle before the ceremony starts.' She slides the paper towards me with a wistful smile, as if she'd like nothing more than to have a drink and mingle. When I don't respond she points me past the staircase, saying, 'Take the lift up to top deck for the welcome party.'

'Thank you.' I take the papers she has offered and try to keep my face as calm and composed as I can, but my excitement is in danger of bubbling over. As I head away from the reception desk I hear the words 'Welcome to *Destiny*' once again, and this time, I don't think it sounds weird. This time I think that she is exactly right. I'm here on the *Destiny*, and ready for mine.

Chapter Two

The Social Sleuth, *extract from blog 39*

> The judge awarded her everything in the divorce, including her soon-to-be ex-husband's beloved yacht. He couldn't have that, so he orchestrated a cruel plan to get what he believed was his.

I stare at myself in the bathroom mirror and smooth down my hair, tucking any mousy-brown strays behind my ears. I readjust my dress, trying and failing to get it to look like it did on the woman from the website. The colour's nice though, the burnt orange suits me.

Exiting the bathroom, I stand behind the glass staircase and slip my phone out of my pocket, determined to immortalise on my blog that I'm here at the Influencer of the Year awards. I hold my phone in the air but the lighting is awful and the opulence of the staircases doesn't translate on my screen. I position myself in front of a window instead, one that has a view over the water. I snap the shot and pull my phone down to inspect it. It's not great. The water below isn't visible through the glass, which has instead turned mirror-like and is reflecting the shadowy image of two people having a conversation. I sigh. I'm nowhere near Influencer of the Year, but it will have to do because above me, a party awaits.

The queue for the lift is long and I abandon the thought of waiting in my eagerness to get stuck in. Instead, I head for the stairs. I bound up the first flight with all the enthusiasm of a novice runner on their first outing but am forced to slow my pace for the remaining five. When I finally reach the sixth floor my cheeks are burning from the effort and I lean against the dark wood interior wall, taking a moment to catch my breath. My year of sitting on my bed writing or at my desk at the law firm has done my fitness no good whatsoever, but I shouldn't be too hard on myself. My blog gave me purpose, it got me through, it got me here.

Ahead of me, through a set of glass doors, the party is in full swing. Crowds of people are gathered in groups, sunglasses on, champagne glasses in hand. Never has the expression 'shiny, happy people' rung so true. They are all shiny. Shiny skin, expensive clothes, white teeth. Drink servers dressed in black flit between the guests, some offering fresh rounds of bubbly, others clearing the empties. Everyone is just as glamorous as Stella Knight, if not more so. I knew an event attended by people who make their living by the faces they show to the world would be fancy, but I didn't realise it would be so intimidating. Under the pretence of scratching the back of my neck, I subtly check that the label I was too scared to remove from my dress remains hidden, my nerves calming a little when I feel that it is.

I head to the bar and order a tonic water with lemon. I don't want alcohol. I want to keep a clear head, to remember everything about today. Perching on one of the high bar stools, I sip my drink, enjoying the bitterness of the tonic.

The open deck is expansive. In one area there is a selection of half-moon-shaped seats covered in squishy orange cushions where several people have already taken up residence, lounging in semi-reclined positions. The rest of the deck is free from seating but dotted with high, slender bar tables covered in crisp, white cloths.

In the far corner of the deck, a DJ snakes his hips in a makeshift booth. The music is recognisable but there are no lyrics, so it's hard to tell. For now, it's not too loud, allowing the guests the ability to hear themselves over it, but once the ceremony is complete this place is going to turn into a nightclub.

Below us, there are three more open decks. On the lowest, chairs are laid out in rows in front of a small stage. A huge banner welcoming us to the Influencer of Year awards spans the full length of the stage, a helpful reminder for those enjoying the liberal flow of alcohol.

The sun, the boat, the people, the music. Everything glitters. London can be called many things: too big, too impersonal, too dirty, too busy, but on a day like today, sitting where I'm sitting, I remember why I love it so much. I remember how it made me feel when I first moved here. It's a city of opportunity, where for generations people have come to make something of themselves. The thrill of what could be shoots through me like electricity.

'Another?' says the bartender as I plonk my empty glass in front of him.

'No,' I say, shaking my head. 'I shouldn't sit here all day.' The bartender nods as if acknowledging that a life lived observing from the outskirts is no life at all. I've been observing for too long. I came here to get involved, and that's what I intend to do.

I slide off the bar stool and as I do so the bottom of my dress rides up. I hastily pull it down, glancing around me to check that no one saw my knickers. The bartender gives me a wry smile but everyone else is deep in conversation, laughing happily like old friends. To them, I'm invisible.

Standing alone with his back leaning against the yacht's railings is a dark-haired man with a well-kempt beard. He is tall and broad with a soft round belly that presses against a baby-blue linen shirt. I drink him all in. If I'm going to talk to someone, I might as well talk to someone attractive.

I walk towards him, but even when I come up next to him he doesn't acknowledge me. His eyes are staring into the crowd, glassy and unfocused.

'Hello,' I say, giving him my most winning smile. The man jolts so violently that beer spills from the glass in his hand and slops on the floor.

'Shit,' he says, looking down at it and then back at the crowd. I give myself a mental kick. What is wrong with me? I've scared the living daylights out of him. I could have given him a heart attack.

'Oh my God, I'm so sorry. I didn't mean to scare you,' I say hastily, looking around to see if anyone saw how much of an idiot I've already made of myself. The man swaps his beer into his left hand and shakes his right to remove further spillage. 'Do you want me to get you a napkin?' I ask.

'No,' he says, waving away my words. 'It's fine, don't worry about it. I was in a world of my own. Which isn't exactly the best way to handle being at a party.' He smiles.

'It depends who's at the party,' I say. 'There are surely some parties where being in a world of your own is far more pleasurable.' I'm thinking of the parties my house-mates have, the ones I avoid like the plague. He nods.

13

'You may have hit the nail on the head there. The people at this party aren't exactly...' he trails off, then clears his throat. 'Well, you know.' He gestures limply in the direction of the people reclining on the orange cushions, as if that somehow explains it.

'This is my first time at an event like this, so no, I don't know.'

'Oh,' he says, scratching his head with his free hand. 'You'll find out soon enough.' He gives a mock shiver, then laughs, a hollow, awkward laugh, and takes a sip of his beer. He looks very nervous. He turns to gaze out at the water.

'Want to know a fun fact?' I ask, hoping to lighten the strange atmosphere he's created.

'Sure,' he says.

'How many bodies do you think they pull out of the Thames each year?'

'What?' he asks, looking at me with a horrified expression.

'Bodies,' I say again, 'how many bodies do they pull out of the Thames each year?' As I'm speaking I realise that he wasn't asking me to reiterate the question, he said *what* because he couldn't quite believe what I asked him. Now the words are out in the open, *I* can't quite believe what I asked him, that this was how I thought I'd put him at ease. 'Thirty-eight,' I answer, ploughing on regardless of his expression. 'I was surprised when I heard that, I'd have thought there would have been many more.' He blinks at me. 'I blog about true crime,' I add hastily.

'Ah,' he says as if that makes it all make sense, then looking back into the dark depths of the river, he adds, 'I wonder how many bodies are still in the Thames, waiting to be pulled out.'

I follow his gaze down to the water and suddenly imagine a hand tangled in slimy green algae, rising up from the swell of the waves. A body desperate to be saved from the murky depths so it's finally allowed to rest. The man shakes his head and turns his back to the water, evidently not wanting to think about what will churn beneath us when we move. I'm about to ask him if he's OK when a voice makes him jolt.

'Hi Noel honey, who's this you're talking to?'

His eyes widen, and I turn too. A petite, red-haired woman bounds towards us. When she's near, she stands by his side and slips her arm into the crook of his. She pointedly twists her left hand to face me so that the sunlight catches the chunky diamond on a gold band wrapped around her fourth finger.

Noel's cheeks flush and he glances nervously from me to the woman by his side.

'I... er... well, we didn't...'

'Hi, I'm Maggie. Maggie Shaw,' I say.

'Maggie,' says the woman, looking me up and down and pulling an expression that makes it clear she thinks her husband wouldn't be at all interested in me. 'Well, Maggie, it was lovely to meet you, albeit briefly.' The woman gives Noel's hand a squeeze and leads him away from me.

A loud horn sounds, and the people on the deck stand alert and look to see where the sound is coming from. Then, as a collective, they cheer. We're off, but as the shudder of the engine moves beneath my feet, I wonder about what Noel just said. What I will soon find out about these people. The people I'm trapped at sea with for the next twelve hours.

Chapter Three

The wedding planner stabbed her employer five times with a kitchen knife before bundling her body into a dress bag, dragging her along the driveway and heaving her into the back of her car. When asked in court why she murdered her employer, the wedding planner said simply, 'It was one tantrum too many, I snapped.'

The movement of the yacht kicks the welcome party up a notch. People press themselves against the railings, jostling with one another to get a good position for a photograph. Others flit from group to group searching for a conversation to retain their interest. The music gets louder, and with it, the chatter and shrieks.

My conversation with Noel unsettled me a little, but I can't let it get to me. I'm out of practice meeting new people, that's all. It shouldn't put me off. I scan the crowd, and this time spot two people I recognise, walking hand in hand: Reiss Rose and Flower Spirit. Reiss Rose is a make-up artist and promoter of all things natural beauty. Flower Spirit is a yoga instructor, vegan cook and general lifestyle guru. I'm not sure how it's possible, but both of them look even more perfect in real life than they do on camera. Reiss is built like a dancer, medium height and lithe, wearing lavender-coloured silk trousers that sit high on his waist, and on his top half he wears a matching corset. His hair is dyed a grey white, the sides cropped close to the scalp and the top blow-dried into a stiff quiff. His eyes are hidden by sunglasses so huge they could be an astronaut's visor. His skin, though pale, has a brightness to it that I can only assume is a subtle layer of spray tan.

Flower Spirit is several inches taller than him and true to brand is in a floral-spattered maxi dress which is sheer enough to see the shape of her long, slender limbs through. Her dark, full cheeks glow with liberal lashings of highlighter. Her hair hangs far past her shoulders in gold-twisted braids and on her head, she wears a black straw hat. Her height and willowy physique and the fact she seems to float rather than walk make her look ethereal, like a goddess or an angel.

Both have huge followings. If they were interested in me or a collaboration, it could be the making of me. A single post could lift me from obscurity. Natural beauty and a boho lifestyle aren't natural bedfellows with true crime, but there must be *some* area of overlap. A yoga retreat gone bad, perhaps. I wipe my damp palms against my dress and approach them.

'Hi,' I say, stepping between them and the bar. They stop and look at me, their faces dropping into expressions of surprise, and I suddenly want the floor to open up and swallow me. 'I'm Maggie, I have a true crime blog. Nice to meet you both.' I blurt the words out in a rush.

Reiss and Flower Spirit glance at each other out of the corner of their eyes. Flower Spirit bites her lip in an attempt to hide a poorly concealed smile.

'Good for you, sweetie,' says Reiss, wrapping his taloned fingers around my arm and giving me a gentle squeeze. Flower Spirit rolls her eyes.

'If you need me, I'll be at the bar.' She saunters off without a care at the awkwardness she leaves behind. The tops of my ears grow warm.

'Sorry about her. She, er, she's quite a shy person.' He shakes away his lie and changes the subject. 'Are you up for an award?'

'No, I'm a guest. First time actually.'

'How exciting,' he says. 'I love true crime.'

'Yes! Me too!' I reply, a little too exuberantly. 'My blog's called The Social Sleuth.'

'Love that. V. clever.'

'I was—'

'Sorry,' he interrupts, his eyes glancing over my right shoulder. 'Isla is beckoning me, she wants to know my drink order. It was a pleasure to meet you. If there's a crime on board, I'll know exactly who to come to.' He winks and chuckles.

'A blog? Seriously, how 2009,' Flower Spirit – Isla – hisses as he approaches her, just loudly enough for me to hear. 'Why are you always so nice to them?'

I scurry away, not wanting to hear Reiss's reply, wanting to allow myself the pretence that he might defend me. He'd seemed genuinely interested, hadn't he? I avert my gaze from anyone who might have observed this exchange, and stare at the floor, blinking back tears, desperate to stave off further embarrassment.

Catching the eye of a gangly teenage boy dressed in black, I wave him over and he lopes towards me carrying his tray of champagne. Against my better judgement, I take a glass. As a general rule, I avoid alcohol, and I especially avoid getting drunk. It's something Jessica imposed on me, but she was right. Alcohol was exacerbating my feelings of being out of control, of having no influence over my own life. When you know what it's like to truly lose control, to have your life path dictated by others, there's no way in hell you'd choose to give the little power you do have over to a substance, even if you do enjoy the taste. But one glass of champagne won't get me drunk, and it might help take the edge off.

The glass is cool in my warm hand and I lift it to my lips. But I overshoot it and tip too much into my mouth. The bubbles fizz and pop, hitting the inside of my nose, crowding my throat and stopping any oxygen from getting in.

Before I can do anything, I splutter and cough. Droplets of liquid dribble down my chin. People turn to look at me and I catch sight of Stella. We lock eyes and her nostrils flare as if appalled that someone like me was allowed to sully this beautiful yacht and her perfect day on it. Her look is short-lived and she turns back to a group that are clearly enjoying everything she's saying.

I wipe my mouth with the back of my hand and return my half-finished glass to another server. I search for somewhere to hide, somewhere to go to give myself a moment to recover from the sting of embarrassment, somewhere to go to lick my wounds.

Since the email from the Influencer of the Year events team landed in my inbox with the cursive words 'You're invited' written across the top, I've been playing over what today would be like. I thought it would be easy, that people would be interested in me. But I've been dismissed, metaphorically thrown overboard without even a conversation.

There's another crowd of people clustered together as a group, but it's not a homogeneous one. Some are yapping away into phones or headsets; others are frantically flicking through notes or scrolling their phones. From the look of them they are probably the influencers' assistants and general staff. They don't have the same glitz and glamour about them as the other guests, and they also look distinctly more stressed.

There's a woman sitting on one of the seats that looks out onto the water, a plate piled high with pastries balanced precariously on her lap. It's the woman that arrived at the event with Stella.

'Is someone sitting here?' I rasp, like I've just run a marathon, not choked on a glass of champagne. She glances at me. Her eyes are rimmed with red, and she hastily wipes at her cheeks.

'No,' she whispers, turning her face away from me, determinedly staring out at the water.

'Were they mean to you too?' I ask, as the woman sniffs loudly.

'What?' she asks, facing me again. A flash of anger in her glance.

'I tried to introduce myself to them,' I say, pointing vaguely in the direction of Reiss and Isla, 'and they didn't want to know. I think they could tell I wasn't one of them. Maybe I should have dressed up a bit more, but I didn't want to go over the top. I was trying to be, you know, true to me. Authentic.'

'There's your first mistake,' she replies. Her tone now hard. 'Never be authentic around these people.'

'I'm Maggie,' I say, changing the subject and offering her my hand. 'Shaw,' I add. The woman looks startled for a moment and then lifts the plate from her lap, places it down on the floor and takes my hand in hers. Her palm is clammy and, as if realising this, she snatches her hand away quickly.

'Anna Nicholls,' she says, trying to subtly wipe her hand on her skirt. 'Nice to meet you.'

'Nice to meet you too,' I say. I lower myself onto the bench next to her. 'So, what are you doing here?'

'I'm an assistant,' she replies. I get the impression she is working to keep her voice steady.

'That's interesting,' I say, and though I already know the answer, I ask, 'Whose?'

'Stella Knight's. If you're here, you probably know who she is. She set up *Fashionsista*.'

'Oh yes, I know who Stella Knight is.'

I glance behind me, to where I saw her before. Stella Knight stands as tall as her tiny frame will allow, surrounded by a cluster of people who are giving her their full attention. She must have said something funny, because everyone is laughing. She's watching them, a small smile of amusement playing on her lips. In the flesh, Stella seems as friendly, warm and approachable as she does on-screen. She has one of those smiles that seems to light up those around her. But there is one person in the group who isn't laughing. The man closest to her looks sullen and bored. He keeps glancing over the heads of the group, searching the crowd, looking for someone. 'Who is that with her?' I ask.

'Her husband,' replies Anna. 'Christopher Clarke.'

'Oh yes, I've seen him in photographs before. From what I've read about him online, he's a silent figure in her life. She's the star, he's the hot arm candy.' I laugh. 'The internet is right about one thing, he is a handsome man.'

'Mmm,' says Anna, noncommittally.

Christopher's search beyond his wife and their group is disrupted by the bartender who served me before. He comes up behind Stella and taps her on the arm. He hands her a lime green drink, his mouth moving excitedly as he talks to her. Stella squeezes his arm affectionately and accepts the drink that matches her dress. The bartender walks away, suppressing a grin. 'She seems to be enjoying herself,' I say with a smile, turning back to Anna.

'Oh yeah, she loves being the life and soul of the party.' Anna's voice quivers and she emits a little bark of sadness. I place a hand on her arm.

'Are you sure you're OK?'

'Yes,' she says swallowing back tears. I don't want to press any further, so we sit for a moment in silence. It's Anna who speaks first. 'Stella isn't happy about her outfit for today. Multiple designers sent her options to wear but one of them had a broken zip. When she saw it was broken, she decided that that was the dress she wanted to wear and then was furious at me that it was broken. I said I'd call the designer and get them to send another one immediately, but she said no, that she'd make do with the remaining options she had. She had nine other dresses to choose from for goodness' sake, and they all looked bloody great because she has the perfect figure. But because things didn't go perfectly she blamed me. She even accused me of trying it on and breaking the zip trying to squeeze into it.'

I screw my face up as Anna speaks. 'That sounds a bit unreasonable.'

'If you looked up "unreasonable" in the dictionary, you'd find a picture of Stella Knight,' says Anna, roughly brushing away the tears that are now rolling down her cheeks. 'This isn't the worst thing she's done to me, nowhere near.'

'What else has she done?' I ask. I'm being nosy and I know it, but I can't help myself. Stella Knight has built a reputation on being the kind and loving girl next door who always reminds us to look after ourselves and others, and yet here is her assistant painting a wildly different picture. Anna's hand flies to her mouth.

'I shouldn't have said anything. She hasn't done anything else to me, this is a one-off,' she says quickly. Her eyes are wild now. 'Please, please don't pass on what I've just said. Stella would kill me if she found out I was gossiping about her.'

'I won't tell anyone. I don't have anyone to tell,' I add with a chuckle. 'It's not like I know anyone here.' A phone trills loudly and Anna mouths an apology before answering it. She walks away, frantically talking to someone on the other end of the line, chewing at her fingernails at each interval. I look up to find Stella again. She isn't immediately apparent; she's moved away from the crowd, and is standing with her back to them, in animated conversation with a figure I can't quite make out from where I am. Her hands are on her hips and her right hip juts out in a pose that from where I'm sitting looks aggressive. She raises her arm and points in the direction of the land and then whirls around, marching away. As Stella storms back towards her group, her lips are pursed and I can tell she's making a distinct effort to relax the tension in her face. The woman she was arguing with slams her hands against the railing, her limp, curly ginger hair shuddering at the violence of her action. Her face is taut with fury, her expression murderous.

My phone buzzes, then again, and again. I send the call to voicemail – doesn't she get that I don't want to speak to her? When I look back up, the ginger-haired woman has gone.

I sit alone looking out as the yacht approaches the skyscrapers of Canary Wharf. The silver spears of London's famous financial district rise into the clouds. A heaviness in my chest replaces the excitement I'd felt about my invitation. I'd been so desperate to meet other influencers and build my brand, maybe even begin to establish my place among them, but today has been a bust. Reiss Rose and Flower Spirit are rude, condescending people and Stella Knight, by the sounds of it, is a complete bitch. I sigh, allowing myself to sink lower into my seat. Appearances can be deceiving; especially on the internet.

Chapter Four

The Social Sleuth, *extract from blog 22*

Nicknamed the Giggling Granny, you'd be forgiven for thinking she was a sweet old lady, but Nannie Doss was anything but. She murdered four out of five of her husbands, reportedly killing one just because he got on her nerves.

The river widens as we sail further out of London, and the shore that we hugged on our journey from Tower Bridge is further away now. The engine quietens down, a signal that the yacht has reached its destination, but for the people at the party, things are only just beginning. The prow points its nose towards the nothingness that is the distant sea, a mass of blue so dark it looks grey. The yacht, which felt huge when it towered over the minute bodies on the red carpet, suddenly feels small when faced with the endless expanse of the ocean.

The sun is still high in the sky and beads of sweat trickle down my calves from behind my knees. We might be edging closer to the sea but I'm yet to experience even a single gust of wind. Clusters of people crowd around me. The heat coming from their bodies intensifies the warmth of my own. My head swims for a second and I grip the rail in front of me, regretting not drinking more water.

I open my eyes and refocus my gaze on the ceremony. On the bottom level, the carefully laid out chairs are now filled. Reiss Rose and Flower Spirit sit next to one another in the third row; Noel and his wife are hand in hand, her knuckles white as she grips his tightly; and Stella's husband, Christopher, and assistant, Anna, sit either side of an empty space. The seat reserved for Stella is unoccupied. The ceremony is about to begin, and Stella isn't there. Where is she? Christopher, evidently wondering the same thing, gets up and leaves his seat. I watch him go, head bowed, not wanting to draw attention to himself. 'Good afternoon, everyone,' says a man wearing fitted linen trousers rolled up at the bottom and a matching linen top, stepping onto the stage. Nobody noticed Christopher's exit – all eyes are on the compere, and a ripple of excitement runs through the people standing close to me as they debate in whispers who will win this afternoon's prestigious awards.

'Welcome to the Influencer of the Year awards,' says the host in a voice like a circus ringmaster. He starts a round of applause which everyone follows obediently. 'I am Dean Charles, you might know me as the fabulous managing director of the Influencer of the Year awards, which I am.' He gives a little bow. 'But today, I will also be your host.' He starts another inexplicable round of applause, but no one in the audience seems to question it. 'All right, let's get this thing started, shall we?'

The audience whoop in response and push themselves towards me to get a better look at the stage. They pen me in on all sides, intensifying the heat. I release my hand from the railing, panicked that I'm going to faint, and turn away from my view of the ceremony.

'Excuse me,' I say to the people clamouring around me. They part to let me pass and immediately fill my spot, not acknowledging the sweat collecting on my brow or the unsteadiness of my legs. I wobble towards the bar. 'Glass of water, please.' The bartender obliges without question. I wipe my forehead with the back of my hand and sit on the bar stool, gratefully gulping the whole thing in one as soon as it's offered. Dean's voice and the ceremony proceedings are audible from my seat and I'm able to applaud along with everyone else, but my arms are heavy. The heat of the day and the rollercoaster of emotions have left me weary.

Thinking it will be cooler inside where there is air conditioning, I get to my feet. The day isn't over yet and I want to make the most of it after the ceremony, but I can't do that if I've passed out from heat exhaustion. The glass doors slide on their tracks as I approach and the icy indoor air allows the tension in my shoulders to loosen. Inside, there's a square waiting area surrounding the lift and I take a seat on one of the sofas. The leather is cool and the gentle breeze pumped from above nips soothingly at my skin. I could almost hiss with relief, like a hot frying pan thrown into cold water.

'This is your own fault, you know that, don't you?'

I jolt upwards, tensing like I've been punched in the gut. Sitting to attention, I twist to see where the voice came from, but there's no one in my vicinity. The words weren't directed at me, they couldn't be directed at me. I slowly get to my feet, trying not to make a noise. My skin burns as it peels away from the leather.

'You brought this on yourself, Stella.'

Stella? My breathing quickens and I creep closer to the stairwell, from where the male voice booms. Standing several stairs down is Stella Knight, resting against the dark panelled wall almost exactly where I stood to catch my breath a few hours ago. Though she is looking up in my direction, she can't see me. Her eyes are glazed over, staring aimlessly in the way that drunk people do, and her cheeks are muddy with thick tracks of mascara. Her husband is standing in front of her with his back to me. Christopher's hands make fists and his shoulders are raised.

Stella pushes off the wall and drapes herself over him. He wraps one arm around her, his fists still clenched. He whispers something in her ear and though his words are inaudible, the tightness of his posture tells me they're not sweet nothings. He then puts his two hands on Stella's upper arms and shakes her hard so her head flops backward and forward like a rag doll, jerking so violently it seems in danger of popping off, but she remains silent, unable to cry out at the assault, unable to tell him to stop it, that he's hurting her. She looks drunk. Very, very drunk.

Before I can intervene, Anna comes scurrying up the stairs behind Stella. I pull back, pressing myself as close to the wall as possible. I don't want them to see me or to know that I've seen this.

'What took you so long?' he asks.

'Sorry, I couldn't find the right staircase,' replies Anna. She sounds out of breath.

'Nobody can see her like this, they'll ask questions. We need to deal with her. Help me get her to the suite as quickly and quietly as possible.'

The coldness of his words chill me far more than any air conditioning could. I peek around the corner again.

'Come on, let's get you to bed,' says Anna kindly, grunting as she places her arm around Stella's waist.

'No,' murmurs Stella. 'Not well.'

The two of them support Stella on unsteady legs and carry her down the stairs and out of sight. My heart beats hard against my chest and I perch on the edge of the leather sofa while Christopher's words replay in my mind.

This is your own fault.

Nobody can see her like this.

We need to deal with her.

When my breathing returns to normal, I head out through the glass doors and try to get a view on those seated downstairs to see if Anna and Christopher have returned to their seats. I muscle my way forward to lean against the railings, tilting myself over them to get a better look. Christopher Clarke is seated and applauding along with everyone else, as if he hasn't just carried his half-conscious wife away. But he's alone; Anna must be dealing with Stella.

The voice of the awards' host, Dean, continues to be projected over the tannoy. He hasn't noticed that one of his nominees is still not in her seat. 'The award for this year's best blogging duo goes to... Sandra and Karen with *BeauTEAs*. Come on up here, Sandra and Karen.' The audience bring their hands together in applause as two women in their seventies dressed in colourful skirts and blouses climb the steps towards the stage. Their sun-beaten faces beam as they approach Dean. Behind them, the wide television screen displays the message *BeauTEAs: sexy septuagenarians serving the perfect cup of tea with a slice of cake and a wee bit of scandal.*

I open my handbag and pull the order of events from it. The Influencer of the Year award comes last, preceded by the Best Blogging Duo. The award Stella is nominated for is next. What will happen if she isn't there to collect it?

The two older women gratefully accept their award and give a rousing speech about age not stopping them from succeeding. As much as it's nice to see that the awards do have some breadth when it comes to their winners – even if these two women are as stunning and glamorous as everyone else – I can't focus. All I can think about it is what will happen when Stella's name is called and she isn't there.

Sandra and Karen step down from the stage and retake their seats on the second row.

'And now,' says Dean into the microphone. 'It's time for our final award. It's time to find out who is the UK's Influencer of the Year.'

'It's bloody obvious who it's going to be,' says the woman standing in front of me to her friend.

'The UK Influencer of the Year Award goes to a woman whom we all love, though not as much as her fans do. A woman who has taught us everything we need to know about living fabulously. Everyone please give a round of applause to...' Dean trails off, but he knows that he doesn't have long to keep the audience in suspense. 'Stella Knight.'

The audience breaks into yet more applause, but there are varying degrees of enthusiasm. Some people are applauding like their lives depend on it, whereas others are slapping their palms together limply like seals at a zoo. Despite the fact that half of them don't even seem that interested everyone around me rises on their tiptoes, ready to watch Stella walk to the stage in her lime green dress. Except she doesn't.

'Stella,' says Dean, his eyes scanning the audience in front of him. 'Come on up here, you absolute babe.' The audience keep applauding, but their heads are twisting even more than before.

The woman next to me turns and mouths, 'What's going on?'

'No idea,' I reply, but my stomach knots remembering Stella's bobbing, limp head.

'Stella,' says Dean once more. 'Is not making an entrance the new way to make an entrance?' His awkward laugh is mirrored by the audience. People are turning towards Christopher, sitting next to the empty seat where Stella should be. Dean glares at Christopher, his face searching for some explanation. Slowly, Christopher gets to his feet and walks onto the stage. The audience is silent, watching him with intrigue.

He stands behind the lectern where the award winners have all stood to give their thank you speeches. His face is tanned and rugged but his fingers are white and they tremble as he wraps them around the lectern's rim. He adjusts the height of the microphone and a high-pitched noise screeches through the tannoy, making the audience recoil.

'Hello. Stella isn't feeling well,' he says. His accent is crisp and clear but every word sounds like an effort, like he's speaking through gritted teeth. 'Seasickness. She's gone to her room.' At that, his fingers unfurl from the lectern and he departs the stage, leaving a dampened atmosphere in the air.

The Stella I saw being shouted at by this man didn't look seasick, she looked drunk – but then again, what else would he announce to a boat full of people? He wouldn't want anyone to think Stella has a drinking problem.

'Well,' says Dean, looking slightly ruffled by the absence of his top prize winner. He surveys the audience with a pleading expression, as if hoping someone will help him loosen the tension. 'Poor Stella might be stuck in her room with a poorly stomach, but we can still give her a round of applause.' Dean starts clapping and the audience follows suit but with significantly less enthusiasm than before. 'Let's keep that applause going for all of our winners.' Dean continues trying to chivvy the audience up. 'And that concludes our ceremony this afternoon. Afternoon tea is now being served in the inside dining room for anyone who's a bit peckish, and later on this evening a buffet dinner will also be available. Check your order of events for more details. The sun is shining, the music is about to start pumping, so grab yourself a drink and get ready to party the night away. Thank you.' At that he leaves the stage.

'Stella got a room?' whispers the woman closest to me.

'I guess,' I reply, hesitantly. That's what Dean implied.

'She got the Blue Diamond suite,' cuts in a young man on my other side. 'It's the fanciest on board.' He doesn't try to hide his scorn. 'Life is great when you're the golden girl, eh?' They both groan and move away.

I glance back down at the seats below and see that Christopher is no longer there.

–

The atmosphere at the awards ceremony wouldn't suggest that anything has gone terribly wrong. People are milling about, glasses of champagne in their hands, chatting to one another and vaguely wondering whether Stella Knight is actually unwell or whether she didn't turn up just to get tongues wagging or, even worse, if she simply couldn't be bothered.

'I know her husband looks worried about her,' says a leggy woman in a minuscule sequinned dress to the short, stocky man on her arm, 'but I don't believe she's sick. This is exactly the type of thing Stella would do. She loves being the centre of attention, and what's more centre of attention than not being there?'

The man laughs and tips the dregs of his champagne glass into his mouth. 'Come on,' he says, 'let's get a top-up and find someone interesting to talk to. The atmosphere here has nosedived. Whether she's ill or not, she's killed the vibe.'

I lean my arms against the railings of the yacht and watch them go, narrowing my eyes. A publicity stunt? It's a rather mean-spirited thing to say, but then again it's not as if anyone I've encountered here so far is particularly nice.

Catching sight of Anna standing on her own in a quiet spot along the side of yacht, I head towards her, hoping to ask how Stella is. Did Anna deposit her safely in her bedroom? What if she just pointed Stella in the right direction and she slipped and toppled over the side? I cast my eyes into the depths, wondering what I'd do if a lime green stiletto were bobbing in the water. My imagination shouldn't be allowed to run as wild as it does.

Before I can reach Anna, Christopher Clarke appears next to her and tilts his head, indicating that he wants to speak to her in private. I shouldn't follow them. I know I shouldn't follow them. I tell myself I won't follow them.

But as they move away, heading along the walkway that encircles the perimeter of the ship, my feet tread lightly in their wake. There's something about the look on his face that makes me want to know what they're going to talk about. I'm drawn to this conversation like a moth unable to resist the pull of a flickering flame.

Reaching the middle of the yacht, Christopher pulls open a door and gestures for Anna to go inside. The door slams shut behind them. I inch closer and peer through the circular window. They're not standing immediately inside the door, so I wrap my fingers round the handle and pull it gently downwards and tug the door open, just wide enough for their words to reach me.

'She's not in a good way,' says Anna.

'I can't imagine she is,' replies Christopher.

'She's been sick everywhere.'

'Fuck's sake.'

'She needs a doctor.'

'No,' barks Christopher. 'Imagine what that would look like. The party will be stopped, the boat will be turned around. No, that would be a huge embarrassment for me and her.'

'But—'

'Leave it, Anna. If you're so worried, you go and sit with her.'

The sound of feet stomping towards me makes my fingers loosen from the handle like it's a hot poker. I sprint away from the door, getting as far as the railings, which I collapse against as if I'm admiring the view. If Christopher takes any notice of me it's impossible to know, because I don't look back at him. My heart pounds against my chest, its beat pulsing in my neck.

There is something going on, and I need to find out what.

Chapter Five

> Despite having killed his mother with
> an overdose of sleeping pills, he wasn't
> sentenced to life in prison. The jury felt
> that the years of abuse he had endured in
> her 'house of tyranny' were enough to drive
> anyone to murder.

The broad, dark wooden door is polished to perfection, the words *Blue Diamond Suite* written across it in gold letters. The conversation I overheard gave me the name and it didn't take long to find. This is the room that Stella was given to get ready for the awards ceremony; where she had the argument with Anna about the dress; and where she was taken when Christopher asked Anna to deal with her. The corridor stretches out either side of me, a soft crimson carpet, walls dotted with gilded lamps. Beautiful but austere. If there is something sinister happening behind the door, it's impossible to tell. I raise my hand and knock twice.

'Anna,' I say to the door when there is no answer. 'Is everything OK?'

The door opens a fraction. 'Who is it?'

'It's Maggie. We met earlier.'

'What are you doing here?'

'I heard Stella was sick and I wanted to check everything was OK. I get a bit seasick myself and wanted to offer some motion sickness tablets, just in case you didn't have any.' Anna looks from me to the packet I'm holding in my hand.

'Oh God,' says Anna. Somehow her face is even paler than it was when we first met, and her fingers grip the door so tightly that her knuckles are white.

'Is everything OK?' I ask again, though things aren't OK – that much is obvious.

'She...' Anna trails off, her lip trembling.

'She what?' I ask.

'She's...'

'Anna,' I bark, hoping that saying her name will get her to focus.

'You best see for yourself.'

Anna steps backward, pulling the door further open to reveal the large suite behind it. Decorated in muted colours with accents of nautical blue, it should scream luxury, but it's the mess that catches my attention. The pale wooden floor is covered with discarded clothing: dresses, shoes, underwear. The white silk bedsheets scattered across the humongous bed are streaked and stained with green. A bottle of nail varnish lies on its side, surrounded by a pool of congealed liquid. Crossing the threshold into the room, the smell of vomit hits me. The sharp, acidic, alcoholic stench is so powerful that it makes me gag. Anna stands in the centre of the room, hopping nervously from foot to foot and staring towards the far corner where another door is ajar, its inside hidden in darkness.

'What's going on?' I ask. Her frenetic energy seems to swell and fill the room with an intensity that grips me by the throat.

Anna walks towards the interior door on unsteady feet and, as if afraid that a ghost might jump out at her from behind it, drags it slowly and tentatively open.

The bathroom is in darkness. The lights flicker as the movement ignites them and brightness is forced through the filaments. Fireworks explode in my vision, a product of the adrenaline and fear coursing through my body. I'm blinded. My only sense is the rhythm of my heart, which rushes like a gale force wind in my ears.

Before I'm prepared the bathroom is illuminated and I see what has sucked the colour from Anna's skin.

'Oh my God,' I whisper, and reach out a hand to grab Anna's to stop myself from toppling over. Where my skin is hot as blood rushes through my veins, Anna's is like ice.

Stella sits on the floor, her body slumped sideways, resting uncomfortably on the tiles. Her usually light-brown skin has lost its radiance and her head tips backward, her mouth hanging open. My own mouth is dry. Horror swirls in my stomach making me nauseous.

'She's dead,' says Anna. She grips the door frame, her chest heaving as she gasps for breath. 'Dead.'

'No!' I say stupidly, unable to process what I'm seeing. The bright, vibrant woman in the lime green dress is gone. I want to scream but I can't. I feel like someone has forced me into a straitjacket and is pulling it tighter and tighter against my chest. It crushes my lungs and steals my breath. I crouch down and place my hands on Stella's cheeks. They're cold to the touch and her skin is unnaturally taut. A shiver runs its cold fingers over my flesh and I recoil, but don't release her. Stella's eyes are closed and her mouth is crusted with white. The front of her dress is dark with damp, wet from the vomit. I wobble, tipping forward until my knees collide with the cold tiled floor, not caring that my own dress has fallen into the pool of sick that encircles her. Stella's chest is still.

'She isn't breathing,' I say. I press my fingertips against the sides of her slim neck. 'I can't feel a pulse.' My hands let go of Stella's face and I stand up sharply. 'We need to get her help. Immediately!'

'Nothing will help her now,' says Anna, staring past me with eyes fixated on Stella. 'It's too late.'

My mouth falls open in disbelief at her words and the coldness with which she delivers them. Anna's conversation with Christopher and his decision to deny his wife the help she desperately needed resurfaces in my memory. 'We have to do something,' I plead.

'Yes, I suppose we do. You go and tell the organisers. I'll stay with her.'

Anna looks at herself in the mirror and neatens her short blonde bob, ensuring no hair is out of place before running the cold tap and pressing her damp hands against her cheeks.

We lock eyes in the mirror. 'Are you sure you're OK to stay here alone?'

'I'm fine,' she says, and to my discomfort she sounds it. She displays none of the horror or panic or shock that is making me feel like the yacht is rising and falling over malicious waves. From what I can see, Anna is sailing on smooth waters. But as I walk towards the door she adds, 'Just so you know, I did everything I could to save her. In case anyone asks.'

Her eyes bore into me, their blue more of a dark, steely grey in the bathroom's dim lighting. She looks possessed, and I fight the urge to flee and scream at the top of my lungs that a woman is dead.

'Why would they think you didn't?' I ask instead.

She smiles in a way that adds no light to her dark eyes. 'Promise me,' she says, not answering my question. I swallow, unsure what to say. Stella is dead, Anna was there when it happened and she wants me to cover for her. It's odd and unnerving.

'I need to go,' I say and walk away from her on shaky legs.

The suite door closes behind me and I rest my back against it, giving myself a moment of pause, trying to collect my thoughts. I raise a hand to my mouth and press it hard, suppressing a whimper. For years, true crime has fascinated me, but nothing that I've researched or written about could have prepared me for this, for seeing a woman go from alive to dead in the blink of an eye. I take deep steadying breaths and try to focus on what I need to do now, because somebody needs to do something.

But in the back of my mind a question lodges itself: what is Anna Nicholls afraid of?

Then I snap out of it, as though somebody has clapped their hands to get my attention. My feet are unable to keep me stationary any longer. I twirl on my heels and sprint from the suite, up the stairs and towards the party. The glass doors fly open under the command of my body hurtling towards them. The sun and the music and the cheeriness of all the guests hits me like a slap to the face and a bubble of laughter almost bursts out of me at the horror of the situation.

Several decks below, a woman lies dead, and everybody here is having the time of their lives. The sound of laughter and clinking glasses runs through the air. It's like I've just emerged from a cinema after watching a horror film, squinting into the daylight, heart still racing. As my body warms in the sun, the image of Stella lifeless on the marble tiles of the bathroom floor swims before my eyes, but the urge to scream and cry is gone and I stand, tense but still, surveying the partygoers before me. Not a single one of them have noticed my panic; not a single one of them knows that Stella Knight is dead.

Dean Charles, the managing director of the awards, stands at a cocktail table, his hand pressed against the base of a champagne glass. He's chatting animatedly to an attractive woman. As I approach him, I imagine the scene unfolding when I tell him the news: Dean's champagne dropping to the floor, the glass shattering, the woman beside him screaming from the shock.

I march towards him. Dean scans my face, desperately trying to place me, maybe wondering whether I'm one of the guests or one of the staff. Maybe his greeting will be dictated by that.

'Dean,' I say, my voice low and urgent. 'I need to speak to you privately.'

His smile falters and he glances at the woman, who raises an arched eyebrow.

'It's an emergency.'

'I'll leave you to it. Find me later, babe.' The blonde woman winks at him, downs her martini in one, and walks off.

'What's going on?' says Dean, evidently trying to keep the panic out of his voice. It isn't working. I can almost see the cogs whirring in his mind. There must be a whole range of emergencies in his line of work, but he won't be prepared for this.

'Stella,' I say. My tongue suddenly feels too big for my mouth and I'm barely able to get the words out. 'Stella Knight. She needs help. She's...' I swallow the panic threatening to overwhelm me. 'She's...' Dean's fingers twitch as he restrains himself from shaking the information out of me. 'She's dead.'

Dean's face drains of colour beneath the multiple layers of fake tan. He sucks in the fleshy parts of his cheeks, exposing the bones and hard angles of his face. The effect is vampiric and discomforting. The hair on my arms pulls my skin into goosebumps.

'Dead? Are you sure?' Dean's expression twists as he gets over his initial shock. He's calculating how much of a problem the death of a guest is for him, assessing what this will mean for his business. The realisation makes me want to slap him. My lips curl; I'm disgusted at how little people care about others in comparison to themselves.

'Anna, her assistant, is with her in her suite. You need to find her husband. You need to tell the captain. You need to call the police.'

'Dead? How?' he asks, wiping his hands against his trousers.

'I don't know, and right now, it doesn't matter. Find her husband, alert the captain, call the police,' I repeat, my voice stern and authoritative, unsure if he is registering what I'm saying. This time he nods frantically and rushes off. At the far end of the deck, he stumbles and is just saved from falling by a passing guest who grabs him by the arm, mocking him loudly for his drunken unsteadiness. An uncomfortable feeling flutters in my stomach. Poor Dean seems ill-equipped to handle a situation of this magnitude. It's understandable; he could never have predicted this, no one could. Dean gives the guest a pained smile and wipes his brow, looking in danger of collapsing. He can't do this, he needs help. I start to make my way towards him when a noise makes me stop.

'Psst.'

I glance around, unsure who signalled to me. The clip-clopping of sturdy heels against decking clatters loudly. Reiss Rose, half-drunk champagne glass in hand, storms towards me with fervent urgency. His eyes are trained on me and he moves closer, pushing his way through the tipsy guests blocking his way, all unaware that a tragedy has occurred.

'Are you—' I start to ask, hoping to clarify that he wanted my attention, but he cuts me off.

'I was only joking,' he says, swaying slightly and darting out a hand to grip the railings.

'Excuse me?'

'I was only joking. When I said if there was a crime on board I'd know to come to you.'

'I'm not following,' I say, tracking my mind back to earlier conversation.

Reiss pulls a slim silver cigarette case from the pocket of his billowing trousers and unclips it. He fumbles with his lighter, failing to get a flame going.

'I'm shivering. Sweetie, would you?' He holds the lighter at me. I ignite the flame and hover it under the cigarette hanging from Reiss's lips. He finishes his champagne and takes a long drag before continuing, 'I didn't know there would be a crime on board. But there has been, and I don't want you to think I knew something, because I didn't.'

'Crime?'

'I just bumped into Stella's assistant, Anna. She's a complete mess. Crying that it's all her fault.'

'What's all her fault?' I ask. I don't know how much Reiss knows. Has word of Stella's death spread already? What's Anna told him? I replay the scene in the bedroom, how pale Anna's face was as she drew back the door to let me in; how she splashed her cheeks with cold water; the lie she asked me to tell. She wanted people to think she tried to save Stella, and now she's saying it's her fault.

'Stella's dead,' answers Reiss. 'Anna told me you knew. I wasn't sure who else to speak to.' He glances around nervously and then shuffles towards me, leaning in to whisper in my ear. The smell of alcohol mingled with cigarette smoke tickles my nostrils. 'I... I...' He swallows. 'I think someone killed her.'

The yacht lurches, sending me sideways and banging my hip painfully against the railing. The jolt loosens Reiss's grip on his champagne glass. It falls from his hand over the side of the yacht. It spins as it drops past deck after deck, so small and insignificant that it doesn't even make a splash before disappearing beneath the crashing waves. I regain my balance and composure. 'What the hell makes you say that?'

'Anna said Stella was behaving drunkenly, was violently sick and then she passed out. Anna said it must have been something she ate or drank. So, there are only three options, aren't there? It was something she ingested by accident, on purpose – or because someone slipped her something.'

He clamps his lips around the cigarette and takes another nervous drag.

'We can rule out something like food poisoning because surely someone else would be unwell too. Besides, Stella never eats at these things, doesn't want to look bloated in pictures. And she doesn't drink or do drugs

43

any more, so we can rule out alcohol poisoning or an accidental overdose. And she didn't kill herself. I know we never truly know what someone's going through inside their own minds, but Stella? If she wanted to take her own life, my gut tells me she wouldn't do it at the awards ceremony. Stella cares about her image. Even if she were so low that she wanted to end things, she'd do it privately and quietly.' He doesn't look at me as he rattles off the scenarios that have led him to his definitive conclusion. He barely stops for breath, giving me no chance to ask how he knows this or why he thinks I need to know it too.

Before I can ask him Dean's voice trembles through one of the speakers next to us.

'Could I have your attention please?' We turn to face the stage from where Dean opened the ceremony, when things were normal. The confidence he displayed earlier is gone and he looks a little shaky as he stands in front of the crowd. As a host, there's probably no worse message to deliver. The award attendees all look towards the stage, still laughing and smiling. The ripple of chatter dies down, but not fully; the inebriated crowd can't quite gather their focus.

'Hello everyone,' continues Dean, 'I'm very sorry to disturb your evening, but this is quite serious.' If people weren't fully paying attention before, they are now. 'There's been an incident.'

'Well, what's so bloody serious about that?' slurs a man who's leaning against the cocktail table in front of him. The man next to him gives him a shove in the ribs and he moans loudly. Dean bites his lip like he can't find the word to describe the situation we are facing.

'A fatality,' says Dean.

'Oh shit,' says the drunk man and, to my horror, the crowd titter at him. This isn't funny, or at least it isn't from where I'm standing. Eventually the realisation that something serious is wrong dawns on the guests, and they gasp in shock.

The questions fly from all angles. I turn back to Reiss. 'So, what are you saying?' I ask him.

'I'm saying that someone did this to her. Someone gave her something and it killed her.' My feet feel as unsteady as if the yacht has pitched atop a wave. Reiss's words ring in my ears.

'The captain has informed the police,' continues Dean, through the speakers. 'We've been instructed to return to London where the Metropolitan Police will meet us. I've been further instructed to tell you that you must stay put. As soon as we arrive in London, the yacht will be secured and none of us will be allowed to leave until the police are satisfied that they have all they need. Please limit your movement around the ship and only go inside if you absolutely must – to use the bathroom, for example. It goes without saying that the bar will now close, and during our three-hour journey back to Shad Thames only soft drinks will be available. If anyone has any questions my staff will be on hand to answer them as best we can. Thank you for your understanding.'

Dean leaves the stage and is instantly pounced upon by people shouting at him. Questions about what this means for them and their plans. Comments about how inconvenient all of this is. I watch in silence as my thoughts collect.

'Sorry,' I say, narrowing my eyes at Reiss. 'You're saying someone murdered Stella Knight?'

He nods, agitatedly. 'As soon as Anna told me I knew.'

'No,' I say, shaking my head and taking a step away from him. I can't believe this is happening. First I find Stella dead, and now her friend is telling me she was murdered. 'Sorry,' I add, though I'm not sure what I'm apologising for. 'Why are you telling me this?'

Reiss exhales streams of smoke through both nostrils and says, 'Because I wanted you to know that I didn't have anything to do with it. That stupid joke about the crime and coming to you. I didn't want you to think my comment was prophetic. But now I think about it...' He trails off and stares over my shoulder with unfocused eyes.

'But now you think about what?' I ask when he doesn't continue. My words snap him back into focus and he lifts his cigarette to his mouth with trembling fingers.

'Now I think about it... there are three hours until we get back to London, and we're stuck on a boat with a killer.'

My muscles tense. Guests mill around us, and I wonder if beneath the veneer of their golden tans, their perfect hair and their tight physiques these are people who would do anything in their ruthless pursuit of fame. Beauty can hide all manner of sins, and all manner of ugliness.

'Someone did this to her,' he insists. 'I know they did.'

I take a deep breath. 'Let's imagine you're right. What do you think we should do about it?'

'We have to find out what happened to her. We have to find out who killed her. Will you help me?' His pearlescent teeth bite at his lips as he waits for me to respond. This is crazy. His reasoning is flawed beyond belief. Yet he's convinced Stella was murdered, and there is evidence that points in that direction. I might be the only person that noticed these things, and if so, maybe I am the only person on this yacht that can prove Reiss is right. An

46

uneasy voice inside my head whispers a warning. *You don't know this man. Do not be led by him.* Reiss bounces on the balls of feet as the pause between us swells like a drumroll climbing towards a crescendo.

'If you're certain, then we have to find out who did this. We have to stop them,' I say.

Reiss squeals in relief and pitches towards me, enveloping me in a tight hug. I reciprocate. My fingers make contact with his bare arms and I feel the discomfort that comes with touching someone you barely know so intimately, but tragedy brings all sorts of people together. His whispered 'thank you' tickles my ear, and I hope to God that I'm making the right choice in helping him. In trusting him.

Chapter Six

The Social Sleuth, *extract from blog 6*

His death was ruled as misadventure, 'boys being boys'. Callum's family agreed with this verdict. It was only his girlfriend who insisted his death was sinister, but her concerns were never investigated.

Reiss asks me what our plan of action is. *Our* plan of action, as if my agreement to see what we can find out cements us together as an investigative team. His conviction that Stella was murdered and the fact that he might have a motive for meddling rings tiny alarms inside my head, but I silence them. It will be hours before we reach land. I won't sit idle when a woman is dead, and someone is crying murder.

'Let's start by speaking to the staff,' I suggest. 'The staff will have been paying more attention to the events of the day and, crucially, weren't drinking alcohol like the rest of the guests.'

'More reliable witnesses,' says Reiss, nodding in agreement, and together we proceed to the reception area, deciding that this loosely abides by Dean's request to only go inside by necessity. The blue-haired woman, still guarding the reception desk, scrambles to her feet as we approach.

'Reiss,' she says. 'How are you?' She tugs at the cuffs of her jacket, pulling them so they graze her wrists, attempting to hide the tattoo that creeps from beneath the fabric.

'As well as can be expected, my love.' He grimaces and places a hand to his chest as if clutching at imaginary pearls, like he's channelling the role of grieving widower. 'How are you?'

'Tired and stressed,' she says with a deep sigh. And she looks it; where this morning her thick make-up hid the shadows beneath her eyes, nothing can conceal her exhaustion now.

'I can only imagine,' says Reiss.

'I'm in complete shock. It's such a tragedy. Poor Stella. Poor Christopher. What an awful thing to happen.' And without warning, the woman bursts into tears. 'Sorry,' she mumbles, bending over to rummage about in a handbag and retrieving a packet of tissues. She swipes one across her face, dragging streaks of mascara as she does so. 'Sorry. I'm making a fool of myself. I only met her once, but she was nice, you know, and...' She sniffs loudly before lowering her voice to a whisper. 'I think if I'd have told someone, I could have saved her.'

'What do you mean?' I snap, unable to stop myself. The woman hiccups loudly and Reiss puts his arm around her, looking at me from over her head and mouthing an *oh my God*.

'There, there,' he coos, running his hand up and down her back, trying to get her to calm down. As her whimpers subside, Reiss speaks to her softly. 'Why do you think you could have saved her?'

The woman stands up straight and gives herself a shake. 'I've said this to Dean already, so I guess there's no harm in telling you?' This is a question, not a statement.

'Of course not.' Reiss is quick to offer the assurance she needs.

'As the senior event manager, I'm always visible in case of any issues. Earlier on this afternoon, one of the bar staff came over and told me that someone should probably keep an eye on one of the guests. He didn't know who she was, but he recognised her as one of the nominees. He pointed her out and it was Stella.'

'Keep an eye on her?' I ask. 'Why?'

She glances over our shoulders, but the reception area is deserted. 'Stella was really drunk. Given she was likely to win the main award, it wouldn't have looked good if she was completely wasted. Plus, if she didn't win… well, drunk people are more volatile.'

'What did you do about it?' I ask.

'I watched her for a bit, but not a sip of alcohol crossed her lips. In fact, I saw her drinking lots of water.' The woman winces. 'She sloshed it all over herself. Maybe she realised she'd had too much to drink, I don't know. She's such a slight woman. I doubt someone so petite can hold their alcohol well. Anyway, I spoke to her husband about it. I didn't want to broach it with her. I was scared about causing a scene.'

'What did her husband say?'

The woman raises both her eyebrows at this. 'He told me that it was in my best interests to mind my own business.' Reiss and I exchange a sideways look. 'Yeah,' says the woman, correctly interpreting our glance. 'He was quite aggressive about it actually.' Her shoulders curl and she lets out a long sigh. 'If I'd have told someone else, or spoken to her myself, perhaps I could have helped her. Maybe even stopped this from happening.'

She crumples into Reiss, a fresh bout of sobs taking hold of her. He leads her away from the reception desk and lowers her into one of the lobby chairs.

'You can't blame yourself,' I tell her softly. 'You weren't to know.'

'No, sweetie. Maggie's right. There might not have been anything you could have done.' We stand and wait while she recomposes herself, both of us reminding her that she wasn't responsible.

'We need to speak to the bartender. He might know what Stella was served,' I say when we are finally able to extricate ourselves from the events manager. We make our way back up the stairs towards the party, if you can call it that. The atmosphere is thick and heavy, as though a veil of fog has descended around us. People are huddled together whispering and wondering. Do they know it's Stella? I wonder.

Behind the bar, a boy who doesn't look even look old enough to buy the alcohol he has been serving all night is piling glasses onto a plastic tray ready for washing. He looks up as we approach and places the tray down on the counter.

'What can I get for you?' he asks, sounding bored. 'I can offer you water, elderflower tonic or freshly squeezed orange juice.'

'Water's fine,' I reply. 'But we're actually more interested in finding out who alerted the management team about Stella needing someone to keep an eye on her.'

'That was me. Why?' His face darkens. 'Am I in trouble or summat? Because if I'm in trouble then my mate Joe should be in much more.'

'What are you talking about?' I ask, tilting my head to one side.

'It was Joe. He was the one who put something in her drink.'

There's a beat or two of silence as the young bartender's revelation hangs in the air. I glance at Reiss, whose face turns a violent shade of red.

'What the fuck?' he roars. 'Put something in her drink. What the *fuck*?' He's shaking his head, unable to believe what he's hearing. As if despite his conviction that someone had done this to Stella he can't fully comprehend that he was right.

'Reiss,' I say under my breath. 'Calm down.' People lift their heads from their conversations, their eagle eyes homing in on new gossip. Reiss needs to keep his voice down, we can't have the whole boat knowing that someone put something in Stella's drink and that her death wasn't an accident. It would be a disaster, trial by mob, Joe thrown over the side of the yacht in retribution.

'Where is he?' snarls Reiss. 'Where is the little bastard?' Reiss leans over the counter, breathing heavily. I grab his arm and pull him back. The boy shrugs as if he couldn't give a shit about Reiss or his anger. But then he slips from behind the bar and walks past us, heading down the stairs to one of the lower decks. We follow him, and I feel the eyes of other guests tracking us as we do, like dogs, as if the scent of intrigue clings to us.

—

It isn't easy to find Joe. He isn't at any of the bars, where he should be. We check the staff room, but he isn't there. Nor is he in any of the toilets we pass. My chest gets tighter and tighter. Joe put something in Stella's drink, and now he's missing. He's either on board or he's not, and there is currently only one way off. Perspiration clings to the hairs on the nape of the young bartender's neck. His concern for his colleague grows with every second it takes for us to find him.

We head inside, stalking the corridors, searching for any hint that he might be here hiding.

'Joe!' shouts the young bartender, sprinting to the end of the corridor. I run behind him, towards the body curled up on the floor, praying that nothing has happened to Joe. The noise of our approach makes the boy stand and I feel myself relaxing as he gets to his feet. 'Jesus, Joe. What are you doing?'

Joe doesn't answer him, but keeps his back pressed against the wall, looking down at us with wide, fearful eyes. He's about the same age as his colleague but taller and fuller, more on the way to manhood.

'These people want to chat to you about the drink. Stella's drink.'

For all Joe's height and muscles, his expression is that of a child's, hauled before the headmistress. He slumps forward and buries his face in his hands, letting out a moan like a wounded animal.

The first bartender takes several steps away from Joe like he's infectious. He clears his throat. 'I should probably get back to the bar,' he says, his voice thick with discomfort. His fear that something has happened to Joe has dissipated, and he's keen to get away now. At my nod, he flees without a second glance.

'Let me handle this,' I say to Reiss, once the three of us are alone. I'm worried he'll scare the boy witless and we won't find out anything. Joe sobs quietly behind his hands, and I wonder what reason he might have had for doing this. It could be a prank cooked up by the lads working behind the bar. Or something more sinister – spike Stella's drink to make her more amenable. Either way, things don't look good for Joe.

'Joe, what did you put in Stella's drink?'

'Dunno,' he says. His head is still in his hands.

'You don't know?' shouts Reiss, unable to hide his incredulity. 'You spiked my friend's drink with an unknown substance. It killed her. Whatever you gave her killed her.'

'You think I don't know that? You think I don't realise what I've done?' Joe releases his hands from his face and slides his back down the wall until he's sitting with his knees pressed up to his chin. He wraps his arms around his legs and rocks backward and forward. 'But you've got to understand. It wasn't me. I was given it. I didn't know what it was. I just did as I was told.'

I try hard to keep my expression straight, but my insides are kicking. This is a lead. A lead in a possible murder investigation. I snatch a glance at Reiss; he nods, encouraging me to continue. I lower myself to the floor and sit cross-legged so my eyes are level with Joe's. Reiss follows my lead. 'Someone put you up to this?' I ask.

'I didn't know it would make her sick.'

'OK,' I say, calmly. 'Start from the beginning, tell me everything that happened this afternoon.' I need to get him to focus. He might be built like a tree, but he's trembling like a leaf. Fear has him fully in its grip. He looks at me, his eyes locking with mine like I'm the only thing stopping him from losing complete control.

'I was working. At the bar on the top deck, making drinks. Then one of the waitresses comes over and she tells me that Stella needs a special drink made for her. Said she needs it for a photograph. Stella's is to be lime green, to match her dress. I said that was no problem, that I could use the Chartreuse as we have it stocked. God knows why, it isn't your usual choice. But she said that Stella doesn't drink alcohol so I should just make a non-alcoholic gin and tonic and add some food colouring. Now that I didn't have. Why would a bar have lime green food colouring? The waitress said she had some already.'

'And you didn't question this?' I ask. Reiss scoffs in disbelief. I place a hand on Reiss's arm, signalling for him to keep quiet.

'Why would I? Client asks, client gets.' Joe folds his arms across his chest. Defensive, telling me not to challenge him, to back off. I take the hint and change direction.

'The waitress who brought the food colouring. What did she look like?'

'Hard to remember. Blonde hair, I think.'

Blonde hair, he thinks? If Joe is your average witness, it's a wonder the police solve any crimes.

'Anything else? Height? Weight? Facial features?'

'I dunno, do I? Wasn't paying attention to her. She wasn't the type of girl that's memorable, if you know what I mean.'

'And by that you mean she wasn't attractive, so you didn't give her a second look. Shallow bastard,' says Reiss, unable to keep the anger out of his voice.

'She was about your height,' he says to me. 'Fa... fuller figure. Blonde hair, it was short, I think. She might have had glasses on.'

'Have you seen her since she asked you to put the colouring in the drink?'

'No.'

'Where is the food colouring bottle now?'

'She took it away, didn't she? Handed it over in a plastic bag. Waited until I'd made the drink and then took it back.' Joe's eyes widen at the realisation of what he has done and he scrambles to his feet and starts pacing the corridor. 'Shit! Am I being set up? Someone wants it to look like I killed Stella Knight. I didn't. I didn't have nothing to do with it.'

'Apart from making the drink that killed her, you mean?' snarls Reiss, storming up behind him.

'What am I gonna do? This is messed up.' Joe runs his hands through his hair, twisting his fingers around the long curls and tugging until the skin on his forehead tightens.

'Joe,' I say, reaching out a hand to stop him from tearing his hair out. 'You need to remember as much as you can about this waitress and what she said to you. When the police arrive, you need to tell them everything.'

'But what's gonna happen to me? What if they can't find this girl? What if the bottle turns up with my fingerprints all over it?'

'Then you'll learn your lesson about putting things in people's drinks when they don't know about it.' Joe has the good grace to look ashamed at Reiss's condemnation.

'One more question. Who gave Stella the drink?' I ask. I think it was him, but I want confirmation.

'I did,' replies Joe. His eyes are wet with tears. 'I was falling over myself to do it and get the chance to speak to her. And it was cool to see Stella's excitement when she received it. The drink looked sick. I was proud I'd made it. Proud. I'm such a fucking idiot.'

Chapter Seven

Mourning fans were popular in the Victorian era, when women were expected to change their wardrobe to indicate they were in mourning. Fans, comprising a wooden frame covered in black silk, allowed a woman to grieve fashionably.

'Murdered, Maggie,' Reiss shouts, the second the door to his suite slams shut behind us. This suite is like Stella's but slightly smaller and much tidier. He marches up and down the length of it, his hands flapping wildly around him. 'Stella was murdered, this confirms it.' He stops suddenly, and whips around to face me. 'We're trapped. We're trapped on a yacht with a killer. A killer who might know that we know it was murder.'

I lower myself down onto the edge of the bed before my knees can give way from under me.

Murder.

That's what we're dealing with. Murder. A murder investigation. We're trapped at sea with someone capable of killing another human being. I feel like someone's coming at me with a knife and I've thrown off my armour, exposing my bare chest to the blade. This isn't like watching a television show or documentary or listening to a podcast. All the times I imagined what I would do if I were the investigator, the one given the reins to find the culprit, I never imagined the unsteadiness of my feet or the way the ground would seem to shift, unrelated to the movement of the boat. How did I think this would be like a fucking *podcast*? I'm almost as stupid as Joe the bartender.

I need some fresh air. I walk towards the balcony and slide back the wide glass door, plonking myself down on the pale blue sofa, which has the most wonderful view of the sea. The sun is slowly beginning its descent and it sparkles off the water below. I slump back against the soft cushions and try to force off the panic that's choking me. I glance at the time; our first interviews and search for Joe took about an hour. That leaves two before we land.

They say the first several hours of an investigation are crucial. That it's the time that people best remember what they saw. Once they've given their account, it's that version of the events that stick with them, and if Joe is representative of witnesses then with every passing moment information is slipping from the guests' brains like sand through an hourglass.

Two hours before the police come aboard and secure the scene. Two hours for the evidence to be trampled on, sullied or thrown overboard. Two hours for Stella's corpse to lie on the cold bathroom floor. A lot can happen in two hours.

Maybe in two hours I can solve this case.

Reiss storms to the bedside table and picks up the telephone that sits atop it. 'I'm going to order myself a drink,' he calls from inside, his voice quivering with nerves. 'Dean said the bar was closed, but he'll make an exception for me if I have to blackmail him for negligence to get it. Do you want one?'

Do you need one? might be the more appropriate question. A drink would be nice, it might ease my panic. But no, I shouldn't let anything cloud my focus, not now I've strengthened my resolve to proceed.

'No,' I reply, 'better not. A coffee would be great though, order me a latte.'

After barking a few words down the phone to the bar staff, he puts it down and grabs the overflowing fruit basket from the side table along with two bottles of water and heads outside. Placing the fruit basket in front of me, he plucks a grape from it and pops it in his mouth.

'Drinks will be five minutes. They refused to give me an espresso martini. Rude. But luckily, I always carry this for emergencies.' He places a hip flask on the table with a flourish that makes me think he's already had a few swigs. 'An Irish coffee is a good compromise.' He takes another grape. 'Help yourself.' I accept and we sit in silence, eating the grapes and thinking.

'Sweetie,' says Reiss, finally breaking the silence. 'Can you believe this? Stella is dead. Dead! My head is spinning. The Interstellars are going to be distraught. The Interstellars, that's what the fans of Stella Knight call themselves. Into Stella.'

'Clever,' I say.

'Yeah, it is rather. Mine call themselves the Rosies. Less clever, but sweet.' There's a loud knock on the door. 'That must be the drinks.' He rises and returns a minute later with a tray.

'A latte for you. A soon-to-be Irish coffee for me.' He uncaps the hip flask and pours a generous serving of golden whisky into his cup. 'What was I saying? Oh yeah, the Interstellars are going to be distraught. The internet will be *awash* with their tears. Gosh, it breaks my heart thinking about them. *So* many people love her.' He takes a sip of his drink. 'This is exactly what I needed.'

The breeze runs over my skin, playful and gentle. It really is a beautiful afternoon; sunny and cloudless, the type of day that promises you nothing bad will happen, because how can tragedy strike in such weather? It's a ludicrous notion.

'We need their help,' I say, looking Reiss square in the eye.

'You've lost me.' He takes another slug of his drink.

'The Interstellars,' I say. It's so obvious I don't know why he isn't following. 'They might have information; they might be able to help us.'

He pauses, chewing over what I've just said. 'I don't know. We'll be publicly announcing Stella's death.'

'How long will it be until everybody at the party knows that Stella is dead?' I ask. 'Once they do it'll be all over the internet, and speculation will be rife. Finding anything useful will be like finding a needle in a haystack. But if we post first with a plea for information and get her followers to come to us, we might be able to get something. Something that will help us find out who killed Stella.'

Reiss waves me away. 'I'm going to have to sit this one out, sweetie. The Interstellars are hard work and I'd... I'd prefer not to be the bearer of bad news.'

'Why?' I ask, confused at his sharp change in demeanour. 'In case they shoot the messenger?'

He gives a short bark of laughter. 'Ha! Or rip the messenger limb from limb.'

I wait for Reiss to say more, and when he doesn't, I take a sip of my coffee. It's rich and warm, and I sink lower into the chair, savouring the taste. Milky coffee always makes me think of my mum. She made a great milky coffee. It was one of the few domestic things she was good at. The taste is comforting despite the fact that my mum wasn't.

'How many followers do you have?' Reiss asks.

'Sorry?' I shake away the image of my mum scooping instant coffee granules into a mug while my sister Jessica told her that the caffeine would stop me sleeping.

'How many followers do you have? On whatever channel it is you're on.'

'Oh,' I say, blushing at his question. My jaw tightens as I waver between feeling embarrassed at how low the number is and defensive in anticipation that he'll judge me. I feel a stab of protectiveness towards the thing I've created. I didn't set my blog up to get followers, I set it up as a distraction. Crime novels, detective shows and documentaries were an escape when my world crumbled around me, and my blog became something for me to channel my energy into. As twisted as it sounds, it saved me. It gave me some control over my life, some influence when I had none.

And, I think, sitting up a little straighter, I'm good at it – researching the crimes, deciding what to say about the victim and the perpetrator, writing the blog. People like my work. I shouldn't be ashamed of what I've accomplished, regardless of how small it is. Plus, there's no point in me concealing it, he could find out for himself quite easily.

'My most viewed blog has 1,220 hits.'

Reiss winces, recovers, and then nods slowly as if I've just told him I have only weeks to live. 'If you were on the right channel, you could get far more. Set up Knock-Knock and post what you want to about Stella there. If

61

you use the right hashtags you should be able to garner some response.'

I pull out my phone, connect to the yacht's Wi-Fi and download the app KnockKnock, pleased to discover that the name 'The Social Sleuth' isn't taken. I find a picture of Stella Knight on the internet and start typing.

WHO KILLED STELLA KNIGHT?

Welcome to The Social Sleuth. It is with sadness that I announce the death of Stella Knight. She died today at the Influencer of the Year awards after someone spiked her drink. I write this from the yacht where the awards took place. We are now on our way back to London, where the police will get involved, but there is still some time before that happens and I want to use it to gather as much information for the police as I can. Reiss Rose is helping me find out who killed his friend.

I have two questions for you, the Interstellars who knew her as well as anyone.

Who would want to harm Stella Knight? And why?

I trust you all to provide me the help that I need to succeed.

Love, Maggie.

I finish my post with all the hashtags that I can think of in relation to Stella Knight and post it.

'Done,' I say, exhaling loudly and feeling like I've just exposed myself to a wild animal. The internet is a creature that nobody can control, no matter how rich they are, how famous they are, how powerful they are. 'This is the right thing to do,' I add, more to myself than Reiss.

'Yeah, they need to know, and as you say, they might be able to help,' he replies.

Barely seconds later, my phone pings, making both of us start. A pop-up appears on my home screen. My heart skips a beat − it's a comment. A comment. A comment on the post I literally just shared. I've never had comments before. My body tenses as I unlock my phone, preparing myself for whatever horrid thing the people of the internet might throw my way.

> STELLAISMYSTAR: My heart is broken, I can't believe this is happening, I can't believe this is real. Who would want to hurt Stella? She is an angel, our angel. Maggie, promise me you'll stop at nothing to find out who killed Stella.

I stare at my phone, momentarily stunned to see the message, and then glance up at Reiss, who gives me a wry smile.

'The Interstellars have found you, and they want your help.'

My phone bleeps again, another comment.

> Knightinshinyprada: This is fake news, no way is Stella dead.

Bleep, comment.

In2stella4lyf: I'm crying, I can't stop crying,
I'll never be able to stop crying.

Bleep, comment.

Kathryn489317283: FAKE NEWS.

Bleep, comment. I silence the app's notifications, annoyed by the sound. Five comments already. Nothing useful so far though. My stomach churns again. Although I've spent a year reviewing true crime cases and discussing them on my channel, I've never actually conducted an investigation. I've never had to ask people questions and search for clues. I'm at risk of making a complete fool of myself on the internet. I review the comments again.

'Reiss,' I ask, deciding to focus on the task at hand and not the hive of activity on my account. 'Who would want to kill Stella Knight? She was beautiful, successful, happily married, surrounded by adoring fans. How does the woman with the perfect life end up being murdered?'

'Sweetie, come on. You're grown up enough to know that life is never perfect.'

I almost laugh at this. No, life is never perfect, I know that better than most.

'What were the imperfections in Stella's life?' I ask.

Reiss picks up his drink and finishes it. 'To be honest, Stella and I have grown apart in recent months, but I always got the impression her career wasn't going quite the way she wanted it to.'

'What made you think that?'

'She was taking risks, trying to be more shocking. More scandalous posts and stuff.'

'Is this why you grew apart?'

'No.'

'So why then?'

'No real reason.' Reiss stands abruptly and brushes his hands along his silk trousers, rearranging them so they fall correctly. 'That coffee has done the trick. Quick, drink up. We have more people to speak to. And this blonde waitress to find.'

I observe his nervous gestures and wonder what he is hiding under his immaculately made-up face. Before I continue along this road with him, I need to know more. Hitching my ride to the first person who has shown interest in me is foolish. No, dangerous.

'How long have you known Stella?'

Evidently sensing that I won't go with him until he has answered my questions, Reiss sits back down.

'I've known Stella for years, sweetie. Years! I first met her when she was still vlogging about jazzing up your wardrobe. There was an event in London, it was called something silly, like "how to get followers and influence people". We were both babies, and so new to the internet game. But we hit it off and several glasses of Prosecco later we became firm friends. The rest is history, as they say.'

'Did you both gain prominence at the same time?'

Reiss's eyebrows narrow almost imperceptibly. 'No. Stella's rise was faster. You could say meteoric. One day she just... whoosh. My career was slower, steadier. But I'm happy with that. Gave me time to learn and grow. It's given me more sticking power.'

Reiss twists the cap on a water bottle, opens his plump lips a fraction and takes a small sip. His sticking power is of no interest to me or this investigation – although a potential rivalry between him and Stella could be.

'And what about Stella's other relationships?' I ask. 'What's her relationship with her assistant, Anna, like for example?'

Reiss snorts at this. 'Stella doesn't have a great track record with assistants. Seriously! From what I've heard, she has a new one almost every six months.'

'Six months? What does she do to them?' Reiss bites his lip, looking reticent. 'This is important!' I add.

'I don't know this for sure. As I said, Stella and I have grown apart but...' He trails off.

'But what? For God's sake, would you just tell me.'

'I've heard she's a bully. She shouts at them, belittles them, throws things at them. Isla told me she even stole one's boyfriend once.'

My mouth falls open. I hadn't expected him to say that. 'Seriously? She treats her assistants like that? Why isn't there more about this on the internet? People are obsessed with Stella and her life. Why hasn't this leaked?'

Reiss shrugs. 'Stella probably makes them sign non-disclosure agreements or something.'

I pause. Multiple disgruntled former assistants gives me numerous motives and numerous potential suspects, but I have to start with the one closest to Stella. The one I know is already on the boat. 'Anna's relationship with Stella didn't seem good,' I tell him. 'I saw her earlier, and she was crying. She told me how awful Stella was to her. Anna was the last person to see Stella alive, and the waitress Joe described could easily match her description. Let's go.' I polish off my coffee in three swigs. 'We need to talk to her.' But Reiss doesn't move. His eagerness to get out there and talk to people seems to have evaporated. 'What?'

'Anna killed her,' he says. 'It's obvious, isn't it? It might be safer to stay here, in the suite, until the police come. Let them deal with it.'

A few questions pointed in his direction, and he doesn't want to investigate any more.

'You've changed your tune.' I struggle to hide my disappointment.

'This is real, Maggie. We could actually be in danger.' He jumps up, rushes away from me and locks the suite door from the inside, pulling the chain across for extra protection. 'We should stay here. We'll be OK here.'

'We will, but what if Anna is the killer, and she decides that Joe is the biggest link to her? She has at least two hours until we get back to land and the police arrive. What if she uses that time to handle him? Do you want his murder on your conscience?' Reiss gulps audibly but avoids my gaze. 'You came to me for help, remember. We interviewed Joe, we got him to tell us about the spiked drink, we could have put him at risk. We can't stop now.'

Reiss flops down on the end of the perfectly made bed. 'No, I guess we can't.' I glance once more at my KnockKnock post and the messages it has garnered. A chill runs through me; there is a short thread that catches my eye.

> Interstellarforever1998: It's not true that everybody loves Stella. She is so gorgeous that loadssss of people are jealous of her.
>
> 4everafanofstella: Yeah and *cough* one of those people is Reiss.

Chapter Eight

The Social Sleuth, extract from blog 43

> It is not uncommon for killers, particularly
> serial killers, to insist their crimes were the
> works of the devil. But this seemed particu-
> larly true in this case.

The sun is lower in the sky, but the temperature is scarcely
more bearable than it was earlier. Reiss and I weave
our way among the other attendees, all of whom are
noticeably more subdued than before. The atmosphere
has wilted like flowers left too long on a hot windowsill
without water. The smiling, happy, polished people from
before are gone, replaced with people who are tired,
anxious and increasingly hungover. Some of the guests are
draped on the orange lounge chairs; others droop over the
yacht's railings. It's like that moment at the end of a night
out when the lights come on in the club, and you see the
people around you in their true forms. It's never glorious
or glamorous, just a mass of bleary-eyed sweaty strangers.
The police will struggle to get anything useful out of this
lot. Everyone is itching to get home and scrub themselves
and their memories clean of this horrid day.

We're now in the Thames Estuary and the land which
had seemed to drift away from us on our way out gets

closer once again. It presses in on us from each side, squeezing the yacht into a narrow channel from which it can't escape.

'Anna isn't here,' says Reiss, re-joining me after pacing a loop of the deck. 'She might have— Isla!' He interrupts his own sentence with a shout and waves to his friend. Isla is standing a little away from us, huddled in a corner of the deck. She has her back to us; her delicate shoulders are hunched forward and her head is bowed low. Beyond the outline of her slender frame, there is another shape. Isla is deep in conversation with someone but the wide brim of her hat and the curve of the ship obscures their face from view.

'Isla, sweetie,' shouts Reiss. Isla draws herself up to her full height and scans the deck.

Registering Reiss she smiles, but she quickly flaps her hands and the person she's talking to slinks off. If this was an attempt to shoo away her confidant subtly, she failed. Further down the deck, one of the heavy yacht doors swings shut with a clunk.

Reiss scurries towards her, his arms outstretched like a child running to their mother. He folds himself into her and squeezes her tightly. 'Isn't it awful, sweetie? So awful.'

She wraps her slender arms around him and rests her chin on the crown of his head. 'Oh Reiss. I know you're upset, but are you really surprised? This was surely inevitable.'

Reiss whimpers but doesn't answer her, so I call her out.

'Inevitable?' I ask. Isla focuses her dark, almond-shaped eyes on me as if only now realising I'm there.

'Stella was a party girl who drank too much and did far too many drugs. Dead in a bathroom? She was probably in there snorting something, had a bad reaction, and died.'

Reiss starts to sob gently into Isla's shoulder, unable to break away from her embrace. I frown. Isla and Reiss are friends, they both knew Stella from the influencer circles they run in, and yet their reactions are a sharp contrast. Reiss ran to me certain in the knowledge that his friend was murdered, Isla doesn't share his concern. Her arms still around him, she rocks him from side to side, making all the necessary noises to soothe his disquiet, but her own expression isn't one of sadness or shock. If anything, Isla looks like she couldn't care less. She looks almost bored by the entire thing.

'It wasn't a bad reaction. She wasn't taking drugs, someone put something in her drink. One of the bartenders told us,' says Reiss, his voice thick with his tears. 'Stella was murdered.'

Isla pushes Reiss off her. She gasps and places a hand to her chest. 'Murdered?' she asks, incredulously.

I watch her reaction. It's a good performance, I'll give her that. It ticks all the boxes of shock, but something isn't right, she isn't being genuine.

'Who were you talking to?' I ask.

'What?' She frowns, feigning confusion.

'Before, when we arrived. Who were you talking to?'

Isla laughs, mockingly. 'I don't remember my personal life being any of your business.'

'Isla James!' says Reiss, in a tone that attempts to scold. 'There's no need to talk to Maggie like that.'

'There's no need for Maggie to be asking me questions.' The agitation with which she speaks makes her hat wobble and she's forced to plant a hand on top of it to stop it falling off.

'What has got into you?' he asks, raising his perfectly plucked eyebrows.

She scoffs. 'What has got into me? Seriously, Reiss. Stella Knight is dead. Murdered, according to you and your new friend, and now you're here asking me questions as if I had something to do with it.'

Reiss looks irritated and mirrors her stance by crossing his own arms, his position in their stand-off clear. 'Maggie wasn't asking if you had something to do with it,' he says. Then he pauses. 'But maybe she should be!'

Isla glares at him with hard, unforgiving eyes. She has one of those faces that makes it impossible to tell what's going on inside her head.

'Who *were* you talking to?' Reiss asks the question this time.

'No one.'

'Fine,' says Reiss. 'Be like that. But be aware – before we moor in London, I will find them, and I'll ask them exactly what you were talking about.'

'You do that. Now if you'll excuse me.' Isla balls part of her dress in her hands and lifts it to reveal legs wrapped in white gladiator-style sandals. She kicks her leg forward and storms off, pushing her shoulder against mine as she walks. Reiss watches her go, his eyes wide like saucers. A woman is dead and already friends are turning on each other, from comrades to combatants in the blink of an eye. It's a reminder of why I never let people get too close. Making friends is like a game of Russian roulette: you never know which one will kill you.

'I have never, ever seen Isla behave like that. Ever.' He looks appalled by her behaviour. When I make no response, he goes on, 'Honestly, she is usually all "peace and love and goodwill to all". It's like a devil's possessed her.'

'Maybe a devil has possessed her,' I say, walking further down the deck and sitting on one of the chairs that face out to sea – or as is now the case, land. The yacht chugs along. The scenery – if you can call it that – is industrial; cranes tower over broad container ships loaded with colourful cubes.

'Do you think Isla is somehow involved in Stella's death?' Based on the conversation we've just had, I have to ask.

'No. Definitely not,' he says without hesitation. 'There could be many reasons that she didn't want us to know who she was chatting to,' he says quickly, then he pauses in a way that signals there's a 'but'. I think he's deciding how loyal wants to be to his friend. He sighs. He's made his decision. 'But she is hiding something, and I want to know what.'

'Why did Isla assume Stella had had a bad reaction to drugs? It's a completely different assumption to the one you made.'

He exhales slowly. 'Isla's right when she says that Stella used to be a party girl. But according to Stella's social media, she's given it all up. She went sober about eighteen months ago.'

'Why?'

'I don't know,' says Reiss with a shrug.

'She didn't tell you, as a friend?'

'Like I said, it's been a while since we were close.'

The subtle change in the way Reiss describes how long it's been since his relationship with Stella started to fall apart doesn't escape my notice, but I decide against bringing that up now. 'You assumed she was murdered because a sober person wouldn't overdo it like that, but Isla thought the opposite. Her first thought was that Stella had simply gone too far. Why?'

Reiss sighs. 'Isla isn't neutral when it comes to Stella or drugs,' he says, carefully. 'There's history there. Isla's younger brother died when she was in her early twenties; he was mixing drugs and alcohol, and she never got over it. It's why she got started in this sphere, her whole brand is based on her advocacy for clean living: no drink, no drugs, no animal products. Isla felt that when Stella went sober in such a public fashion, it was a PR stunt, not something she believed in, certainly not in the way that Isla did. I know you've not seen it so far, but Isla is a good person; a damaged person, but a good one. Her career was born out of pain and anger; she felt that Stella's sobriety was a fad.'

'Do you think Stella was still drinking?'

'I think that Stella had many faults, but she was ruthless when it came to setting goals and achieving them. When she publicly announced she was quitting, I believed her.' Reiss turns to me. 'Do you think that the waitress or whoever asked the waitress to make the drink wasn't trying to kill Stella, but they wanted to make her look drunk for some prank, or to get back at her?'

'You mean did Isla spike her drink to make Stella look like a fraud?'

'Yeah, maybe, but it sounds ridiculous now you say it aloud.'

'We don't have enough to go on,' I say, and therein lies our biggest problem. We have no evidence to point us towards a culprit, and our conversation about Isla is based on nothing but conjecture. 'We need more information,

Reiss. About Stella, about her life, about who would have cause to harm her.'

'How?' he asks, looking at me blankly.

'I'm going to look for Anna Nicholls. Unless she's thrown herself overboard she has to be around somewhere. But I think we should split up and you should try and talk to Stella's husband.'

Reiss's face twists. 'Do you think he'll talk to me? His wife has just died, remember?'

I want to say that I remember that perfectly well, that it's the reason I'm doing this with him, but I hold back; he meant no harm. 'I'm sure you'll find a way to persuade him, but make it seem casual. Not like an interrogation.'

Reiss gives me a salute. 'Sleuthing,' he says, 'but make it social.'

–

Reiss and I part ways: him in search of Christopher Clarke, me in pursuit of Anna Nicholls. I stalk the open decks, but she is nowhere to be found among the guests and no one I ask has seen her recently. Maybe she's gone in search of some space and fresh air, away from the prying eyes and questions of the other guests. I head along the side of the ship, wondering what is going through Anna's mind right now. She was with Stella when she died; she was upset and hurt by Stella's behaviour towards her; and she fits the description of the waitress who asked Joe to spike Stella's drink. I reach the front of the yacht, where the walkway widens to create another outdoor space. There, leaning against the prow, is Anna, staring out to sea. She doesn't turn as I approach.

'Anna,' I say. She startles and turns to face me. She wipes her eyes with her sleeve and sniffs loudly. 'Sorry, I didn't mean to disturb your...' I trail off, not sure what word to use. Contemplation? Fear? Moment of regret?

I take her in, my first real suspect. Everything about her seems at odds with her boss. Anna's hair is white-blonde and cut into a bob that is slightly too short to frame her face properly. It's not a good colour on her – it's only just possible to see where her pale skin ends and her hair begins. Although she's probably average height, the outfit she's chosen makes her seem shorter. She's wearing a white shirt that looks at least one size too small, a calf-length skirt that skims her wide hips, and black slip-on trainers favoured among nurses... or waitresses.

Anna is nothing like her whippet-thin fashionista boss. What on earth Anna was doing working for someone like Stella is beyond me. Why would Anna, a woman who doesn't appear to care about fashion and seems – from my brief encounter with her – to be down to earth and normal, want to work for Stella Knight? And why would someone as image-obsessed as Stella have hired her? The two of them are an incongruous pair. It feels very *The Devil Wears Prada*.

'If you don't mind, I'd like to be alone,' she says, turning away to face the water again.

'I'm so sorry, Anna. This must be horrible for you.' I can tell that she isn't really listening. I draw closer to her and lower my voice. 'Do you have any idea what happened?'

'What do you mean? Stella is dead, that's what happened. What else is there?'

'There's the fact that Stella was murdered.'

Anna's head spins round, her blonde hair splaying out with the movement. 'What did you just say?'

'Stella was murdered,' I repeat.

'She... she was... she was murdered?' Anna stammers 'No. That's not possible. You're lying.' She flaps a hand in front of her face, desperately wafting air towards her. 'How do you... Are you sure?'

'Quite sure.'

'No? No!' A question, swiftly followed by a statement.

'Yes,' I say. 'I spoke to a bartender who told us that he was asked to make a drink for Stella and was given something to put into it.'

Anna starts tugging at her shirt. 'I can't breathe. This isn't happening. Murdered? Impossible.'

'And the waitress who asked the bartender to make the drink and gave him the substance fits your description almost exactly.'

Anna stops flapping, her hands drop to her sides and she stares at me straight.

'Excuse me?'

'The waitress that spiked Stella's drink was average height, with shoulder-length blonde hair.'

'No, I heard you. My brain is just trying to catch up with the fact that you're telling me Stella was murdered, and that you're accusing me of murdering her. Unbelievable.' Anna shakes her head and goes to sidestep me, but I move to block her. The waitress fits her description, I'm not letting her get away that easily, especially not given the conversation the two of us had earlier today. Anna and Stella were far from the best of friends.

'You didn't have anything to do with it?'

Anna's face darkens and she squares up to me. 'What a ludicrous suggestion. Of course I didn't have anything to do with it.'

'Then you won't mind answering some questions.'

'That's not how things work. Just because I don't want to answer the questions of a self-appointed investigator doesn't make me a murderer. You're an amateur. You're not the police. I don't have to talk to you at all.' Anna swerves around me and starts to march away.

'Yes, you're right,' I say, keeping pace with her strides, which are longer and speedier than one would expect. Anna pumps her hands by her sides as she drives forward, trying to get away. 'But when the police arrive, I will be telling them about the waitress, and that you were the last person to see Stella alive. And I'll tell them about the argument you had with her.'

Anna stops dead, still refusing to look at me. Her cheeks redden. 'My argument with Stella has nothing – *nothing* – to do with her death,' she says through gritted teeth.

'Then tell me. What do you think does have to do with her death?'

'Why? What has any of this got to do with you?'

'We won't be back to land for at least an hour, and in the time it takes us to get back, people with vital information might forget it. I'm trying to help the police.'

'I'm sure they're perfectly capable of doing the job themselves.' Her words are short and sharp.

'Maybe. But there's also the fact that we're trapped on a boat with a murderer. I don't know about you, but I'd rather know who they are than not.'

Anna's shoulders hunch forward. 'Fine. If I answer your questions, will you let me tell the police about my argument with Stella? I'd rather it comes from me than you.'

Knowing there is no way she can hold me to this I say, 'Sure.'

She points to a bench a little further along the deck. 'Let's go and sit there. I'll answer some questions. Some.'

Chapter Nine

The Social Sleuth, *extract from blog 39*

This wasn't the first time she had stolen from friends. The police discovered a pattern going back years of Paige befriending people, worming her way into their lives and then taking as much as she could.

Once seated, I pose my first question. 'From the beginning, can you tell me what happened today?'

Anna closes her eyes and massages her forehead as if trying to smooth out a lump.

'I barely saw Stella during the party. She was busy talking to people and having a good time. I was working, ensuring that her social media was updated and making some changes to her schedule for next week. It was only when I took my seat for the ceremony that I realised something was amiss. Christopher was there, but Stella wasn't. When the ceremony started and she still hadn't joined us he went to look for her. Then ten minutes or so later, Christopher texted me to say that he'd found her. She was completely wasted, and he needed me to help him get her to the suite.'

'Why couldn't he do that alone?' I ask.

'Things aren't great between them at the moment. She wouldn't go because he was asking her to.' Anna sounds mildly fed up. Obviously the strain on Christopher and Stella's marriage had had an impact on her as well.

'Go on,' I say, aware that I interrupted her flow.

'We both took her to the suite. She isn't heavy, but she was so out of it that it was difficult to manoeuvre her. When we got inside the room, she stumbled straight to the bathroom. Christopher told me to watch her and that he'd handle the ceremony, he said he'd tell everyone she was unwell. He left and I went to check on her. The bathroom stank, she'd been sick. It was everywhere: on her hands, in her hair, all over her dress. It was gross, unnatural even, for a person to be that sick. I went to Christopher to tell him I thought she needed a doctor but he said she didn't, that she'd be embarrassed if anyone saw her in that state.' Anna suddenly clamps a hand over her mouth. 'Do you think he knew?'

'Knew what?' I ask. Anna looks over her shoulder to check no one could be listening to us, but the deck is deserted.

'Knew that what she'd taken would kill her, and he wanted it to happen? No, that's ridiculous. It's ridiculous, isn't it?' Her whole body shakes and I'm reminded of my childhood dog, Pebble, on bonfire night, the way she'd skitter at every explosion. She was such a nervous little thing. My mum didn't want her but eventually she relented when she realised that it was enough to keep me contented in her absence. Pebble made it all bearable; with her my childhood was marginally less lonely.

'Statistically, the husband is the prime suspect,' I say, pushing away the thoughts of my past. 'So your thought isn't ridiculous. But do you have any evidence to back it up? Why would he want to kill his wife?'

Anna twists her hands in her lap. 'From what I saw, Stella was difficult to be married to.'

'How so?'

'She was... difficult to be around.'

'How long have you worked for her?'

'Eighteen months.'

'What was she like to work for?'

'Our earlier conversation made it clear what it was like to work for her.' She speaks softly, but her tone is at odds with her words. Anna sighs and wipes a tear from her cheek. 'Stella was difficult, demanding, and frankly, rude most of the time.'

'And yet even with all that, you've lasted longer than most of her other assistants. Why do you think that is?'

Anna's forehead creases. 'Who told you that?'

'Reiss Rose.'

'How would he know?'

'Reiss and Stella were friends.'

'Is that what he told you?' she asks. Anna's usually soft, innocent expression hardens a fraction. 'I wouldn't trust a word that comes out of the man's mouth.' She shakes her head and the glint of anger in her eyes disappears. 'Sorry, the people in this world. No matter how much they try to live up to their online personas, they can't do it. None of these people are who they say they are. They're not even who they think they are. It's complicated.'

There's an awkward silence between us, and I'm reminded of the comment Noel made earlier about people not being what they seem. I suddenly feel as if I've been thrown behind the scenes of a movie and the actors are no longer in character.

'But have you lasted longer than her other assistants?'

'From what I've gathered, yes.'

'Why?'

'Because I don't have the luxury of quitting my job when it gets tough. I have responsibilities.'

'Unlike the assistants before you?' I ask, annoyed at her tone. There's a touch of self-righteousness to Anna that doesn't sit well with me. She chose to work in this world, so I don't know when she climbed onto this high horse. Anna brushes imaginary crumbs from her skirt and sniffs before continuing.

'Stella went through a phase of hiring younger versions of herself. Rich, beautiful, entitled. The type of girl born with a silver spoon in their mouth. The girls weren't cut out to work with her, they were weak and would always eventually be broken by her... expectations.'

Of all the words one could use to describe the woman sitting next to me, strong isn't one of the ones I'd have used. Everything about her looks soft and gentle, one of those women who look maternal for no apparent reason. But then I think of Stella. She had the entire world fooled. Appearances can be deceiving.

'What responsibilities are so important that you stayed working for a boss who was horrible to you?' I'm not judging her for being in a job she doesn't like, my own job doesn't exactly make me want to jump for joy every morning. I stay in it because I have to pay rent, but it is at least bearable. I don't think any amount of money would make me endure the daily bullying it sounds like Anna put up with from Stella.

'My responsibilities are irrelevant,' replies Anna with a hint of steel. There again, a glimpse of something more underneath the soft exterior. Though strong and hardened might look the same at first glance.

'So every assistant that worked for Stella quit after several months and she didn't realise she was the problem?' I shake my head in disbelief at how ignorant people can be.

'They didn't *all* quit. She fired a fair number too,' says Anna.

'Do you think any of the assistants she fired still hold a grudge?'

'I have no idea,' says Anna. 'It seems extreme. And I know I said I need this job, and I do, but I think if she fired me part of me would be relieved, like she was putting me out of my misery. Maybe they felt the same.'

I raise my eyebrow. She talks about being fired like people talk about euthanasia.

'Reiss told me that Stella gave up drinking and drugs about eighteen months ago. Did you have anything to do with that?'

'No, but maybe that's another reason why I stayed as long as I have in comparison to earlier assistants. Stella isn't – wasn't – the most reasonable person at the best of times. Add alcohol into that mix and I can see it getting very messy.'

'Was there a reason she stopped drinking?'

Anna pauses and takes a deep breath. 'There was, but it isn't my place to tell you. When I found her today, I assumed she'd fallen off the wagon. It wasn't that surprising. Not after all she's been through.'

'What do you mean?' I ask. My tone and unmistakable curiosity seems to scare Anna and she leans away from me, crosses one leg over the other and busies herself with smoothing out her skirt. 'Anna,' I press. 'This might be important.'

'Even though Stella's dead, I'm still not sure if I should tell you. I don't want to draw attention to it.'

'Don't you want to find out what happened to Stella?'

Anna sighs heavily. 'Stella was...' Anna looks behind her once again. Content that we are alone, she leans towards me. 'She was worried about some messages she saw about herself.'

'Like what? Death threats?'

'No, they weren't death threats. The messages weren't sent to her. There's this website called *hashtagnofilter*. It's half blog, half forum, sort of like *Gossip Girl* for influencers. The blog usually publishes articles about influencers and the forum is for people with nothing better to do in their lives than bitch about the celeb du jour.'

'I've never heard of it,' I say. 'What was on there that was worrying her?'

'There was one user on there called...' Anna clicks her fingers, trying to remember. 'I can't remember the name. Anyway, this user was always starting threads about Stella, saying that they would stop at nothing to bring her down.'

'Bloody hell, that's horrible.'

'You clearly haven't spent enough time on the internet. People are awful. Honestly, the internet is a burning hellfire of shit. For every ten people who say the sun shines out of Stella's arse, there's one person who says she's a Russian spy or goes into grotesque detail about the stuff they'd like to do to her. It really is quite horrible. But this particular user said that the truth about her would bring her down.'

'And what's the truth?' I ask her.

'I don't know.'

'Is it the reason she stopped drinking?' I ask Anna.

'I doubt it,' she replies. 'Stella was beside herself about it all. A few months ago, she asked me to contact the website about it. She was threatening to take them to court over it.'

'Did it work?' I ask.

Anna laughs. 'No! In fact, it made it worse. The website then posted an article called "The thread Stella Knight doesn't want you to see".'

'So did the article give any more information?'

'It wasn't anything specific. Just that Stella was a dangerous influence, that she was a fraud, that she should be banned from the internet, and that this user knew the truth of what she really was.'

'But the article didn't give any more specifics?' I'm repeating myself now but I'm desperate. Someone out there has information about Stella and it could be vital to this case. It could change everything.

'No, but even so, Stella was frantic, and she remained touchy about it. She asked me to do a daily sweep of the forums in case the threads started again.'

'And did they?' I ask.

'Yes, once a week or so, the user would post a new thread or comment on other threads. Why can't I remember the name? I read it so many times. Sorry, it will come to me.'

'What did Stella say about the posts?'

'She said she was worried they'd try to bring her down. I say worried, but what she actually said was that she needed to find a way to stop this, or we'd both be out of a fucking job. Stella liked to swear. I offered to look into it but she didn't want that. She said I'd already fucked up trying to contact the website, completely forgetting the fact that it was her idea to contact them, not mine. So I didn't dig any deeper and left it at that. Working for her was… well, I just did as I was asked and didn't ask any questions. It was easier that way. It was the only way to get through it. Do you think this has something to do with her death?'

I don't answer Anna's question – I'm not here to speculate with her. Instead I change the subject. 'Aside from that, how was she?' I ask.

'It's really hard for me to say. She was always the same with me, but she was getting more obsessed with what was being said about her on this website.' Anna suddenly claps her hands together, making me jump. 'Make it, don't fake it,' she exclaims.

'Excuse me?'

'Make It, Don't Fake It, that's the name of the user on the forum. Make It, Don't Fake It, they were the one who kept posting saying that Stella was a dangerous influence and should be stopped.'

Make It, Don't Fake It.

'I don't want to take much more of your time, Anna,' I say, realising how long we've been chatting and how many more people I want to talk to. 'But I saw Stella in conversation with a woman earlier today and it looked like they were arguing. Do you know anything about that?'

Anna purses her lips. 'No idea, sorry.'

'OK. Well, thank you for your time.' She knows she is being dismissed and stands, about to walk away. But then she stops and looks down at me, her face serious.

'I just want to say again, like I said at the beginning, I wouldn't have done anything to hurt Stella. I needed this job, so I wouldn't have killed her.' Anna's eyes burn into mine and she shudders. Then she turns on her heels and stalks off. I watch her disappear. I'm convinced there is more to Anna than meets the eye, and I need to keep mine firmly on her.

–

Reiss and I stand side by side looking out as the yacht curves its way back up the Thames and towards Canary Wharf. The evening sunlight peeks through the gaps between the giant towers that compete with each other to be the biggest, the tallest. It's a reminder that there is a world that exists outside this boat, beyond the investigation that has consumed my focus. A reminder that there are still billions of people in the world, going about their lives like it's an ordinary day.

The buildings still stand sentinel, protecting the stressed, frantic people inside, enabling them to make as much money as they possibly can for faceless corporations. What would they do if one of their number was murdered? Hush it up, probably. The management would say things like, 'That sort of thing doesn't happen here. Not at Gerald, Hugh and Wiseman,' or whatever man's name, man's name and man's name applies. The company where I waste a nauseating number of my hours – also named after a man for whom none of us except maybe the partners feel any personal attachment – would do the same. They are lawyers, after all. I've always thought lawyers would make the best criminals; it takes one to know one, as they say.

'So, Christopher wouldn't speak to you?' I ask, shaking away the thought of my day job.

'No,' says Reiss. 'But it is understandable. His wife is barely cold and I'm asking him what happened. I did tell him about her drink being spiked though.'

'What did he say to that?'

'That I was a disgusting human being for spreading rumours and using his wife's death to raise my own profile.'

My face creases when I hear of Christopher's reaction. 'If someone came to me and told me my wife's drink had been spiked, I'd be horrified. I wouldn't instantly dismiss it as a rumour.'

Reiss nods, solemnly. 'I thought exactly the same thing. Do you think Christopher Clarke should be suspect numero uno?'

I purse my lips. Christopher's reaction is unnatural, bordering on cruel, and he is painting himself as a man who couldn't care less about his wife. It would be so easy to say yes, let's close all other lines of enquiry and focus our efforts on the person statistically most likely to have done this. But I have to be smarter than that. I have to consider all the possibilities, not just follow the easiest, most obvious path. I shake my head. 'No, not yet. There are other suspects – Anna Nicholls for one. That said, we should keep a close eye on him.'

'What do you make of Anna?' asks Reiss.

I think of the way Anna shook nervously, and how her eyes looked almost dead with exhaustion; of her quickness to anger and defensiveness; of what she said and what she didn't say.

'She didn't try to make herself look good when she answered my questions. She didn't pretend to like Stella or pretend that she didn't have reasons for killing her. She said she needed the job and that she wouldn't kill Stella because of that. I want to believe she's telling the truth, but all I know about her is what she has told me. She could be lying about everything, and she was cagey about a few points. Once we're off the boat I want to investigate Anna more, see if we can't find out what she doesn't want to tell us. There isn't much time until the yacht moors in London and we will be overrun with police officers, but there's still so much I want to find out.'

'What should I do?' asks Reiss. He rocks backward and forward on his heeled shoes, displaying a nervous energy I hadn't noticed before.

'There's a website, *hashtagnofilter*, do you know it?'

Reiss's nostrils flare and he shivers as if he's just found a spider in his hair. 'Urgh, yes! I've been featured a number of times. It's vicious stuff.'

'Well, there was someone called Make It, Don't Fake It on there who was apparently trying to bring Stella down.'

'Bring her down? What does that even mean?'

'Not sure yet, but do you think you could find out what was being said about Stella by this user on the forums?'

Reiss nods. 'I'm sure I can. But you do know there is probably a whole section of the website just dedicated to slagging her off. I say that because there's a whole area dedicated to slagging me off,' he adds at my raised eyebrow.

I could ask what is being said about him on these forums, but I don't. 'Could you get onto that now?' I ask instead. Reiss gives me a fake salute, whips out his phone and starts typing away. Then he stops suddenly and looks up at me.

'And what will you do?' he asks.

'I'm going to find the woman I saw earlier, the one who was arguing with Stella.'

The other guests have barely moved since I was last on top deck. This time a few of them eye me as I wander among them but quickly turn away when I glance in their direction. Maybe they know I'm asking questions, maybe they know I've posted about my investigation. But I'm not interested in any of them, I'm looking for a woman who looks nothing like these people, a woman who looks more like me – who lacks poise and polish. The woman who was arguing with Stella, like me, isn't one of the beautiful ones.

As I walk away from the group, a head turns, following me. Their stare burns into my skin and I glance towards it out of the corner of my eye. The face doesn't shy away like the others did; the eyes don't flicker in a different direction but drink me in before narrowing. My breath catches in my throat as the face scowls and the nostrils flare. My feet want to drag me away but I force myself to move slowly to show I'm not scared. I'm determined to continue my search for the ginger-haired woman, and I push from my mind the fact that Christopher Clarke is watching my every move.

Chapter Ten

The Social Sleuth, *extract from blog 9*

The moral of this tragic story is that bullying kills.

It takes a while for me to find the ginger-haired woman, but eventually I do. She's nestled in one of the deep windowsills behind the glass staircase I'd taken a picture beside earlier. Her forehead is pressed against the glass of the window, her knees drawn up close to her body. Her dress is a deep crimson, made from cheap chiffon material. Around her wedding finger there's a silver ring nestled below an engagement ring with a small diamond. Her nails are bare and frayed. She's a nail-biter, an awful habit that I'm guilty of too. As a teenager my mum used to slap my hand away from my mouth every time she caught me doing it, chastising me for adopting such 'disgusting' behaviour. I never told her she was the reason I did it, but then she never asked.

'Hello?' I say, taking a step closer to the window. The woman's body jolts violently at my words, nearly toppling her off the sill. 'Sorry, I didn't mean to make you jump.' She puts her legs on the floor and stands up. She's so short in stature that her height barely changes. Her round face is blotchy, flushes of pink and red splattered across her cheeks, and she's breathing heavily. 'Are you OK?'

'Fine. Just want to get home. Terrible business.' The woman keeps her head bowed as she speaks to me, her broad shoulders curled inwards.

'I wanted to ask you a few questions. Can I sit down?' I ask, and gesture to the window seat she just vacated. She shakes her head and goes to walk past me, but I don't move to let her.

'I don't want to answer any questions,' she says, trying to sidestep me. I block her once more.

'I saw you arguing with Stella Knight earlier.'

The woman looks up at me with narrowed eyes. She's close enough now for me to see the sheen of sweat dotted along her upper lip and for me to smell the musty body odour coming from her, but this part of the yacht it isn't warm enough to sweat this profusely – quite the opposite; in here it's cold.

'I don't know what you're talking about,' she says, avoiding my eye. Her accent is local, born and raised London.

'What you argued about might be important.' She does know what I'm talking about, despite what she says.

'She's dead,' replies the woman.

'Yes, but—'

The woman cuts me off. 'Nothing I can do or say can change that.'

'No, you can't change the fact that Stella is dead, but Stella was murdered by someone on this boat, and I intend to find out who.'

'If someone decided to murder Stella Knight, that's their decision. It's nothing to do with me.' This time she doesn't try to sidestep me but raises her hand and shoves me out of the way. The force of her push takes me by surprise, and I trip over my own feet, toppling with a thump to the floor. Pain shoots through my arm from the hand that stretched out to soften my fall. The woman storms away, the chiffon of her dress billowing behind her like flames. I scramble back to a standing position.

'Hey,' I call after her, but she doesn't turn back around. 'Come back!' I hurry behind her, calling out again. The woman runs along the corridor towards the ladies' toilets at the end. She presses her hand against the door handle and rushes in. The wooden door swings shut in my face, making a heavy clunk as it collides with the frame, shortly followed by the click of a lock. I raise my fist and knock against it a few times.

'What were you arguing with Stella about?' I call through the door. She doesn't answer me and there is no sound coming from inside the toilet. I knock again. 'The police will want to know the same thing, because I will be telling them about you.' Frustration at her lack of cooperation rises in me. This woman was arguing with Stella an hour before she was found dead, and now she is refusing to speak to me. She's suspicious, and I want to know what she is hiding. I knock and call again, but my threats have no effect on her. She is unmoved. The door remains resolutely shut, keeping me from vital information.

Someone grabs my arm, their fingers pinching hard into the skin. My heart jolts in panic; I didn't hear or see anyone approaching me.

'Ouch!' I yelp, yanking my arm away and spinning round to face my attacker. I raise my fists in front of my face, ready to defend myself from this ambush.

'Sorry,' says Reiss. He steps away from me and the door, his cheeks flushing. 'That was harder than I meant it to be.' He bites his lip. 'Did I hurt you?'

'What the hell? What are you doing sneaking up on me like that?' I rub my upper arm. The stinging subsides faster than my heartbeat.

'I wasn't sneaking up on you. You were too focused on banging on the toilet door to notice me. Anyway, you can tell me what that was all about later.' He nods towards the door that he doesn't know is hiding the ginger-haired woman. 'There's something I want to show you,' he says, suddenly serious. 'Come with me.'

–

Reiss and I sit on the balcony of his suite with his laptop and the website *hashtagnofilter* open in front of us. Darkness is here; it was slow and almost imperceptible at first but like a hand smothering a candle, the day is snuffed out. The yacht chugs slowly along the Thames, the lights of the buildings flickering alongside us like the flashes of paparazzi cameras. A taste of what will await us when we dock, perhaps. There can't be much time until we do. There isn't much time until the head start I had on the police dwindles away and my suspects scatter across London.

'It wasn't difficult to find,' says Reiss. 'It only took a simple search. I hope you're prepared, it makes for uncomfortable reading.'

The laptop screen shines brightly in the darkness, the light bouncing off Reiss's face. He looks ghostly, illuminated like this. His nails clack as he taps on the keyboard, typing 'Make It, Don't Fake It'. The whole page fills with search results. Whoever this person is, they've been busy. He selects the latest post, created less than a week ago. It already has pages and pages of replies, but it's the title of the thread that feels like a kick in the stomach:

> Stella Knight is a pill-popping whore and
> it's time someone ripped her clothes off and
> exposed who she really is.

'Jesus,' I say.

'Oh yeah,' says Reiss, giving me a sideways look. 'It ain't cute and it ain't pretty.'

'Why do people write this stuff?'

'No idea, but it's gross.'

'What do they say about you?' I ask.

'I stopped reading it years ago,' he says, and I frown, unsure whether I believe him. 'Honestly sweetie, it is *so* addictive, and there's a huge part of you that wants to reason with these people. These people who spend their free time conducting character assassinations all over the internet. But there's no point, so I learned to let it go.'

We continue to scroll down the page. It's full of comment after comment about how fake Stella is; about how she doesn't deserve to be as successful as she is; about how annoying her voice is; about how idiotic her husband is. The comments are indescribably horrible and vindictive and, worst of all, anonymous. Everything is posted under pseudonyms like KisslikeCyanide and Hereforthethrill/inforthekill. If every single commenter here hated Stella as much as they say they do, then this opens up at least a hundred other suspects.

'Go back to the top,' I say, pressing my finger against the screen. My heart pounds against my chest as I see the name that Anna had told me to look out for.

> Make It, Don't Fake It: Need to update
> the thread title from pill-popping whore to
> DEAD pill-popping whore... LOL

Make It, Don't Fake It: Stella has been so
desperado to stay relevant. I bet she'd be quite
happy with being murdered.

Reiss clutches his stomach. 'We only spoke to a few
people; I can't believe the news that Stella is dead has made
it off the yacht so quickly.'

'Maybe it has or maybe it hasn't,' I say, turning from
the screen to stare at the side of Reiss's spotlighted face.
'I don't have that many followers, it can't have all come
from my post. What if this Make It, Don't Fake It is on
the yacht with us?'

Beneath the light of the laptop screen, Reiss's eyes
flicker and he shudders. 'Do you think Make It, Don't
Fake It is the killer?'

'They seem to hate Stella, whoever they are.' I think of
the thread's title. 'Expose who she really is. What could
they expose?'

Reiss places the laptop down and crosses one of his
legs over the other before answering. 'Her treatment of
her assistants? Do you think Anna is Make It, Don't Fake
It?'

I contemplate this. Would Anna have pointed in this
direction if she was to blame? I get to my feet. 'I don't
know, but I think we ought to ask her.'

Without warning, the floor beneath my feet shifts
position and my shoulder smacks against the glass of the
balcony. My hands reach out, searching for something to
hold on to, the muscles in my legs tense and my feet grip
the floor, terrified another jolt will send me tipping off
the edge and into the dark waters below. Lights from the
shore bulge and swell in my vision.

'Shit! What was that?' I ask, but as the words tumble
from my mouth, I realise that I know the answer to the

question. 'Come on,' I say, flying from the balcony and through Reiss's room. A second bump sends me sideways, but I regain my balance quickly. I bound up the stairs and head back onto the top deck to see what is waiting for us.

–

'Please can I have your attention?' Dean's voice comes through the speakers to my left and right. 'We have now docked in Shad Thames. I've been instructed to ask you to please stay where you are.'

'Oh my God,' cries a voice from somewhere in the darkness. The people around me swivel to see what's caused the shout. Seconds later, a wave of the same sentiment crashes through the crowd. Ignoring Dean's words, there's a stampede to the side of the yacht nearest to the land.

'What is it?' Reiss asks. I push my way through the throngs of people and clamber up onto one of the benches. Reiss climbs up beside me and we both crane our necks to get a better look over the mass of whispering heads. Reiss's hand darts out and grabs my arm, squeezing it tightly. His taloned fingers dig into my skin, making my eyes water, but the pain is nothing compared to the shock that courses through my body when I see what caused him to squeeze my arm in the first place.

'Bloody hell,' I whisper.

The scene alongside the yacht is one that you'd only expect to see in a high-octane police drama. It's surreal to see it here before my eyes. Lights are flashing, sirens are pipping and people are shouting. But among all the hubbub of activity, there are two people standing still like statues: a male and a female police officer, positioned shoulder to shoulder, their faces pointed directly towards the ship. For them, the investigation is just about to begin. One that will be followed by an army of online warriors who scrutinise their every move, waiting with bated breath to find out what happened to their precious leader. My teeth press against my bottom lip so hard I'm in danger of drawing blood. Now that I'm here, I suddenly wonder if I've made a huge mistake by inserting myself into this investigation.

–

Reiss and I face Shad Thames and the flurry of activity below. A camera flashes in the darkness, setting off the others until the sky is ablaze. Two men with their heads bowed walk either side of a stretcher upon which rests a body bag, inky black despite the flash photography. Reiss intertwines his fingers with mine and clasps my hand.

'Goodbye, Stella,' he whispers. His words are like a knife to the chest, and I tighten my grip, hoping to convey my support. As the stretcher is loaded into the back of a waiting car, I tug Reiss away, back to the activity encircling us on the deck.

The deck is now crawling with officers, moving around the guests, taking names, addresses and initial statements. Their movements are slow and methodical, like sharks haunting schools of fish. Two plainclothes detectives, notebooks in hand, stand talking to Dean, who hops from foot to foot, twitching like he's just snorted a line of cocaine.

'Excuse me a minute,' I say to Reiss. I slip away from him, moving closer to Dean and the detectives. One of them, a pale-faced woman, poses a question to Dean. Her male colleague, as dark as she is pale, stands beside her, nodding as Dean speaks. It's impossible to fight my desire to hear what is being said. I grab an empty drinks tray from behind the bar and head towards the cocktail table nearest to them. None of the waiting staff have wanted to get close, perhaps for fear of intruding, but the table needs clearing so, waiter's tray in hand, I edge closer.

'Just remind me of the timings,' says the male officer. His voice is soft, at odds with his stern expression.

'From about two thirty p.m. I was inside, preparing for the ceremony. Reviewing my lines and the nominees, the usual stuff. Came onstage at a couple of minutes to four.'

The threesome doesn't notice my approach. The officers are too interested in Dean, who continues to twitch like they have him on the rack. I set the tray down gently on the table closest to the officers and, with my back to them, start slowly picking up glasses.

'And then,' the officer prompts.

'Pretty normal, I called all the award categories. Got to Stella, called her name, she didn't come up. Found her husband in the crowd, the seat next to him was empty. He got up and said she was feeling seasick and had gone to bed.'

'Then what?'

'Then I'm being told Stella has been found dead.'

The table I'm clearing is small, the number of glasses left dwindles, and with it my excuse for loitering. But there's another not too far away. I pick up the tray; it's laden now and difficult to manoeuvre, but I grip the edge tightly and take slow, steady steps, keeping an ear tilted towards the conversation.

'We'll need room numbers,' says the female officer. She doesn't sound as gentle as her colleague. 'Who found the body?'

'Her assistant, Anna, was with her when she died, I think. But it was one of the guests that informed me.'

'OK. We'll want to speak with both of them.'

'Yes, of course,' replies Dean.

'Thank you,' says the female police officer. I chance a glance over my shoulder in time to see her nod her head to Dean in a way that suggests she wants the details now.

'Oh. Yes. Sure. I... I'll tell them to meet you in the lobby,' he says, and scuttles off, thankfully not noticing me. I turn back to the table and occupy myself with rearranging the glasses.

'What now, boss?' the female officer asks.

'Let's speak to the husband first,' he says. 'He'll be able to give us a more accurate idea of Stella's movements.'

'Can we help you?' the female officer barks. I look around so sharply that I knock over three half-filled champagne flutes. The liquid splatters over the white tablecloth, darkening it with damp. One of the glasses then rolls sideways and falls, fracturing in half upon impact with the floor. The noise is like a gunshot and people turn to look in my direction.

'Sorry, sorry,' I say, picking up the toppled glasses and placing them on my tray. The eyes of the detectives are on me, making the hairs on the back of my neck prick up. I lift the tray and hurry from them, keeping my head bowed, praying they'll just think I'm a curious bystander. They must encounter lots of those in their job. People can be so nosy, especially when something as dramatic as this happens.

I reach the bar and heave the tray upwards, setting it in front of a bartender who's loading them into plastic racks ready for the dishwasher. He doesn't question why I'm helping. Under the pretence that I'm stretching my neck, I rest my chin on my shoulder and glance at the officers. The ashen face of the female officer is staring right at me, and for a fraction of second we lock eyes. Before I can pull my gaze away, she frowns, as if making a mental note to keep an eye on me.

Chapter Eleven

The Social Sleuth, *extract from blog 1*

> Karen Frond is the genius behind netsleuths.com and the inspiration for The Social Sleuth. Her work has helped the police on numerous occasions.

Reiss and I sit in chairs in the yacht's lobby and watch the two detectives talk in hushed tones with their heads tilted together. It's almost ten o'clock in the evening now and still not the end of what has been a very long day. I should be exhausted but I'm not – the adrenaline that courses through my body pushes off any tiredness. Stella Knight, the queen of the internet, is dead, and I was there. Today has been like none I've ever had before in my life, and none I hope to ever have again.

The hair on my arms stands on end as a chill runs over my skin, but despite this my hands are clammy and heat swells in my armpits. My knees bounce up and down with the same nervous tic that Dean displayed. I press my hands against them to keep them still. The officers glance over – their eyes are on me and my eyes are on them. They don't look away, so neither do I. They might intimidate me, but I'm not showing them that. Their feelings towards me will change when they hear what I've discovered and how much I've helped them.

They each grab a green velvet chair and plonk them in front of us. The male officer smiles, showing large, straight teeth. He has a kind face, and the small amount of excess weight he carries fills his cheeks, giving him a gentleness that his colleague doesn't possess. She doesn't smile and her cheekbones, angular and sharp, threaten us like a knife-edge. Smile, frown. Soft, hard. Good cop, bad cop personified.

'Good evening. I'm Detective Inspector Matthew Alebiosu, and this is my colleague, Detective Sergeant Angela Swain.'

'Nice to meet you both,' I say. Angela raises an eyebrow and I want to kick myself. I shouldn't say it's nice to meet them when a woman is dead. For a moment there's a silence; it hangs between us, oppressive, pushing me to fill it, but I shouldn't. They are the true investigators of this case, not me, and I'm suddenly gripped with a fear of being reprimanded for sticking my nose into their business. 'What a terrible thing to happen. Have you investigated many deaths on boats before? Sorry, I don't know why I asked that. I've got to admit, this whole business is making me nervous.'

Reiss's eyes bore into the side of my head. He's silently asking me what the fuck I'm twittering on about. What *am* I twittering on about?

'Nervous? Why does it make you nervous?' asks Angela in a way that seems to suggest I've given her a vital clue to the case. My heart quickens and I scramble to answer her.

'I'd never seen a dead body before today,' I say, truthfully, 'and I've never been interviewed by the police before. Seeing her, Stella I mean, lying there, it was horrible. So, so horrible.' I don't add that I'm nervous they'll find out about my social media post or that I've been asking questions. Angela's snappy questions and evident short-temperedness have convinced me they won't want my help, and that if they find out I've been investigating I'll be in trouble. Angela's long, pale fingers flick open her notebook and she holds her pen poised over the paper. Her piercing blue eyes bore into mine and she makes a note of something. I shiver. This woman is cold in every sense of the word.

She's only doing her job, I remind myself, and she wouldn't be doing her job if she didn't treat everyone with suspicion. She isn't here to be my friend. I take in her posture and poise: how content she is to sit in silence; how she doesn't rush into asking her first question; how her eyes take in every part of me, from my head to my toes; how she seems to be assessing everything. I'm sure I could learn a thing or two from her.

'Maggie, is it?' she asks. I nod and she follows suit. 'Great, could you tell us a little bit more about yourself, Maggie?'

I draw back in my seat. I wasn't expecting that question. I clear my throat.

'Of course. I'm Maggie, Margaret Shaw. I'm twenty-eight years old, soon to be twenty-nine. I'm from Kent but live in London now.'

'What were you doing at the Influencer of the Year awards, were you up for an award?'

'Gosh no, it'll be a long time before I'm up for any awards. No, I was invited.'

'By whom?'

'The organisers. They sent me an email, do you want to see it?'

'Please.'

My cheeks warm as I scramble about in my bag to find my phone. 'Here.' I hold the screen towards them and Matthew scrolls down as he reads.

'You say it will be a long time before you're up for any awards. Did the invitation come as a surprise?'

'Absolutely,' I reply. 'I'd heard that they reserve spots for newcomers, so it's a huge honour to be considered. Obviously, until all this happened.'

Both the officers note this down. It's Matthew's turn to speak now. He leans forward and points his pen at Reiss. 'And you?'

'I'm Reiss Rose, I'm twenty-six years old, and I'm originally from Birmingham but I now live about ten minutes that way.' He points his finger towards one of the windows in the direction of the historic warehouses I saw earlier today.

'Reiss,' says Angela. 'You were invited to the awards ceremony as a nominee?'

'Yes. No. I mean I was, but I pulled out of the running.'

'You pulled out?' I ask, surprised. DS Angela Swain purses her lips but refrains from reminding me that she is the one asking the questions.

'I've been nominated for the best make-up artist award for the last five years, but it's an *always the bridesmaid, never the bride* situation. Couldn't face another failure this year so I took myself out of the running.'

'And you have how many followers?'

'One million, twenty thousand and forty-seven, at my last count.'

Detective Sergeant Angela Swain attempts to hide her scoff as a cough.

'And how long have you two been friends?'

'Hours, we only met today at the event. Why?' I reply.

'We'll ask the questions, if you don't mind,' cuts in Angela.

'Of course, sorry,' I hastily reply, but inside I'm cursing her. The tone she's decided to take with me isn't necessary. It's not a crime to find a dead body, and she's hardly making either of us want to tell her anything. I wanted to help them, but now I'm not so sure if I should.

'What time did you arrive at the yacht today?' asks Matthew.

'I arrived around twelve o'clock, in time for the welcome drinks,' I say.

'I was here much earlier; I was allocated a room for the day. So, I got here at ten-ish,' says Reiss. He has barely moved a muscle since the officers sat down. It's like he is purposefully not moving, as if he's worried any fidget will be misconstrued as guilt.

Matthew's pen scratches against his notepad, his hand flowing in calm, deft movements. He looks up and I snatch my eyes away.

'And when did you realise that something had happened to Stella?' he asks.

I glance at Reiss, and he nods curtly, offering me the floor to answer.

'I heard she was unwell at the same time as everyone else,' I say. 'When she didn't come to collect her award and her husband got up and said she was seasick. But just before that, I accidentally overheard a conversation between Stella and her husband. She seemed to have had too much to drink and he was livid about it. He was rough with her. I was about to intervene when Stella's assistant Anna appeared. Stella's husband told Anna to get rid of her. Get rid of Stella. Something in his tone worried me, so I went to Stella's room to check everything was OK.

When Anna answered, Stella was already dead. Dead in the bathroom, her body slumped against the toilet bowl.'

'To confirm, Stella was dead when you found her?' asks Matthew.

'Yes, I think so. I'm not a doctor or a medical expert, so I couldn't say with certainty, but she wasn't breathing, and I couldn't feel a pulse. That was when I went to tell Dean, the managing director.'

'This was murder,' chips in Reiss. Two pairs of eyes zoom in on him and he gulps, audibly. 'We chatted to one of the bartenders. He told us that he put something in Stella's drink.'

'What did he look like?'

'Tall, young. He was called Joe. He said that someone asked him to put something in Stella's drink.'

Matthew's nostrils flare, a minimal reaction to the news that this won't be an open and shut case. Both he and Angela make notes and I imagine the words *This was murder* scrawled across the page in large letters.

'What made you talk to the bartender about this?'

Before I can say anything, Reiss answers. 'It was me. I encouraged the conversation. I spoke to Maggie because something felt off about Stella's death. I was convinced of... er... foul play.' He reddens and hurries to give the same explanation he gave me about Stella's sobriety and appearance-driven personality. His rosy cheeks and fervent chatter make him look like a child weaving an elaborate tale about why his homework is late; I'm reminded of a book Jessica used to read to me about a little girl full of stories about how she cut her knee, each of them more fanciful than the last.

'Did you notice anything suspicious at the ceremony?' The detective inspector directs his question towards me.

'Er...' I trail off, unsure how to answer his question. Suspicious is a wide spectrum, an adjective that has the ability to change even the most harmless of interactions. There's Noel and his overbearing wife; Anna telling me how awful Stella was to work for; the woman arguing with Stella; the *hashtagnofilter* forum. All of these things are suspicious to varying degrees, given the circumstances.

'Anna told me that she wanted to get a doctor for Stella, that she knew she needed help, but that Stella's husband said no, his wife would be fine. He was quite serious about it; he didn't want the ceremony stopping on her account. I thought he looked like a nice man, but appearances can be deceiving.'

'He also didn't seem shocked when I told him her drink had been spiked,' adds Reiss.

'Thank for your sharing that,' says Matthew as both officers make notes in their books. 'Is there anything else we might need to know?'

I waver. I'd intended to tell the police everything and position myself as someone who could help them, but the detective sergeant has spooked me. I bite my lip.

'Maggie?' presses Matthew, correctly sensing I have more.

'Stella and her assistant Anna didn't have a good relationship,' I say, deciding that the information I've uncovered is important and I might get in more trouble for withholding it. 'From what we've been told Stella was a bully. And she was being trolled on an online forum called *hashtagnofilter*. Oh, and she had an argument with a short, ginger-haired woman. I don't know what they argued about but Stella looked pissed about it and the woman locked herself in a toilet to avoid talking to me about it.'

The words fall out of me, like my lips are floodgates and I've opened them wide. The officers raise their eyebrows in unison, their hands scrambling to keep track of revelations.

'How did you find out all of this?' asks Angela.

'I wanted to be helpful,' I say with conviction, choosing to ignore how Angela's lips curl.

'And Maggie, what's your, er, area of business?' asks Matthew, giving away how unsure he is about how to properly phrase any questions related to influencer culture.

'True crime,' I say. Angela can't stop herself from rolling her eyes at my words. But I don't let her disdain affect me. Millions of people find crime interesting – it makes up a huge bulk of the books we read, the films we watch, the stories in our newspapers. She's wrong to judge me, to dismiss me.

'I see,' she replies, in a way that suggests she doesn't see. She glances at her watch.

'Is there anything else you think we ought to know?' asks Matthew.

I glance at Reiss, who shakes his head. 'No,' I say, 'I think that's everything.'

'Well then, you're free to leave the yacht. Thank you for everything you've done so far.' He rips a piece of paper from his notebook and scribbles something down. 'Here's my mobile number.' He hands me the piece of paper. 'If you do remember anything else that will help this investigation, please don't hesitate to contact me.' Matthew gives us both a smile.

'Also, it would be best if you left this investigation to us from now on. How does that sound?' says Angela, in as condescending a manner as she can.

'Thank you, officers.' I accept the paper Matthew is holding. The two of them rise and put the chairs back where they got them from. As they turn to walk away I add, 'I understand. I'll leave this investigation to the professionals.'

–

Reiss is in his room packing while I wait for him in the lobby. After the two police officers left us, I gave Reiss my assurances that our pursuit of justice for Stella wouldn't end here. It would be wrong to abandon what we've started. He suggested we go back to his apartment, since it's nearby, and we have much to discuss. It's late and I should've said I needed to go home, but I didn't. I have nothing to go home for.

I don't how long it will take Reiss to organise himself, so I decide to make good use of the time available and read more of the *hashtagnofilter* threads. Plonking myself in one of the lobby chairs, I pull my phone out of my handbag and press the home screen, but nothing happens. Bollocks – the battery has died. I untangle my charger from the bottom of my bag and plug it into a nearby socket. The cord isn't long enough to reach the chair, so I perch on the edge of the deep windowsill where the ginger-haired woman had hidden herself before. While my phone fires up, I look out to the shore below. It isn't the circus it was before; there are still several police cars parked up, but their sirens are off now. The people are little more than black dots scurrying around like ants on a lollipop. Then, the cameras flash. I press my forehead against the glass as the camera's subject is given the limelight.

'Oh my God,' I whisper. I frantically try to turn my phone on, desperate to capture this moment myself, but it doesn't have enough life in it yet. All I can do is watch as Anna and Christopher are escorted by officers from the yacht, along what was once the red carpet, and guided into the back of a police car. The car's beams flick on and the paparazzi step back to allow it to drive its charges away.

Buzz. Buzz. Buzz. My phone awakens from the dead, bringing with it all the notifications I've missed since it's been off. Before I even have the chance to review then, it vibrates again as a call from my sister, Jessica, comes in.

Can't she ever leave me alone?

I swipe the call away, forcing it to go to voicemail. I'm not answering her. If it's important she'll leave a message, she always does. A notification pops up barely seconds later informing me that I have one new voicemail. I sigh and, giving up my fight to avoid her, I dial in to listen.

'M,' she barks as soon as the message begins. 'Where the hell are you? I've been calling and texting all day and I've not heard from you. I am *sick* with worry. Why aren't you replying to my texts or my calls? Call me as soon as you get this.'

I take a deep steadying breath, reminding myself that Jessica is a wonderful woman and an extraordinary sister. But it's impossible to shrug off how tense she makes me, and it's difficult not to associate her with hard times. When I was a child she was my caregiver, forced to take the role that Mum should have occupied. Barely fifteen years old and giving up her childhood to care for me, her five-year-old sister. If she resents me for her sacrifice she hides it well. Better than I do.

It's not that I'm not grateful for everything she's done, but sometimes she takes it too far. A day when I don't check in sees her catastrophising, imagining my demise.

Jessica and I are the type of sisters that the expression chalk and cheese was created for: she's a doctor, married to another doctor that she met at university. They live together in a four-bedroom house with their two children and their dog, all three of whom I adore in equal measure. From where I'm sitting, her life is perfect. The fourth bedroom is mine to stay in whenever I want it and there's always a space for me at the dinner table at a moment's notice. Jessica's worried expression comes into sharp focus in my mind. Her warm brown eyes, rich like a mug of hot chocolate; the lines that have etched her forehead since before I can remember. My initial frustration at her hounding me melts away. I've given her cause to worry in the past and I don't want to do that to her, she doesn't deserve it. I type a quick message.

> I'm fine, just been a busy day. I'll call you tomorrow. Xxx

The sound of it whizzing off into the ether coincides with a crash of tiredness and a feeling of disappointment in myself for my impatience towards Jessica. She deserves better than me. Just as I'm wondering if it's better if I just go home and sleep a voice makes me look up.

'Hey sweetie, sorry I took such a long time.' Reiss stands before me, his hand wrapped around the handle of a suitcase so large you could hide a body in it. 'Are you ready?'

I give him a weary smile and nod, pushing away any thoughts of sleep. This investigation comes first. I can sleep when I'm dead.

Chapter Twelve

The Social Sleuth, *extract from blog 3*

> Jack the Ripper's crimes took place in a small
> area of London over the course of one year,
> but the memory of those crimes spans the
> globe and hundreds of years.

We walk along the narrow streets. They're darker than before, the blackness exacerbated by the bursts and flashes still popping in my eyes, an after-effect of the waiting cameras. Reiss and I were captured leaving the ship together; it won't be long until the Interstellars put two and two together. I've hitched my wagon to him now, and the success of my investigation hinges on his support.

We turn down a side street. The old warehouses press closer on each side, reaching high above us, cutting off any moonlight. It's noticeably colder here than on the main street and I shiver. I feel like I've stepped back in time to Victorian London. It's possible to imagine Jack the Ripper lurking here, his black hat pulled low, his sharp knife held tightly in his murderous hand while he lies in wait for his next victim. An image of one of the women he viciously attacked flashes into my mind, a body lying dead and mutilated on the cobblestones, blood seeping into the gaps between the smooth round stones.

The area is silent, but the sound of Reiss's case against the cobbles breaks it. The case is heavy, and he makes slow progress over the lumps and bumps of the old roads. I pull my phone out and look again at my KnockKnock post. My stomach dips as I scroll through the numerous comments it's now garnered. It's more visibility than I was expecting, and it sits uneasily, like an undigested meal.

Many of the comments beg me to continue with my investigation, saying that they trust me to keep them posted in a way the police won't. I'm pleased the fans are on board, that goes some way to calming my nerves, but my heart tightens a little at more than one comment telling me to be careful, that there's a killer on the loose somewhere and I could be in grave danger. I think of Christopher's eyes trailing me as I walked on the top deck, and the fact that he's been taken away by the police. I must remain vigilant.

'Here we are,' says Reiss, stopping at a double-fronted red iron door. He lifts a flat disc from his pocket and presses it against the pad. When the buzzer sounds, I push open the heavy door and hold it open for him to drag his case behind him. The entrance hall is dimly lit but I can make out the glow of the lift sign. The lift doors screech open; it's a tight squeeze. Reiss presses the button for the top floor and with another screech the lift trundles upwards while visions of snapping ropes and us plummeting rocket around in my mind.

We survive the journey, and when I cross the threshold of Reiss's penthouse flat, it's hard to keep my jaw from dropping.

'Welcome, sweetie,' says Reiss, fanning his hands out wide. 'Glad we got here in the end, wasn't a far walk but I'm exhausted.' He leans over to look in a mirror hanging next to the front door. 'Argh, I look frazzled, and you do too, no offence. Let me get us a glass of wine and we can discuss.'

The flat's living space is vast and open plan. Two baby-blue art deco sofas sit opposite each other near a door to a balcony. The kitchen is on the other side, where Reiss is busying himself placing wine glasses onto a white marble countertop. I look around at the exposed brick walls and the beams that line the ceiling. Next to the kitchen there's a staircase leading to what I assume will be the bedroom. I walk towards the sofas but can't resist peeking out at the balcony. It's huge – there's enough space for a six-seater dining table, sun loungers and a vast array of plants, but it's the view that really takes my breath away. From Reiss's balcony, I can see Tower Bridge, its tall columns lit up and sparkling in the night. Shad Thames, being central and historic, is a coveted area to live – coveted meaning seriously expensive, and though I'm no expert when it comes to real estate, Reiss's flat looks like it cost a fortune. I have an investigation to focus on, but I'd be lying to myself if I didn't admit that seeing this world is a little exciting.

'Good idea, sweetie,' says Reiss, coming up behind me and making me jump. He holds a glass of wine in each hand. 'It might be almost midnight, but it's warm enough. Let's sit out here. If you get cold there are blankets in that box.' Reiss lowers himself into one of the sun loungers and, once I'm seated, hands me the glass of wine. 'Hope you like Chardonnay,' he adds.

The golden liquid is cool inside my mouth, and I close my eyes, enjoying the buttery taste of it. The smoothness with which it slides down my throat makes it clear that it's streets ahead of anything I've drunk before.

When I open my eyes, I find that Reiss is watching me expectantly. He doesn't say anything but there's an energy coming from him that gives him away.

'What?' I ask.

'Are we going to continue investigating?'

'Do you think we should?' I'm genuinely interested in his opinion.

'Abso-fucking-lutely. Don't you?' He flops back against the seat and takes a large gulp of his wine. I can't deny that it's comforting to have someone to talk to, to not have to do it alone. It's nice to not be alone, full stop. A voice in my head whispers to me to not let him get too close, that this is a murder investigation and everyone should be a suspect, but I take a sip of wine too and the voice quietens down.

I nod. 'I think I have to.'

'What's your plan?'

I don't answer him immediately, because what *is* my plan? Everything is muddled in my head and I'm suddenly a little woozy. It's dangerous to drink on an empty stomach.

A shrill buzzing makes me jolt and some of the wine sloshes from my glass onto my lap. I glance at Reiss. His eyes widen, and he shakes his head at me.

'Were you expecting anyone?' I ask.

'No,' says Reiss, sounding a little fearful. He rises slowly and heads inside to the intercom. 'Hello?'

There's a garbled response from the person waiting outside, but I'm not close enough to hear what they say.

'Oh my God, you scared the bejesus out of me. Come up, sweetie.' Reiss appears behind me, a wide smile now on his face. 'I completely forgot I told Isla to join us. She's a little drunk. I hope you don't mind her being here.' Reiss grimaces, as if remembering our previous encounter with her. She was rude and tetchy and developed a swift dislike for me. I should mind, but I don't. Quite the contrary, I'm pleased she's here, because Flower Spirit Isla is lining up to be a potentially interesting suspect.

There's a thunk against the front door and Reiss pulls it open to reveal Isla. She topples inside and catches sight of me.

'Oh, it's you. What are you doing here?' she asks, her voice as breathy as it was when I last met her.

'Maggie and I are investigating Stella's murder. I told you that,' says Reiss, directing her to one of the sofas. I stop hovering by the balcony door and sit on the sofa opposite.

'Investigating Stella's murder?' she asks as if she's completely forgotten our earlier conversation. 'Why would you do that?' She doesn't wait for an answer before adding. 'Reiss, I wouldn't get yourself involved.' Isla sounds serious now. 'Not given your relationship with her.'

'I need to do this *because* of my relationship with her,' he snaps back.

Isla's eyes are suddenly more focused that they were before. 'That isn't wise. It could be dangerous. It *is* dangerous. You're talking about catching a murderer.'

They glare at each other, unspoken words flying between them.

'Isla,' I say, sitting down opposite her. 'What was your relationship with Stella?'

Isla grimaces. 'We didn't have one.' Reiss frowns and she adds, 'Not really.'

'Why? You moved in the same circles.'

Isla huffs. 'I, personally, have never been drawn to Stella's work or her style, and I find her success somewhat disheartening.' Before I can ask what she means Isla continues, 'I don't like, didn't like, the message she sent out to beautiful young people. I try my best to make actual valuable content that people can use in their lives or to improve their lives. I help people exercise, cook healthy food, I share information about the world and how to make it a better place.' She throws her arms out beside her and it's apparent she's had too much to drink. She's talking like a drunk person, barely pausing for air, the words running from her mouth like water from a tap. 'I don't make content that requires people to watch me living my life in a way that adds no value to their own. I've always worried about how many young girls and women, gorgeous in their own way, watch her channel and feel like their lives aren't good enough. She started in her late teens or early twenties but she's now almost thirty years old. And yet, her fanbase is much younger. They have naïve, impressionable minds. Sometimes I wonder how many teenagers look at Stella and ask themselves, why can't I be like her? Be as slim as her, as beautiful as her, as famous as her? I've always worried about how damaging a channel like *Fashionsista* is.' Isla takes a big gulp of her wine. I glance at Reiss – I'm not sure it was the best idea to give her more alcohol. She turns to him. 'Got any snacks?'

Reiss nods and gets up, heading to the kitchen. I fold my arms across my chest. Isla hasn't told me anything helpful – I could have surmised everything she's said from looking at Stella's channel, it doesn't tell me anything new or shine a light under a bushel.

'But what was your relationship with her?' I ask.

'We didn't have one.'

'That's not entirely true, Isla.' Reiss puts a large bowl of popcorn on the oak coffee table between Isla and me.

'What's that supposed to mean?' Her voice is harsher than before, the breathiness of the yoga teacher is gone.

'Well, you didn't like her at all. Did you?'

Isla snorts. 'Not many people did like her.' She turns to me. 'You only need to know one thing about Stella Knight. It's the most important thing about her, and about her death.'

I hold my breath and lean in towards her. 'What's that?' I whisper.

'Stella Knight wasn't a good person, and there are loads, literally loads of reasons why people might have a motive to kill her.' She points at Reiss. 'And you can add him to that list.'

'Isla! You're drunk and you don't know what you're saying,' snaps Reiss, trying and failing to keep his voice low. 'It's late. Why don't we all just finish this bottle and carry on our discussion in the morning when we've slept and are a bit more sober?' Reiss struggles to keep his tone light. He tops up Isla's glass, then his own, and goes to top up mine but I block it with my hand.

'Why would Reiss want to kill Stella?' I say to Isla. The two of them exchange a look. Reiss's jaw is tight and he gives an infinitesimal shake of the head.

'Were you not listening to anything I just said?' Isla scoffs again, trying to recover from her slip of the tongue. 'Stella was a bad person. She hurt people. She stole things.'

'Who did she hurt? Why did she steal from them?'

Reiss opens a box on his coffee table and pulls out a cigarette.

'You shouldn't,' says Isla, ignoring my previous question. 'I thought you were quitting.' Reiss rolls his eyes and balances the end of the cigarette on his lips.

'Today has been a day.' The cigarette flaps as he talks, like a fish thrashing about on the end of a fisherman's hook. He flips the cap of a leather-bound lighter and with a deft flick a flame springs up. The smoke rises in swirls and fills my nostrils, herbal and heady. The potent aroma of tobacco fills the room. I used to smoke a handful of Marlboro Lights a day, Vogues if I was at a party. Delicious, dirty, sexy cigarettes. Another thing from my old life that I gave up. Jessica wouldn't allow me to smoke in the house or anywhere near the children and it meant that I was forced to walk to the end of the road each time I wanted one. When winter came, it became less and less appealing to stand on a street corner in the pissing rain, all for a cigarette that I only smoked to keep me alert at work and because I thought it was cool.

Still, one puff won't do me any harm. I reach forward and accept the cigarette from Reiss's outstretched fingers. I take a long, slow drag, holding the swirling smoke it in my mouth, and I take another deep breath in. I release it slowly through my mouth, savouring every moment. The impact hits me almost immediately, harder than I remember. My body, unused to the rush, sways as the nicotine hits my brain and the tension my muscles have carried for years loosens a fraction. I hand the cigarette back to Reiss. Once is enough for now.

'What's it like?' I ask.

'What's what like?' replies Reiss.

'Being famous.'

Isla and Reiss look at each other. 'We're not famous,' replies Isla.

'You have thousands of followers. That's famous by my standards.'

'Ask Reiss, he has far more followers than me. I almost, *almost*, have five hundred thousand. He has double that and then some!'

'Our channels are very different, my love.'

She shrugs as though not bothered by the difference.

Reiss continues, 'Well, to answer your question, it's weird. I don't know what it's like to be movie-star famous, but being internet famous is quite random.' He offers me another drag on the cigarette but I refuse, still feeling the effects of my last go.

'Random in what way?' I ask.

'It's not like you're a household name, so you're not being chased by paparazzi everywhere you go. Most people have no idea who you are, which I guess is a good thing.'

'Yeah, but you have a following. Any picture you post will be seen by millions of people. People go to restaurants because you went there. They'll buy things because you recommend them. What's it like having that much influence?'

'Ha, you make it sound like we're really powerful. It isn't like that, not really. There are so many wonderful benefits – obviously the income is pretty good, and I get invited to lots of nice places. Spa retreats, holidays, launch parties. But the thing I love the most is my fans. None of this would be possible without them.'

I watch him as he speaks a line that many, many people have recited before. Even when spoken by someone sitting opposite me it still sounds as strange as it always has. My fans, who make all of this possible. I remember seeing an interview once where one of the members of a girl band said that they loved it when their fans connected with each other; to me it seemed odd to celebrate that groups of people were meeting to honour you. I've always found that level of follower dedication slightly unnerving, like you were the possession of others.

'Isn't it strange having fans?'

'Ha,' says Isla. 'It is *so* strange having fans, although mine would probably be considered loyal followers. Most of them are great, but then there are some...' She trails off and shakes her head, leaning forward to pick up some more popcorn.

'Some of them are what?'

'Weird,' she says, matter-of-factly. 'Some people on the internet are weird. That's not news.'

'What's the weirdest thing that's happened to you?'

'Nothing especially *weird* has happened to me, but some horrid stuff has. Disgusting comments from random people. Racist comments; sexist comments. Some of it can be really nasty.'

'Oh my God, I'm so sorry.'

'It's fine, you get used to it and the channels are getting much better at removing that kind of stuff now. Plus, it's been such a long time since I've properly read any of the comments.'

'What about you, Reiss?'

'Yeah, I've had the mean stuff, like what you saw on *hashtagnofilter*, but I've also had strange stuff. Stella had a lot of creepy stuff too.'

'Like what?'

'I'm trying to remember. Like...' He bites his lip. 'Oh yeah, I remember when her channel started getting lots more followers, there was one fan who'd followed her from the beginning and used to message her and tell her how proud she was of her. Proud that she was living her dream and so on.' Reiss flicks his wrist and ash falls from the end of the cigarette onto his trousers, but he doesn't seem to notice. 'When Stella got even more followers, these messages continued, the fan even sent her letters. Stella messaged her once to say she was grateful for the attention but basically asking her to stop.' Reiss grimaces. 'Well, that was the wrong thing to do. This girl started following her in real life, taking photographs of Stella without Stella noticing and posting them on the internet. There was one of Stella's front door. I remember Stella was very upset about it.'

My lip curls, horrified and disgusted in equal measure. 'Did anything happen to the girl? Was she arrested or something?' Stella had a stalker – is she another suspect to add to my list?

'Don't think so. But I didn't hear much about it after that.'

'It's like bees,' says Isla, tipping the last of her wine into her mouth. 'The queen bee is surrounded by her worker bees, who dote on her. The worker bees do everything, they clean away her waste, they pre-digest her food and feed it to her. But if she isn't doing a good enough job...' Isla trails off and draws one of her heavily ringed fingers in a line across her neck.

'Do you think Stella was killed by an obsessive fan?' I ask, assuming that is what Isla is saying.

'Stranger things have happened,' says Isla with a nonchalance that shows she can't be bothered hiding how little she cares.

'Oh God, I've just remembered. Wasn't there that girl who died?' Reiss asks Isla.

'A girl who died?' Isla repeats. 'I don't know anything about a girl who died.'

'Yeah you do. Oh, was ages ago. Can't remember the details,' says Reiss. He's slurring a little bit now. I want to know more, but before I can ask him to try to remember anything Isla cuts in.

'I don't want to talk about Stella any more. Let the police do the investigation and let me drink a glass of wine in peace.'

She gets up and connects her phone to Reiss's speakers, pressing buttons on a slim remote control until reggae music fills the room, so loud I can barely hear myself think, let alone speak. I'm not going to get anything else out of them today. Isla sways from side to side in time with the music. I should go home. Reiss looms towards me with a fresh bottle of wine. He pours some in my glass, and this time, I don't stop him.

I shouldn't really drink, it isn't good for me or my stability. For the last few years, I've tried to stay away from anything that might cloud my judgement or influence my decisions. But the result seems to have cut me off from any fun as well. I think of Jessica, her texts and her worry. It's all right for her, she already has a job she loves and a wife who loves her, she already has the children she always wanted and the dog and the four-bedroom house with the garden she tends to at the weekend. What do I have? Unbidden, anger rises in me. Not anger at her. It isn't Jessica's fault. Anger at myself, for letting myself get so far away from the life I want. I know this glass of wine, this party, this investigation isn't the answer, but it's a start.

Isla holds up her glass for more wine and sways around Reiss's living room, drops of Chardonnay splashing onto the floor as she does.

Reiss mouths an apology to me. I sigh. It looks like I won't find out much more this evening. I drain my glass and help myself to another top-up. Might as well give into the night and the music.

–

Hours later, when I crash out on Reiss's sofa and close my eyes, my dreams are filled with Stella. She stands in front of me in her lime green dress. A bee flies in and lands on her shoulder. She winces, her face contorted in pain and fear. Another bee comes, then another, until Stella is surrounded by an army of them. They swarm around her, crawling over each other to take up position on her skin. She screams and cries for them to stop but they don't. From head to toe, they engulf her. A once loyal army has turned on their queen.

Chapter Thirteen

The Social Sleuth, *extract from blog 2*

It's well known that there are three main things that investigators need to uncover about potential suspects: the ability or capability to commit the crime (means); a reason to commit it (motive); and the chance to commit it (opportunity).

Sunday

Sunlight streams across my face and I peel my eyes open. It takes me a moment to remember where I am and why I'm still wearing yesterday's dress. Pushing myself into a sitting position, I scan Reiss's apartment. My head is pounding and my mouth is as dry as the ashtray on the table in front of me. Cigarettes stick out of it at odd angles. The stench of them is as unappealing now as it was appealing last night.

'Good morning, Sleeping Beauty,' says Reiss's voice from the kitchen. I plant my bare feet on the wooden floor and turn to look at him. He comes into focus as he walks towards me. 'Correction,' he says, placing a large glass of water and two paracetamol in front of me. 'Good afternoon.'

'Afternoon?' I croak, looking up at him. Frustration tightens in my stomach. I've slept through the whole morning, lost hours of possible investigation time. If you can call being sedated by alcohol sleep.

'Just,' he says.

'This is a disaster.' I speak the words that I want to shout. 'I've an investigation to conduct. I shouldn't be sitting on your couch, hungover.' I start to stand but the room spins. Reiss gives me a pained expression.

'Sit down, sweetie. Drink the water and take the paracetamol. I'll make you a coffee, and then we can plan.'

Flopping back down, I resign myself to following Reiss's instructions. My stomach knots in anger at my own stupidity, at how carried away I got last night. I can't let my budding friendship with Reiss interfere with my work. I shouldn't let him influence me into getting carried away.

'Where's Isla?' I ask.

'She's gone home. Why? Did you want to speak to her?'

'Maybe later.' I rub my hands over my eyes; crusts of sleep rub rough against my skin. 'You don't happen to have a whiteboard, do you?' I ask.

Reiss laughs. 'The whiteboard: the hangover cure you need to know about.' I look up at him with a grim expression and his smile drops. I'm not in a joking mood. 'As a matter of fact I do. I use it to decide what days I'm going to release certain videos. Shall I get it?'

'Yes, that'd be great.'

I crunch the paracetamol between my teeth, the powder bitter and sharp against my tongue, and then swallow them down with the water. I never was good at swallowing tablets. By the time I've moved on to the coffee, Reiss is wheeling the whiteboard in front of me.

The mug is warm and fragrant in my hand and I breathe in its aroma. A breakfast of over-the-counter drugs and black coffee, quite the party girl diet.

'OK,' I say to him. 'Joe, the bartender, confirmed your suspicion that Stella Knight was murdered. So we need to establish who the suspects are.' I stand up and accept the whiteboard pen from him. In the middle of the board, I scrawl Stella's name in thick black capital letters. I circle her name and from the circle draw a line, writing the words *Christopher, husband* at the end of it.

Turning, I say to Reiss, 'Her husband is the most obvious suspect, and it is likely the police investigation will begin with him. In fact, I forgot to tell you, I saw the police taking Christopher and Anna away yesterday. Probably for more questioning, because they were closest to Stella,' I add in response to his shocked expression. 'Anyway, as I was saying, they *always* look to the husband first, because statistically it's most likely to be him. But I don't want to be as clichéd as that. From what you and Isla have told me, there was a lot going on in Stella's life.'

A lot going on, my euphemism for what Isla said last night about there being lots of reasons people might want to kill Stella. I draw another line and at its end write Anna's name. Another line with 'obsessed fan' written at the end; another line for Isla. I draw one final line and write one final name.

'Me?' asks Reiss, narrowing his eyes. 'I'm a suspect in this case? The decline of my friendship with Stella isn't exactly a motive for murder. And if it was, why kill her now?'

'I don't think you had anything to do with this,' I say, truthfully. 'But I have to be thorough.'

'Fine,' says Reiss, his features relaxing.

'So we have Christopher, Isla, you, Anna, a crazy fan. Oh, and Make It, Don't Fake It.' I twirl the fat whiteboard pen between my fingers, the plastic smooth and cold, and survey the names. 'That doesn't seem like that many people to speak to, especially since we don't even know if this crazy fan actually exists, and we don't know who Make It, Don't Fake It is.'

Reiss walks up and down the length of his flat. 'So what do we do? What are the next steps?'

The names stare out at me from the board. We still lack any useful information on which to pin our investigation. 'Means, motive, opportunity,' I say. 'Means is relatively straightforward – something was given to Joe to put in her drink. It's substance dependent, but I don't think it's that difficult for people to get their hands on elicit stuff, and there are so many household liquids that are lethal.'

Reiss nods solemnly, agreeing with my logic, so I continue.

'Opportunity will need a bit of figuring out. I need to understand where everyone was during the awards cere-mony. Did any of these people slip away from the party or organise a rendezvous with Stella? All of them apart from the unknown crazy fan and Make It, Don't Fake It were definitely at the ceremony, which gives them the opportunity.'

I reach forward and grab my coffee, holding it in my hand like a bigwig business exec delivering a presentation, energised and in control.

'Now the big one. Motive. Motive is much harder to establish. Anna was clearly angry at Stella, but being angry at your boss hardly seems like a strong enough motive for murder. Isla has made her opinions about Stella quite plain, but Isla wasn't close with Stella, and you said it yourself: she lives her life by a motto of love and light. There's Christopher, Stella's husband, but if he wanted to kill her, why do it at the awards? He could easily have pushed her down the stairs at home and made it look like an accident. If he is to be considered a proper suspect, I need to establish why he'd choose to kill her at the event.' I take a deep breath. 'And then there's you.'

Reiss stops pacing. 'I don't have a motive, so you can discount me.'

I want to believe him, I do. He's been nothing but nice to me since Stella died and I think he genuinely wants to help me solve this case, but I shouldn't ignore the voice inside my head that tells me to be careful and not let him get too close. He joins me at the board and surveys the names.

'We need to figure out the basics – means, motive and opportunity – for all of these people. Then you'll see I had no reason to kill Stella. She was my friend.'

My memories of last night as a little hazy, but there is one thing that Reiss said that has stuck in my mind. 'Last night you mentioned a girl who died. What was all that about?'

He looks momentarily confused, then he clicks his fingers, 'Oh yes, the girl who died.' He rubs his forehead as if trying to resurface the memory. 'She was young, obsessed with *Fashionsista*. I don't know many of the details as it was kept out of the press. I chatted to Stella about it at the time and she said that the girl's family were furious and were trying to pursue criminal charges against her, but that they didn't get far with them. That's the reason it was kept out of the press. Hang on, let me see if I can find something about it.' He swoops for his phone and quickly types something. I take sip of coffee while he searches but I barely have time to swallow the warm, bitter liquid before he holds the phone towards me. 'Here's the story. Stella isn't mentioned because she was never implicated. The pills that this girl bought were fake.'

'Huh?' I frown.

'Stella partnered with a wellness brand who made pills to boost your metabolism or some shit like that. The pills sold out quickly and this girl bought some knock-offs. She got hooked on them and eventually died.' Reiss's face crumples and for a second I think he's about to cry. 'There'll always be people wanting to make a quick quid, and these knock-off pills aren't regulated, they're usually sold in a very dark part of the internet. Poor, poor girl and her poor family.'

I take Reiss's phone from him and read the headline: 'Family of teenage girl killed on Christmas Day by illegal diet pills "heartbroken" that more isn't being done to protect young people.'

I stare at the image that sits below the headline: a mum, a dad, a boy and a girl in her early teens all stand in front of what looks like the Magic Kingdom at Disney World. Their mouths are pulled wide in smiles and their arms are looped around one another. It's a picture of familial bliss if ever there was one. I scroll down, my eyes skimming over the description of a Christmas Day turned horror story and stop on a second image taken outside a courthouse: the same man and woman are walking towards the camera. He has his head bowed, not looking into the lens, but the face of the woman, the mother, is contorted. Her lips are clamped together so tightly they're almost white. She glares out of the photograph so she makes eye contact with the viewer. It's as if she is about to leap from the frame and wrap her two hands around your throat. I shiver; despite the distance in time and place, her anger radiates from the image.

'Oh my God.' My fingernails dig into the squishy case of Reiss's phone as my hand grips it tighter.

'What?' asks Reiss, stepping towards me and glancing at the image from over my shoulder.

'It's her.'

'It's who?' asks Reiss. My heart beats against my chest faster than before. I can't believe what I'm seeing – what was she doing on the yacht? Her ginger hair, her round face, her sallow skin is no different in the photo than in real life. 'Who, Maggie?' he implores me.

'It's the woman I saw arguing with Stella yesterday.' I hand the phone back to Reiss. He expands the image, his long nails clipping against the plastic screen.

'She was at the ceremony yesterday?' He looks closely at the image, his eyes narrow, his shoulders tense.

'Do you recognise her?' I ask.

'No.' He shakes his head. 'But if anyone wanted to kill Stella, it'd be her.'

'We need to speak to her,' I say. 'She was on the yacht. She was seen arguing with Stella. She has a motive, a rather significant motive.'

Reiss doesn't take his eyes off the screen but nods to show that he's listening. 'She looks devastated.'

'What's her name?' I ask, pen poised once again over the whiteboard.

'Clare Owen,' replies Reiss, and I scribble it down along with a note about her potential motive.

'So we've got seven suspects, assuming we count the unidentified crazy fan and Make It, Don't Fake It. Five were definitely on the yacht at the time of the murder, and one of those five has a very strong motive.'

Clare Owen would be perfect candidate to speak to first, but finding her won't be easy. I perch on the arm of the sofa and stare at her name. It's there in black and white, as is her motive, but how can I find her? And, perhaps more challenging, how can I get her to talk to me?

This detective work is much more difficult than it looks. All my experience watching crime shows, reading crime books and blogging about crime cases made me think I'd know exactly what to do, but I don't have the access that the police do to interview people or gather evidence.

Reiss takes the pen from me and adds *tall, dark, handsome, couldn't possibly be killer* next to his own name.

'Hey!' I say. 'Scrub that out. For starters, you aren't that tall.' He clicks his tongue against his teeth but does as he's told. 'We need to speak to Clare Owen, but how?'

'Well, I don't know where she lives. But,' he says, giving me a cheeky smile, 'that is one benefit of having followers who spend their lives on the internet. They're pretty good at finding information for you.' He reaches for his phone.

'Hang on,' I say. 'Before we announce to the world that Clare Owen is a suspect in an unofficial murder inquiry, we need to think carefully.' I get to my feet and pace around Reiss's living room. 'I might be jumping to massive assumptions here, but do you think Make It, Don't Fake It could be Clare Owen? The messages on the forum, saying that Stella is dangerous and a bad influence, it fits, right?'

Reiss hums, thinking about my question, and I wonder if it does fit or if I'm just twisting things to suit the story I want to tell.

'There's only one way to find out, I guess,' says Reiss.

'Ask her,' I reply.

'Bingo.'

–

We sit on Reiss's balcony. Shouts of laughter come from the streets below and the air is thick with the tang of barbecuing meat. Sunday funday, as the line goes. People going about their normal lives, unaware that above them two civilians are conducting a murder investigation.

Reiss's laptop is in front of me, the cursor blinking as it waits patiently for my instruction.

'How do we, er, contact her? Assuming Make It, Don't Fake It is Clare Owen.'

Reiss pours more coffee from the French press into his mug and brings it to his lips. He takes a deep breath, drawing in the steam that swirls atop the dark, viscous liquid. Then he puts the mug down. 'We could message her? Send her a direct message.'

I think of how she ran from me on the yacht. How easy it was for her to slam the door in my face and be deaf to my calls. 'No,' I say, deciding that that isn't the best course of action. 'She might ignore us. But if we call her out publicly, she might be more inclined to reply.'

'Sweetie, we aren't even certain Make It, Don't Fake It is Clare.'

I shrug. 'We have to do something, something big.'

'I guess so. God, if it is Clare, then you're a fucking genius.'

'And if it isn't, we'll have to find another way.'

'OK,' says Reiss. 'I have a *hashtagnofilter* account, I'll do it. Also, there's the added benefit of users knowing it's me, so that might make her more likely to reply.'

'Thought you said you didn't read this stuff any more,' I say, twisting to look at him.

'I don't,' he says, sounding scandalised. 'I haven't logged on in ages. I haven't!' He adds when he sees my raised eyebrow. 'Honestly, this place is so dangerous, it's like a black hole crossed with hell.' I'm not sure if I believe him, but I don't push it. He taps at the keyboard and logs himself into the forum of doom. Then he stops and bites his bottom lip.

'What?' I ask.

'I don't know,' says Reiss. 'Calling her out publicly. Is it really fair?'

I scowl at him. 'You've seen what was written about Stella. Even if Clare-slash-Make It, Don't Fake It didn't kill her, it could easily be considered a call to action to whoever did.'

Reiss shifts in his seat. 'Even so. I'm slightly scared of poking the beast.' I ignore him and drag the laptop towards me. Reiss's name sits next to an empty rectangular box and a blue cursor blinks, waiting for me to start typing. What should I say? I brush the tips of my fingers against the keyboard as if that will give me the inspiration I need, but it won't. I need to write something. I start typing.

Hi Clare, I'd love to hear more... I press delete, that doesn't sound right, it's a weirdly formal message on a chat site where someone has written *She's sober but still a twat.*

Clare, I want to know what... I press delete again, that's too aggressive, I don't want to scare her off.

Hi Make It, Don't Fake It, are you Clare Owen? I'm sorry for what happened to your daughter. Would you be up for talking about it with me? I'm investigating Stella's death and think you might be able to help me shed some light on it.

It isn't a perfect message, but I have to send something. If she doesn't respond, then I'll have to think of something else. I don't give myself another moment to doubt; I press send.

Chapter Fourteen

The Social Sleuth, *extract from blog 1*

The problem with the success of the website netsleuths.com was that not only were the detectives following the online discussion about the case, so was the chief suspect.

'How long do you think it will be until she replies?' I ask.

'Who knows, could be minutes, could be days,' says Reiss, lifting his arms into the air and stretching like a cat in the sun.

'Days,' I say, unable to hide my disappointment. 'I hope it isn't days, this will hardly be an all-guns-blazing investigation if our first lead doesn't materialise for days.'

'The internet is a cruel mistress.' Reiss drinks some more of his coffee, as if for him this is a lazy Sunday morning occupation, no different than reading the newspaper. He doesn't have the itch inside him that I do. It's gnawing at my stomach, calling me to do something, to be active.

'Well, while we wait, would you mind if I took a shower?' I ask. It'll be impossible for me to sit in front of the computer screen waiting without tearing off all of my fingernails. Also, it's been over twenty-four hours since I last washed myself properly and my body is sticky from sweat. I'm even still wearing the dress I wore to the awards ceremony.

'Of course, sweetie. Bathroom's upstairs. Let me get you a towel and I'll even leave some fresh clothes outside the door.'

I tilt my head to look at him.

'I often buy women's clothes,' he continues, answering a question I didn't ask. 'Not bound by labels, me. And as you can see I'm a slip of a thing, so I'm sure I have some things that will fit you.'

He turns away and walks inside. I follow him up the stairs; it's true, his body is as slender and slight as my own. He points me to the bathroom and places a towel in my hands. A towel that's not like any that I have at home: it's bright white and bouncy and soft in my hands, just like I imagine a towel feels at a posh spa. I thank him and enter the bathroom, which like the rest of his flat is modern and cool. I step out of my dress and switch on the shower. The contrast between this bathroom and my own is so stark that it makes me want to cry. There's no trace of mould creeping in between the gaps in the chipped and cracked tiles; there's no dank, saggy shower curtain. The windows are double glazed and tightly sealed. I'm used to windows framed with wood that's splintered from age and rot, full of gaps which, in the winter, the icy wind blows straight through.

I step into the shower and my head sways a little from the vestiges of my hangover. I need to wash off the night of drinking and get my head in a place where I can meet the suspects and do this properly.

The water rains over my shoulders and down my back. The heat allows my muscles to unwind. I think about the news article and the picture of Clare Owen. There's something that draws me to her, her face lined with sadness, her eyes burning with anger.

Hair and body washed, I turn off the shower and step out of it onto the plush bath mat, the thick threads weaving themselves in between my toes. I unfold the towel to wrap around my body and, as I do, a smaller one falls out. I wrap that around my head. The towel feels luxurious against my skin. I could so get used to this, but I shouldn't let myself. This isn't my life, not yet.

I open the bathroom door and retrieve the clothes Reiss has placed outside. He's even left a toothbrush set complete with mini tube of toothpaste on the top of the pile. He is certainly the host with the most. I quickly pull on the clean clothes – nothing special, light blue jeans and a grey T-shirt, but the material is expensive. I wipe away the steam clinging to the bathroom mirror and look at myself. The clothes say off-duty model in a way that my own cheap jeans and T-shirts never could.

There's a comb on the countertop. I quickly run it through my hair and, still wet, slick it back into a low bun using a hair tie from a clear plastic box of them sitting next to the comb.

'Sweetie, you look great,' says Reiss as I walk down the stairs.

'Any word from Make It?'

'Nothing. Want me to do your make-up while you wait? It is my speciality.'

'Sure,' I say with a shrug. It would be ridiculous of me to turn down the offer of a makeover from Reiss Rose.

–

I sit in front of the dressing table in Reiss's bedroom. The room is light and airy. The white walls and furniture are elevated by artwork of intense colour. On the bed a huge vanity case is open, revealing more make-up than I've ever owned in my life. He brushes his hands over it, muttering to himself.

'Tell me about yourself, Reiss. How did you get started doing what you're doing?'

He glances up at me and rolls his eyes. 'Always the investigator, eh?'

'Just interested.'

'I've always loved make-up, used to steal it from my mum when she was out at work.' He dots moisturiser across my forehead and cheeks. The palms of his hands are soft as he massages the cream in and I close my eyes.

'Then one day she said she was sick of her favourites being used up, so she took me to Boots and bought me my own collection. I was only about twelve. Such an awkward, chubby little thing.'

'I can't imagine that,' I say.

'We all have things in our past we'd like to keep there.' A shadow passes over his face, but he doesn't give me the chance to question it; it's gone almost as quickly as it appeared. 'Anyway,' he continues breathily. 'For my eighteenth birthday, my parents enrolled me in an evening beauty course at the local community college. It was a dream come true. It was like finding myself – I knew it was where I belonged, where I fitted in. Once I'd finished the course, I wanted to keep learning and share what I'd learnt with others, so I started my channel. My goodness, sweetie, you should see the quality of those videos. HOR-REN-DOUS, but they had a good number of viewers and, after about a year, I had several thousand for each one I released.'

Reiss squirts foundation onto the back of his hand and with a round orange sponge starts pressing it into my face. The gentle pressure relieves the tension that's collected on my temples and along my jawline.

'And it snowballed from there?' I ask.

'Not exactly. I noticed that viewers were commenting asking me to do this celebrity or that celebrity, and it made me realise how much people look up to celebrities and want to emulate them. It really frustrated me, because these celebrities have access to plastic surgeons, Botox, facials and the most expensive creams money can buy. It isn't fair that people, especially young women, want to look like them.'

I don't say that you could quite easily apply the same logic to Reiss himself – a man who has beauty products coming out of his ears and a lifestyle many would envy.

'So I recorded a vlog where I pointed out what surgery or help I thought certain celebrities had had. It was my most viewed video by a lot. It hit me that people want to know what is real and what isn't, so they know what they're comparing themselves to. We look at images on social media or in the newspaper or magazines and we compare ourselves to the glossy people we see there. Proving that these celebrities weren't naturally as beautiful or perfect as they made out provided comfort for people, I think. So that became my brand, celebrating natural beauty and exposing lies. I'm not against people having work done or professional help, I'm against them pretending they woke up looking like that, or that it's their genes and not Botox that means their forehead hasn't moved an inch in years.'

'Are celebrities lying about getting work done? I assumed they just didn't advertise it.'

'It comes to the same, sweetie. We compare ourselves, and I don't like that. I want people to feel good about themselves and make the best of what they have. Like I'm doing with you.'

Reiss swirls a brush into a palette of blusher and sweeps it over my cheeks. 'What channels do you use?' I ask.

'Well I'm on all the usual suspects, so to speak, but I've had most success on KnockKnock.'

'What is so great about KnockKnock?' I ask, wrinkling my forehead, which receives a tap from Reiss to keep my face straight.

'It's the app that saw Stella skyrocket to fame. She started her career about ten years ago but when Knock-Knock launched four years ago, and she moved onto it. Whoosh! I did pretty well there too. The focus on video meant I could find really fun ways to do my plastic surgery exposés. My website is still where my main content is, by which I mean my make-up videos, but KnockKnock has really brought in the viewers. They're less loyal, which is why I still dedicate a lot of time to longer videos on my own site.'

He swivels me around so I'm once again facing the mirror. I take a sharp intake of breath at what he's managed: my skin is flawless, my cheeks are rosy, my eyes more defined from the lashings of eyeliner and mascara, my lips plump and glossy. I haven't looked like this in years. All I need now is to bleach my hair to a blonde that doesn't suit me, intensify the eye make-up, the bronzer and the blusher and I'd be staring at the twenty-three year old me. While it is possible to use make-up as a disguise, my lack of interest in my appearance has become just as much of a mask. My plainness keeps me hidden from the world, protected because no one notices me.

'You like it?'

I'm about to say that I love it when my stomach growls.

'I'm going to choose to take that as a compliment. Let's get something to eat. I'm pretty hungry too. Does avo on sourdough suit?'

'Sounds delicious,' I say. He's being incredibly accommodating, and as much as I'm enjoying it the question of *why* is nagging at me. I shake it away. He wants to help, there's nothing wrong with that, and he *is* being helpful. He has a much bigger platform than me, he can help my cause. As he pops two large slices of white sourdough into the toaster, I grab his laptop and take a position on one of the bar stools in the kitchen. While Reiss slices open a hefty forest green avocado, I check our messages.

'Oh my God,' I say aloud to the laptop as much to myself. There is one new unread message in Reiss's inbox.

'Oh my God, what?' asks Reiss, looking up at me. I shake my head, not wanting to answer, not until I know if it's from her. The toast pops up, making me jump, and I only just stop myself from crying out in fright. My fingers tremble as they drag over the trackpad to open the message.

My breath catches in my throat. I was wrong. Clare Owen isn't Make It, Don't Fake It. I didn't find her – but my call to arms ensured she found me.

The message sits in the inbox. The font, round and soft, doesn't match the tone of the message at all. Every fibre of my being is desperate to reply, begging her to tell me what happened, but I stop myself. I need to respond calmly and rationally.

Reiss butters the toast and spreads the mashed avocado across it in thick, gooey chunks before sliding two plates towards me. He moves around the island and sits on one of the vacant bar stools.

He's staring at me, desperate for an answer. 'She's replied to us privately,' I say. 'At least, I think she has. It's a different username. Someone called Oneangrymum. But this has to be her, it has to be. Who else would it be?'

'What does the message say?'

'It says: "Take your post down immediately".'

Reiss lets out a low whistle. I take a bite of the toast, giving my mind a moment to compose itself. Then I start typing, reading aloud as I do for Reiss to hear.

> Hi Clare, we will take the message down, but only if you talk to us. I'm sorry that you lost your daughter, and I want to know everything, because if there's more to your story, there may be others like you.

My finger hits send and I exhale. I feel like a hostage negotiator; every word I type has the ability to tip the balance one way or another. I take another bite of toast and though it's dry and brittle in my mouth I force myself to swallow it. I need to eat, fainting halfway through an investigation wouldn't be wise.

A new message notification starts flashing at the top of the page. Another private message from Oneangrymum.

> I'm sure there are others like me. Stella Knight was a beacon of immorality whose only goal was to make herself richer.

Clare? Are you Clare Owen? I type in reply. I can't stop myself, I want her to know that I know who she is.

What does it matter who I am? is her response.

> I'm investigating Stella's murder, and I think you might be able to tell me who would have a motive for killing her.

> Aside from myself, you mean?

Reiss inhales sharply at that comment and immediately starts coughing. 'Toast went down the wrong way,' he says between coughs.

Yes, I type in reply, *aside from yourself.*

> If I talk to you, will you take the message down?

> I'll take it down immediately if you tell me where you live so we can chat.

> It isn't safe to have my name up there. You promise you will delete it?

> I promise.

I wrench my phone from where it's plugged in and take a picture of the address Clare sends. I can barely hold the phone straight, I'm shaking so much. I found a lead, I followed it and it led somewhere. It led me to Clare Owen.

'Reiss,' I say, 'could you delete the message we posted on the main thread?'

'Sure,' he says, pulling the laptop across the marble worktop so it's sitting in front of him. 'It might too late to *delete* delete, meaning people will have already seen it and possibly screenshotted it.' I pull a face, I hope that won't cause problems for Clare. She said she might be in danger, and I don't want to cause her any harm. 'All done,' says Reiss. 'But... oh. There's another message. From someone else.'

He slides his fingers over the trackpad and clicks. Reiss stands so abruptly that his stool topples over. I jump backward to save my toes being squished as it clatters to the ground.

'Shit,' I say in alarm, and he scrambles to pick it up. 'Reiss, what is it?'

He doesn't answer me, so I move towards the laptop myself. There's one message at the top of the inbox. One new message from Make It, Don't Fake It.

If I were you, I'd leave Clare alone. Unless of course you want to end up in the same position Stella did.

Chapter Fifteen

The Social Sleuth, *extract from blog 13*

> There has been significant research into what
> makes mothers completely disregard their
> own safety or the law when protecting their
> children.

Oneangrymum lives in north-west London, meaning that it isn't the easiest journey to get to her from Shad Thames, but I could hardly say no. Not after how lucky it was that I found her. I wanted to go alone but Reiss insisted he should come with me.

'She could be dangerous, sweetie,' he said. 'That message says it all. Look at it.'

I don't need to look at the message. I've read it several times at this point. I know Make It, Don't Fake It's message by heart and I still can't work out whether they are telling me to stay away from Clare because she's dangerous, or if *they* might be the dangerous one. If they were threatening me.

'We don't know that,' I reply. 'And if we don't go and see her, we'll never know.'

Reiss shakes his head and mouths '*wow*' as though what I'm suggesting is the bravest thing in the world. It isn't, I'm simply following the investigation where it leads me.

Logical next step after logical next step, and now, the logical next step is to speak to Clare Owen.

We arrive in her borough at about four p.m. after a disjointed journey during which we have to change trains multiple times. The sun beams down on us like a spotlight, intense and focused, and the temperature matches it, swiftly dispelling the benefits of my earlier shower.

I glance behind to check no one saw us getting off the train. I'm not sure why I'm looking, or who I'm looking for. It's not as if anyone would be following us.

Clare Owen's street is typical of suburban London. The houses press their sides against one another and cars line both sides of the road. It's like when someone wears an outfit with a few too many accessories – every piece is fighting for position. The front gardens are tidy and well cared for, the parked cars are all in good condition but the congestion is overwhelming and my stomach flips as if the street is going to gobble me up.

Clare lives at number fifty. The numbers ascend on my left, starting from two. Every step closer to Clare's house makes me more nervous and questions that I hadn't thought of before surface.

What if this isn't Clare?

What if this is some serial killer lurking about on the internet and I've walked straight into their trap?

I give Reiss a sideways glance; his head twitches from side to side, constantly surveying our surroundings. He's on edge too. Does he sense danger?

Reaching Clare's house, we pause. My fingers are tingling and I bounce on the balls of my feet, readying myself to flee if I have to. Reiss looks at me, blinking more rapidly than is natural. I place a hand on his arm and give him a stern nod. It *will* be OK.

The house is perfectly ordinary. A low fence separates it from the houses either side and a neat square hedge rims the front. There's a broad window on the ground floor through which a border terrier is watching me. His dark, round eyes narrow as I hover in front of the black, waist-high gate. He doesn't bark immediately but waits for a moment, sizing me up, deciding how much of a threat I pose. The second my fingers touch the gate he's up on his feet, his position wobbly as he stands on the back of a sofa. His head is thrown back as he barks. Behind him, a figure comes to the window. She looks through the pane and sees me. She nods and retreats. I push the gate open and walk down the short pathway. The door opens and the border terrier races out like a bullet from a pistol, yapping but wagging his tail.

'He's friendly,' says Clare, watching him with a smile playing on her lips. 'He likes to think he's the protector of the house, but all he wants is a cuddle and a biscuit.'

'Food and love,' I say, 'that's all anyone wants really.' Clare nods. 'I'm Maggie,' I add, 'Maggie Shaw. This is Reiss Rose. Thank you so much for agreeing to speak with us.'

Clare frowns at Reiss, her eyes scanning him a little suspiciously, as if she recognises him but isn't pleased that he's here. Perhaps she knows him from his channel, but if she does, she doesn't pass any comment.

'Come in,' says Clare, and I follow her into her house. We walk down a narrow hallway and turn right into the living room, where two grey sofas are positioned perpendicular to one another. Like the street, Clare's house is ordinary but cramped. The sofas are too large for the room and the television is squashed into one of the corners. Clare gestures for us to sit and we oblige.

'Can I get you anything? Tea or coffee? I actually made some lemonade today if you fancy any?'

'Lemonade would be lovely, thank you.' Clare acknowledges this and leaves us alone. The dog, whose collar tells me he's called Reggie, hops up onto the sofa to sniff me and my belongings.

I lean towards Reiss and whisper, 'Homemade lemonade doesn't scream cold-blooded killer, does it?'

'Someone with the time on their hands to make homemade lemonade might have enough time on their hands to plan a murder,' he says. 'Plus it could very well be poisoned. It was a drink that killed Stella, let's not forget that.'

'She won't kill us in her own home.'

'If you say so,' he trills. 'Bit eclectic, interior design-wise.'

I laugh – he's not wrong. On first inspection everything looks like a normal front room. Grey sofas covered in throws; light grey painted walls hung with family pictures in silver frames; discarded newspapers on a wooden coffee table. But look closer and there are items that don't fit, items that jar with the suburban aesthetic. There's a golden tree about the size of a bonsai covered with multi-coloured leaves, and a black wooden yoga wheel etched with geometric flowers resting on top of an unrolled exercise mat.

'Leave her alone, Reggie,' says Clare, returning with a tray carrying a big jug of pale-yellow lemonade and three glasses. Clare sets it down on a side table and pours us both a glass before taking a seat on the other sofa.

'What's that?' I ask, pointing at the tree.

'It's a healing tree. The leaves are crystals, they represent different chakras.'

'Oh,' I say, sounding more surprised than I meant to. Clare didn't strike me as someone who would be into that sort of stuff.

'My husband thinks it's all bollocks,' she says gruffly. 'And it might be. I don't care.'

Clare doesn't elaborate but sits expectantly, her hair hanging over her shoulders in limp curls. She wears a baggy T-shirt that tents itself over her chest and round belly. She pulls at it so it arranges itself as loosely as possible. I take a sip of my lemonade to give myself something to do. I clear my throat and draw myself up a little straighter; it's time to show what I'm made of.

'As I said, I'm Maggie Shaw, and I'm investigating the murder of Stella Knight.'

'I thought you wanted to hear about my daughter Abbie, not talk about Stella.' Clare twists her fingers together. Her movements are agitated, suggesting a need for me to tread carefully.

'I do want to hear about Abbie,' I say. Clare cuts in, barely letting me finish.

'Because to be frank with you, I don't care that Stella is dead. In fact, I'd go so far as to say she got what was coming to her.'

The matter-of-fact tone with which Clare speaks is disarming. She could just as easily be telling me it was lasagne and garlic bread for dinner. Looking at her now, I'm fascinated by the character she presents. If I had passed her on the street I'd probably have thought she was an ordinary woman; nice enough, maybe a bit of a gossip, probably involved in some church committee-related drama. I wouldn't have expected her to tell me that Stella deserved to die or that she believed in the power of healing crystals. Yet there's an undercurrent to her, as if she's battling against the anger and hatred that bubbles beneath her suburban exterior.

'Why did you say Stella got what was coming to her?' I ask, deciding there's no point tiptoeing around the issue.

Clare slams her glass down hard, making the tray wobble. 'Stella Knight killed my daughter.'

I stare at her, startled by the suddenness of the statement and the fury in her voice. For a moment I find I can't speak. Reiss fiddles with the chain around his neck, pulling it away from his chest and running the purple pendant along the links. The whirring sound of metal against metal is the only sound in the now deathly silent room. Clare glares back at me, a defiant expression pasted on her face. Her chest heaves as she furiously tries to catch the breath that has run away from her.

'How did she kill your daughter?' Clare looks away, her eyes bright with the early signs of tears. 'Please, Clare,' I urge.

Clare keeps looking away from us, her eyes lingering on the healing tree. Light streams from the broad bay window and the tree shines as if lit from within. Clare takes a deep steadying breath. 'I'll tell you everything, but I want you to promise me that when I tell you, you won't dismiss my accusations like the police did. People think my daughter died because of the pills she took and, yeah, technically that's right, but Stella was never held accountable, she was considered completely faultless. But I know the truth, Stella Knight has blood on her hands. She's the reason Abbie's dead.'

Before I even really know what I'm saying or what I'm committing to, my mouth opens. 'I promise, I'll take your accusations seriously.'

'OK,' says Clare after I've given my word. 'Stella Knight was predominantly followed and loved by young girls – at least she was several years ago. She started her career when she was in her late teens, but I always found it slightly uncomfortable how she continued to behave quite childishly well into her twenties. It was soon after Abbie died that Stella changed her aesthetic to be more adult. Anyway, as I was saying, her channel *Fashionsista* was hugely popular with young girls, and my daughter Abbie was one of them. After school, once we'd eaten and she'd done her homework, she'd retreat to her bedroom to watch the latest video. Whether it was a make-up tutorial, a review of all the things she'd bought that day, or a video about her night-time skin routine, it didn't matter, Abbie just loved to watch.' Clare sighs and shakes her head. 'Honestly, even now my mind cannot grasp why my daughter wanted to watch the inane day-to-day life of another person.'

Reiss fusses with his trousers, a move I've come to recognise as the tell he displays when he's uncomfortable. A comment a little too close to home, perhaps.

'But I didn't stop her, of course, she was a wonderful girl and if that made her happy then who was I to judge? I think she saw Stella as the big sister she didn't have. All of her friends liked watching Stella's channel and it was something for them to discuss.

'Then, Abbie started becoming quieter and more reserved than usual. I also noticed her getting thinner. I tried to speak to her about it, but she didn't want to talk to me. I thought it was just usual teenage stuff, so I vowed to keep an eye on it but didn't do any more.'

Clare gives a little hiccup and, as if drawn to his mistress by a sixth sense, Reggie pads towards her and springs onto the couch to sit next to her. She reaches her hand to him and strokes his wiry head.

'On Christmas Day, a few months after she had started retreating into herself, she didn't come downstairs to open her gifts. I looked in on her and thought she was asleep. We waited for her, even laughed about her being an awkward teenager now, but an hour later she still hadn't come down. I went upstairs to get her.' Clare pauses and shakily lifts the lemonade to her mouth and takes a drink. She clears her throat. 'As soon as I opened her bedroom door, I knew something was wrong. There was vomit all over the bedsheets. I ran to her, her skin was on fire. I screamed for John to call an ambulance. I thought that she had a fever or something. When the paramedics arrived, they rushed her to hospital, but in the end, it was too late to save her. She died on Christmas Day.' Clare wipes a tear away from her eye and sniffs loudly. 'She was only thirteen years old.'

It's like all the air has been sucked out of the room. Reiss and I sit still like statues, unable to respond as Clare composes herself.

'There was an inquest, and what was discovered then was that Abbie had started taking diet pills. I don't how much you know about diet pills, but they burn fat, and I don't mean in the gimmicky way that people say grapefruit burns fat, I mean literally. They raise your body temperature. My daughter was cooked from the inside out.'

My stomach convulses and I grip my pen a little tighter, willing myself not to throw up. Next to me, Reiss's hands squeeze the sofa, his knuckles white.

Clare continues, despite our horror. 'There was a trial, because my daughter had been buying the pills online using John's credit card. He wasn't in the habit of checking his statements. Poor John, I thought he was going to have a heart attack and die himself. It would have served the smug, unfeeling judge right. Anyway, because she'd used a credit card the sellers were traceable. The pills were illegal, of course, so they were liable for selling them. I remember the medical examiner saying that diet pills are like a game of Russian roulette, any single one of them could kill you, or at the very least do you serious harm. We discovered that Abbie was taking them with some regularity. She was addicted, and we never even knew. You have no idea how horrible it is to learn details about your child's life at a criminal trial.'

My mind spins, trying to keep up with the key bits of information that Clare is sharing. Abbie Owen, a huge fan of Stella's, died at thirteen years old, four years ago, after developing an addiction to diet pills. Clare's eyes are glazed, covered in a film of tears, and my heart aches for her. It's hard to imagine what she must have gone through.

'Forgive me,' I say gently, not wanting to upset her further. 'But where does Stella Knight come into all of this?'

Clare's lips purse, as if the answer to that question is blindingly obvious. 'Stella was always on a diet. Stella was taking diet pills. Stella was promoting diet pills.'

'Stella was promoting the diet pills that killed Abbie?'

I glance sideways at Reiss. It seems highly unlikely that Stella was encouraging her followers to buy illegal pills off the internet.

'No, she wasn't promoting those exact pills, but she was promoting taking pills. She's an influencer, for fuck's sake, every word that comes out of her mouth has the power to *influence* her followers' behaviour.' Clare is shouting now and her face is contorted, displaying the ugly anger seething beneath her heartbreak. 'Most of her followers are impressionable young women and girls. It was irresponsible of her to be encouraging her followers to even go on a diet, let alone take supplements.'

'What did the police say? Did they think she was responsible?'

'I told the police, but I don't know the extent to which they investigated it. Stella was maybe, *maybe*, given a slap on the wrist, but was found not to be responsible. The videos where she had talked about dieting and the benefits of diet pills were removed, and while I buried my baby girl she lived and breathed and walked among us worshipped like a God, when in my eyes she was Satan.'

Clare folds her arms across her chest defensively, as if trying to contain the fury raging inside her. If Clare whipped herself up into a frenzy, is it unreasonable to assume she could turn violent? It is there within her, I see it. But then, for someone who believes Stella killed her daughter, I don't feel like she has a lot to go on. Before I can ask her another question, one that would likely provoke her, Reiss speaks, saving me from myself.

'Stella was absolutely in the wrong.' I shift in my seat to look at him. 'She was,' he says to me this time. 'When you have a voice like she had, or I have, you have a responsibility to think about what you're saying. Look at politicians and celebrities — for the most part they're careful about what they say, they don't just mouth off about any old thing. Although Stella promoting diet pills was unlikely to hit the front page of a newspaper, that doesn't mean her words didn't matter. They matter more, even, because she and I have built relationships with the people who follow us. They listen to us, and they believe us when we say something.'

Clare raises her arm towards Reiss. 'See,' she says.

I nod, acknowledging what both of them are saying, but it doesn't matter to me whether Stella was responsible for Abbie's death or not; what matters to me is that Clare blames Stella, and Clare was at the awards ceremony.

'Moving on to yesterday,' I say, and Clare winces at my abruptness. 'I have to ask. What were you doing at the event?'

'I was invited,' replies Clare curtly.

'Who were you invited by?'

The front door opens with a rattle that makes Clare jolt and sends Reggie into another round of yapping.

'That will be my husband,' she mutters, urgently. 'It's time you left.'

Chapter Sixteen

The Social Sleuth, *extract from blog 18*

> Depending on who you asked at the time, Joan Creed either willingly participated in the murders her husband committed or she did what she did out of fear for her own life.

Clare gets to her feet as Reggie jumps from the couch and skitters from the room. She looms over us. Her expression is stern but her flushed cheeks give away that she is nervous more than anything.

'We—' I try to say, but she interrupts me.

'I have nothing more to say to you. I didn't kill Stella, and it's up to you to believe me or not.'

Reiss doesn't need to be asked twice. He gets up, his hazel eyes signalling to me to do the same, but I don't move. I have more questions to ask her and I'm not giving up that easily. A man pops his head around the living room door, and I turn to face him.

'Oh hello,' he says, and steps into the room, a smile plastered on his face. It's the sort of smile I recognise, one I've given many times before. A smile that has been perfected to look like happiness, that attempts happiness, rather than is happiness itself. Like Clare, he seems weary. An aura of crumpled sorrow hovers around him, not visible to the naked eye but there all the same. 'You didn't tell me we were having visitors, love?'

Clare interjects before I can say anything. 'We're not having visitors. They were just leaving, weren't you?' Clare glowers at us, her face a picture of determination. Her husband comes and sits on the opposite sofa, his movement towards us making Clare's cheeks flush further. With every fibre of her being she wants us to leave, but her husband didn't know we were coming over, he might give something away that could prove vital. I can't leave now.

'Well actually, I can stay a little longer.' I push my bum further to the back of the sofa, settling myself in. 'There was one more question I wanted to ask you.' Clare, her husband and I are positioned in an awkward triangle with Clare in the middle, wringing her hands.

'You can ask me another time, Maggie.' Clare keeps her voice as calm as she is able. 'You told me you needed to leave. Didn't you say you needed to feed your cat?' The words come out stilted and false. Reiss hovers near the sofa, he hasn't moved from the spot where he first stood up, and Clare's husband is looking from her to me to Reiss, his forehead creasing.

'How do you three know each other?' he asks. My mouth is dry and I swallow to moisten it, wavering over whether I should answer him truthfully. His frown deepens. 'What's going on, love?' He stands and takes a step towards her; he's not paying any attention to me or Reiss now, only his wife. He lowers his voice. 'Please tell me this isn't anything to do with her?'

My stomach does a flip. *Her?* Who is her?

'No,' snaps Clare, 'it isn't anything to do with her.' Clare charges at me and practically pulls me from the sofa, chivvying me towards the door.

'With who?' I ask.

'No one,' hisses Clare in my ear, now trying to shoo me out, waving her arms like I'm a wasp bouncing against the window.

Reggie bounds up and down the room making short, shrill barks. His barks aren't aimed at anyone in particular but at the atmosphere itself, which has become thick and clammy. My heart is thundering in my chest. I have to say it, I have to ask, but I also can't predict what direction it will drag this big, burly man.

'Do you know that Stella Knight is dead?' I say to him. Clare lets out a little squeal, her eyes darting from her husband to me, like we're both unexploded bombs and one of us will set off the other. 'She was murdered yesterday at the Influencer of the Year awards. We're investigating her death.' Clare's husband's mouth falls open and it flaps up and down like a fish out of water.

'She was murdered?' he finally manages to say.

'She was. Someone spiked her drink.'

'Clare, love, what the hell is going on? Who is this woman?' He gestures limply towards me.

'She just told you, John. She's investigating Stella's death.'

John turns to face me, his eyes wide and his mouth still agape.

'You can't seriously think my Clare has anything to do with it. She wasn't anywhere near Stella. She was with her friends for a drink, weren't you, love? I remember, you got back and were a little worse for wear.' He attempts a chuckle at this but it falls flat. Both John and I are looking at Clare, who is wearing the expression that I imagine Reggie would probably pull if he'd been found after eating something he shouldn't have. Her T-shirt flaps around her belly as her stomach swells and contracts with her heavy breathing. She's weighing up what to tell him. 'You *were* at a friend's, weren't you?' asks John, sounding more than a little desperate. 'Clare, say something.' The blood is draining from John's face and he's staring at his wife like her life depends upon it.

Clare sighs and flops back down on the sofa. 'Well, you might as well know.'

I perch on the edge of the sofa and lean forward, ready to hang on each and every word about to come from Clare's mouth.

'Might as well know what?' says John, who remains standing, his fists clenched and his body rigid.

'I… I didn't go to my friend's,' stutters Clare. 'I was at the awards ceremony.'

'What the hell? You were at the awards ceremony where Stella died? Jesus fucking Christ,' cries John, and I raise my hand to silence him.

'Sit down, John,' I bark at him, not feeling a trace of discomfort that I'm telling a stranger to sit down in their own home.

'You told us you were invited, who invited you?' I ask, my voice low and gentle. Clare looks down at the hands that she's twisting over and over in her lap. She shakes her head slowly from side to side.

'What were you doing at the awards ceremony, Clare?'

'I was invited,' says Clare, glancing at her husband. 'I was invited by a friend. Someone who also thinks it's a crime that she keeps Abbie's death a secret. We wanted her to come clean so decided we would go to the event to tell her she needs to do more to support the physical and mental health of the young women who follow her.' John listens to his wife speak as if mesmerised by her words. 'I thought I'd go there, confront her and she'd be jolted into action. I knew she hated the messages on the forum, I thought she might be scared enough to change…' Clare trails off and wipes away the solitary tear running down her cheek.

I expect John to cut in at this point, but he doesn't. He's completely still. His face has glazed over as if he's running all the possibilities and implications of this situation in his head.

'What happened when you got on the yacht?' I ask.

'Nothing happened. I immediately looked for Stella. It wasn't hard to find her, she was there, centre stage on the top deck in that teeny tiny lime green dress, looking every inch the celebrity.' Clare's voice is stronger now, the memory of Stella living her life to the fullest apparently filling her with an anger that's more powerful than her fear of being implicated. 'Surrounded by people looking at her like she had come down from heaven to grace them with her presence. I marched right up to her, tapped her on the arm and I told her who I was and that I wanted to chat with her. The look on her face when she saw me, it was like I'd opened a vein and drained her of blood. But she recovered quickly and plastered a smile on her face and took me to one side. Then she told me in no uncertain terms to get off the boat immediately or she'd have me dragged off. She had no intention of apologising.'

'And what did you do then?'

'I drank several glasses of champagne and cried a bit in the toilets. When I heard Stella was dead I tried to keep myself out of the way. That's when you came to speak to me and I locked myself in the toilet. I slipped off the ship soon after we docked and rushed home. I didn't kill her. God knows I'd have loved to, and I'll happily shake the hand of whoever did it, but it wasn't me.'

'My wife wouldn't hurt anyone. She shouldn't be a suspect, Detective,' says John.

'She's not a detective – well, not a police one anyway,' says Clare, placing a calming hand on his arm.

'What do you mean she's not a detective?'

My cheeks flush as John's jaw stiffens.

'I'm investigating Stella's murder. I'm assisting the police.' My voice dips in tandem with my stomach and I sound flustered and unprofessional.

'Did they ask for your assistance?' asks John, getting to his feet and bearing down on me.

He looks at Clare, whose expression is blank. She says, 'She said she's doing her investigation as an online thing for Stella's fans.'

I don't like where this is going, so I too get to my feet. Reiss jumps up beside me, but John blocks our path.

'Why did you agree to speak to her?' John tries to keep his voice steady.

'I must go,' I say.

'What you discussed cannot go any further,' says John. He wraps his fingers around my upper arm and squeezes. 'D'you understand me?'

'No,' I reply. 'Your wife consented to being interviewed.'

'You took advantage of a grieving woman,' he growls, and bits of his spit land on my face.

'I've done nothing wrong, and what you're doing right now is bordering on assault. Want me to add that to the list of things I tell the police?'

'Assuming I let you go so you can call them.'

'John!' cries Clare. 'Stop this right now. Let her go. There's no evidence that I killed Stella, and once the police check the guest list they'll probably be around here anyway. Don't make things worse than they already are.'

John's fingers don't loosen. Instead he raises his other hand and grabs Reiss's arm. He is much bigger than us both and it isn't difficult for him to drag us from the living room, along the hallway and out of the front door.

'Stay the fuck out of our lives,' he says, slamming the door shut behind us.

Chapter Seventeen

The Social Sleuth, *extract from blog 21*

When interviewed by the police, the exper-
imental physicist insisted that he didn't kill
his brother, explaining that he would never
have used drugs to do it. 'Too unreliable, too
messy. Would've pushed him off a bridge,' he
said.

Back in Reiss's flat, I recline on one of the sun loungers
on his balcony. The sun is coming to the end of its slow
descent from the sky, but it's forgotten to take its burning
heat with it. The air is clammy, and my limbs feel swollen
and bloated from it. Reiss is in the kitchen whipping up
some hummus and crudités. I occupy myself by scrolling
through KnockKnock and reading the new comments
that were posted while I was interviewing Clare.

My finger slides across the screen and then stops.
There's one new comment that makes my heart jump into
my throat.

How the hell could you have missed this?
And why are you still working with him?

I frown and read it again. What is the 'this' the commenter
is referring to? And the comment isn't a one-off, it isn't
an isolated incident, there are more.

Reiss is looking mighty guilty from where I'm sitting.

My head snaps up. I can see Reiss through the windows which run the length of the balcony; he winks and raises his hand in greeting. My heart thumps against my chest and I suddenly become aware that I'm on the balcony of a penthouse apartment with a man I don't know at all. I return his wave, not wanting to let him know that anything is wrong. There might be nothing wrong. I do a quick search on the internet browser on my phone, clicking on news articles and ordering them by latest.

'Oh God,' I whisper, unable to keep it inside. The skin on my arm prickles my eyes hover over a new article from *hashtagnofilter*. An article that I know, from the headline alone, changes everything. I dive in and read.

> Hashtagnofilter – you're thinking it, we're saying it
>
> Place your bets. Ours is on Reiss Rose, on the yacht, with the Gamma-hydroxybutyrate.
>
> According to more reputable news sources than mine, the police have confirmed that they're treating Stella Knight's death as suspicious. But what I lack in reputability I'll make up for with an inside scoop. Who cares if I got the info from a policeman I shagged once?
>
> According to our police source, it was GHB what done her in. I speak from experience when I say that GHB (also known as G

or liquid ecstasy) is most often used among people engaging in what is affectionately called chemsex. Since the police are treating Stella's death as suspicious, she mustn't have chosen to take it. Wonder if her husband told the police she was too much of a bore to want to use it in the bedroom? As far as murder weapons go, GHB isn't a bad choice: a splash too much and you're in a coma or, in Stella's case, dead.

So we know where Stella died, we know how she died, might we also know who killed her?

Thing is, GHB has been mentioned on this site before. Back when I reported on Reiss Rose being rushed to hospital after overdosing on the stuff. Maybe things weren't as rosy between the two friends as they'd like us to believe!

The article stares at me and I stare back at it. Something catches in my throat. It claws at the back of it, making me splutter and cough.

'Sweetie, are you OK?' asks Reiss, his voice sounding miles away. I feel like a razorblade is sliding up and down my throat as my body works to get rid of it. 'I'll get you a glass of water.' Tears stream from my eyes and heat burns in my cheeks as the coughing continues. Is this what Stella felt like as the GHB infected her system? Was her throat raw as she hacked her guts up, as her body tried to save itself? The thought makes me dizzy.

A glass of clear liquid is shoved towards me. I hesitate over whether to accept it after what I've just read but another round of coughing forces me to. I swallow it down gulp after gulp, not caring that it spills down my chin. 'Must have been pollen,' he says. 'Happens to me sometimes.' He takes the empty water glass from me and heads inside. I wrap my fingers around my throat and try to catch my breath. Sweat trickles down my back and my breathing remains ragged and panicked.

'A present for your swift recovery, sweetie. Deliciously tahini-laden hummus.' Reiss returns to the balcony, setting down a blue-edged bowl and a wide platter of carrot and pepper and celery. I shake my head, I couldn't possibly eat anything right now.

He picks up a wedge of carrot and slides it through the bowl. Clumps of beige mush cling to it as he raises it to his plump lips. 'For something that looks so gross, it sure does taste fabulous. Come over and grab something, you've barely eaten today.' He waves me to join him at the table but I'm cemented to the spot. 'What?' he asks when I don't move.

'What have you done?' My voice is low and gravelly, the tension rising inside me exacerbated by my recent fear of choking. It was dangerous to let myself get close to him. I took a risk and it's backfiring.

'What have I done?' Reiss asks. Something tells me he has no idea what's coming.

'A fatal dose of GHB killed Stella.'

The piece of carrot in Reiss's hand drops, splattering hummus on the table. 'But that doesn't have anything to do with me.' He sounds shaky, like he's trying to make himself believe his own words.

'Doesn't it? It isn't a drug you use?'

Reiss rises to his feet. He walks towards me, his eyes wide and pleading. 'I use it, occasionally. Recreationally only. I didn't use it to kill Stella. Why would I?'

Means. Tick.

Opportunity. Tick.

Motive. To be confirmed.

'People think you killed Stella.'

'People? Who's people?'

'*Hashtagnofilter*. They've written an article implying it.'

'I didn't kill Stella. I didn't!' His voice is so high it could break glass. My jaw tightens, my teeth grinding against one another. 'I didn't,' he repeats.

'Then why did you keep it secret?'

'I didn't keep this a secret. I didn't know my drug habit was relevant until this very moment. What does the article say?'

'Look for yourself.' I hand him my phone. He reads, spluttering words of disbelief as he does.

'They mention reporting on my overdose. Why would I kill Stella with a drug that I'm publicly linked to? It doesn't make any sense.'

My breathing starts to slow – he's right, it doesn't make any sense. Killing a friend with a drug you are known to take would be monumentally stupid, and Reiss isn't stupid.

'Could be a double bluff?' I challenge. 'Use a drug that is linked to you to purposefully change the focus of the investigation.'

'It could be, but it isn't. *If* I wanted to kill Stella, there is no way I'd take that sort of risk.' He paces the length of the balcony. 'Oh my God, will the police see it that way? Is this grounds to arrest me? I can't go to prison.'

There's a shrill pip and he jumps backward. His hand upsets the tray of crudités, flipping the bowl of hummus and sending the whole thing crashing to the floor.

'Shit, shit, shit.' Reiss's hands tremble as he picks up the shattered pieces and places them on the table. The noise comes again and Reiss lurches to his feet. 'Someone's at the door.' My heartbeat quickens and I follow him as he skitters towards the intercom. 'Do you think...' he starts to say before trailing off. He stands beside it staring at it like it's the barrel of a loaded gun, convinced it's the police here to arrest him for a crime he says didn't commit. The intercom beeps again and Reiss leans against the wall. He looks in danger of collapse. I go to him and pick the phone up.

'Hello, who's calling?' I ask.

'Where's Reiss?' asks a breathy voice.

Reiss snatches the phone from me and presses it to his ear. 'Isla, it's you. Thank God, I thought you were... well, it doesn't matter. Come on up, sweetie.'

His shoulders sag from relief as he buzzes her in, making me aware of just how tense he was when he thought it was the police. More tense than the article should warrant. There's something he isn't telling me.

Reiss pulls the door open and wraps his arms around Isla, collapsing into her. Isla rocks him gently from side to side. 'Darling, I came as soon as I saw what was posted. I can't believe they wrote that about you, you should sue. Have you spoken to your lawyer? I think you should.'

I stand awkwardly beside them, contemplating whether accusing Reiss was the best thing to do. But I didn't have a choice. I must follow the investigation where it takes me, however hard that might be. Reiss rests his head on Isla's collarbone, his shoulders shaking, and she strokes his back, telling him it will all be all right. I fold my arms across my chest and narrow my eyes at her. I can't put my finger on it but there's something about Isla that I just don't like. She puts me on edge.

'Shall we sit?' I ask, my tone curt, unable to hide my annoyance at her interruption. Isla ushers Reiss to the sofa, giving the whiteboard a glance as she walks past it.

'These are your suspects?' she asks, settling Reiss down on the couch and offering to make him a tea.

'Yes,' I reply, not elaborating.

'I think it's a bit shit of you to ask for Reiss's help but still have his name up there on the board.' Her eyes are daggers as she puts several scoops of tea leaves into a pot. My nostrils flare. Has Reiss said something to her about me?

'Firstly, he asked for my help,' I snipe. 'And secondly, we need to be thorough. Reiss agrees, don't you?'

Reiss sniffs and wipes his damp cheeks with a tissue. He nods, showing me despite his tears he is in agreement.

'Like it or not, Reiss had the opportunity and the means to pull it off. I don't think he killed Stella, but it would hurt our investigation to not cover all bases.'

Isla huffs and carries a tray laden with the teapot and mugs towards us. Her eyes are hard and unforgiving. Then she says, 'Let me help you. What can I do?' She picks up the teapot and pours steaming, fragrant tea into three mugs, locking eyes with me as she offers me mine. She doesn't trust me, it's written all over her face, but Reiss evidently takes comfort from her being here, so I have to work with that.

I bring the tea to my lips and blow on it. Swirls of aromatic steam rise from it, helping me unwind. Then I put the mug down and press my palms to my aching eyes.

'Are you OK?' asks Reiss.

'Just drained. I've not been sleeping well recently.' Recently is a stretch, I haven't slept well in years.

'I've got something that will help,' he says. Reiss goes upstairs, leaving Isla and me sitting opposite each other. The silence swells between us. Her years of meditation and yoga have clearly made her more comfortable with silence than I am. I get up and move towards the whiteboard.

'Now we're talking about it, there are some more details I need to add.' I scrawl John Owen's name next to Clare's and add the fact that Clare had opportunity.

'If I were you,' says Isla, 'Anna Nicholls would be my prime suspect.'

'Why?' I ask. I don't disagree with Isla – Anna is a suspect, and a high-priority one at that. My focus has been on Clare and Make It, Don't Fake It, but I know I need to pick things up with her again.

Isla takes a sip of tea, her dark eyes staring at me over the rim of the mug. She places it down in front of her. These slow, considered movements must be part of an act. Surely you can't get through life at this snail's pace. I clench my jaw, resisting the urge to ask her the question again. I don't want to give her the satisfaction of knowing I'm interested in her opinion.

'Stella wasn't a good person. You only have to look at the list of suspects to know that. Imagine what it would do to someone, being surrounded by that level of toxicity every single day. I think it would drive most people to murder.'

'What *is* your issue with Stella?'

'No issue,' she says, answering much quicker this time. 'I'm simply helping you be thorough.' It takes an effort to stop my lip from curling. Isla has a way of getting under my skin, and I wonder if it's because she reminds me of my mum. My mum liked to think she was different; a free spirit whose birthright it was to stick it to the man and have fun at all times. That's why Jessica is as strait-laced as she is, for all that my mum was alternative and unbound; Jessica straitjacketed herself with normality and stability. Isla displays the same hypocrisy that I came to associate with Mum, criticising the man for taking, but snatching at everything that came her way and giving very little back. Maybe I'm being unfair, but the little I know of Isla unsettles me and the ground feels shaky with her around.

'Here sweetie, I've found it.' I break my eye contact with Isla. Reiss is coming down the stairs holding out a thick, padded eye mask. 'I'll just heat it up for you.' He chucks it in the microwave. 'Isla doesn't like Stella because of how she rose to prominence. Remember how angry you were when you came back from that date?'

'What date?' I ask.

'Isla went on a date with Stella's cousin, didn't you sweetie? He told her all about how he was instrumental in Stella's rise to fame.'

'In what sense?'

'He worked at KnockKnock at the time. He tweaked the algorithm to promote Stella more. She was featured a lot, it took her stratospheric.'

'And he confessed all of this to you?' I ask Isla. Isla's expression is thunderous. She nods.

'Told her he'd promote her too, if she'd let him in his pants.' Reiss winks at her. Isla sets her mug down on the table forcefully.

'What did you say to that?' I ask, aghast. The look on Isla's face is almost enough to make me want to duck for cover.

'To be absolutely clear,' she says, her voice shaking. 'You're asking me if I whored myself out for fame?'

'I...' My mind searches desperately for something that will save me from her stare.

'I said no.'

'You were furious, weren't you babe?' says Reiss. Isla shoots him a look but he doesn't seem to notice her annoyance – he seems almost gleeful to be sharing such gossip. Isla crosses one of her long legs over the other and clasps her hands around her knee, positioning herself like a politician about give a television interview.

'I value fairness a lot, and the way Stella's cousin helped her felt very unfair. We were all playing in the same sandbox, but she'd been given an advantage over the rest of us. And then to have the same advantage dangled in front of me by this repulsive man in exchange for sleeping with him. Well, that was very upsetting.'

'Wow,' I say, unsure how to compute this information. I don't know if it has any bearing on this case. My eyes itch from tiredness and I rub at them with my knuckles.

'Oh, the eye mask,' says Reiss 'I forgot. Lie back, sweetie, and I'll get it for you.'

My legs sink into the deep, soft cushions and I place my head against the arm of the couch. Reiss hands me the eye mask and helps me secure it at the back. The heat sinks into my skin and the muscles around my eyes sing with relief. The tightness loosens as the pain is smothered. My phone digs into my back and I pull it out from under me, placing it on the table.

'Like I said, my priority suspect would be Anna Nicholls. Working every day with a woman who cheated her way to the top, who practically killed a little girl. If I were her, I'd want a way out.'

'Isla,' says Reiss. 'You don't know anything about Anna. You can't just invent things because you think you would behave a certain way in a certain scenario.'

Isla huffs. There's a deep droning sound as my phone vibrates against the wooden coffee table.

'Oh my God,' says Reiss. I sit up and pull the eye mask off my face. Reiss stares down at my mobile phone.

'What?' The screen is still glowing from the incoming message. Isla and Reiss both look at it. I lean in closer to see that it's from Oneangrymum.

> Maggie. I'm sorry about before. It might be stupid of me to tell you this because it doesn't look good for me, but keeping it a secret could hinder the investigation. I hated Stella, but her killer should be punished. I was invited to the ceremony by someone who goes by the persona of Make It Don't Fake It and I think they could have something to do with Stella's death.

'Fuck,' I say under my breath, snatching my phone up from the table and swiping to open it up.

'Who's Oneangrymum?' asks Isla.

I ignore Isla's question and type back to Clare: *Who are they?*

'Her name's Clare Owen,' says Reiss, pointing at the whiteboard. 'She's the mum of Abbie Owen, the girl that died from overdosing on diet pills,' says Reiss.

Clare answers almost immediately.

> It's better if you come round. I'd prefer to
> tell you in person. My husband is out with a
> client tomorrow afternoon, come over then.

OK, I reply and place my phone back down on the table.

'She wants me to go and see her tomorrow when her husband's at work. She says she has information.'

'About what?' asks Isla.

'About Stella's death. What else would it be about?' I snap at Isla. Her incessant questions are annoying. She isn't involved in this investigation, I wish she'd go away and leave Reiss and me to it. As if reading my mind Isla stands, her face contorted in a grimace of anger.

'It's clear I'm not wanted here. I'll leave.'

'Oh Isla, don't be like that,' says Reiss, getting up to stand next to her.

'No, I'll leave you and your new friend alone. If you'd be so kind as to let me use the bathroom before I go. I assume that's still fine.'

'Of course it is, you're being ridiculous.' Reiss opens his arms to embrace her, but she jerks her body away from him and storms up the stairs.

Reiss plonks himself down on the couch and shakes his head. The need to apologise wells up inside me but I swallow it down. She's the problem, not me.

'I think she's jealous.' He tips his head towards the stairs, talking more in Isla's direction than to me. 'Of our new friendship.'

'Yes, and she doesn't hide it well.'

Isla comes thundering down the stairs, her braids bouncing off her shoulders. She picks up her tie-dye linen bag from the floor, throws her head through the strap and, without a second glance backward, flies through the door. It bangs shut behind her. Reiss blows a raspberry and crosses his legs in front of him before grabbing his mug of tea.

'Where were we?' he asks. Where we were before Isla arrived was him trying to convince me that he had nothing to do with Stella Knight's death. He was so keen to tell me about the secret Isla knew about Stella's fame, a piece of information that could potentially attribute blame to his friend – like he was trying to shift the focus onto someone else. He's hiding something, and I want to know what.

'Why were you so keen for me to solve Stella's murder?' I ask the question I should have asked from the beginning.

Reiss looks uncomfortable and begins to busy himself with tidying up the tea before either of us have had a chance to finish it.

'I told you in the beginning,' he says. 'I suspected foul play, and she was my friend.' The tea splashes as Reiss lifts the teapot above the sink. I edge closer to him. 'But why did you suspect foul play? You were so certain.' Reiss turns on the tap and starts noisily swilling out the mugs. He's blocking out my words with his clatter. 'Reiss!'

He whirls around to face me. He grips the counter tight with both hands.

'Because you heard what Isla said, Stella wasn't always a good person. I thought someone might have wanted to hurt her, and I was right, but it wasn't me. You have to believe me.'

I glare at him. Why do people say this? Do I? Do I *have* to believe him? It isn't about whether or not I believe him.

It's about logic and reason. And it is logical and reasonable for me to be suspicious of his motives.

'It's late. It's time I went home.' He starts to speak but I silence him with a wave. 'Let's talk tomorrow.'

I hurry from Reiss's flat, still undecided about what I should do about him.

–

I let myself into my house. It's in complete darkness despite the thumping music and shrieks of laughter coming from the back garden. I stalk along the hallway, where white paint flakes off the skirting boards onto the carpet. Built in the Victorian period, the house has high ceilings and odd period features that create shadowy shapes in the twilight. The sole of my shoe slides on a piece of paper that's fallen from the makeshift recycling bin, which overflows with discarded junk mail and empty boxes of cereal. Cereal has been my staple food the past year, which probably explains why my skin has paled and I've lost so much weight. Funny that – for years I tried many different ways to get rid of my puppy fat. Who knew all it would take was for something awful to happen? And when it happened, *poof*! My appetite left me as quickly as my interest in life.

I slip off my shoes and pad up the wooden stairs to my bedroom on the first floor. The floor is cold, and the clammy soles of my feet stick to it as I walk.

My bedroom is small, but it's brightened by the cream bedspread and colourful art that Jessica helped me hang on the wall when I first arrived. She was determined to help me 'make it my own'. What she didn't understand was that I didn't want it to be my own. I'd had my own and then it was gone. I didn't want anything else.

There's a full-length mirror balancing on the radiator because I never got around to hanging it on the wall. The wardrobe is off-white, yellowing with age. Its distorted doors don't close properly, so they hang open, casting long shadows on the floor.

The heat inside my room is stifling and the air still. I slide the window open and welcome the fresh breeze that comes floating in. The sun has now set but club music, shouts of laughter and the smell of something burning are coming from the garden below. One of my housemates is attempting to have a barbecue. People in swimwear are crammed together on the square inch of grass that constitutes our garden. Hands run up and down bare legs and one couple is intertwined, practically eating each other's faces, completely unashamed that they're surrounded by onlookers. The music is awful and loud. I grab my ear plugs and push them into my ears. Though the sound is dulled, the vibrations still penetrate the building and enter my bones, but I need the breeze more than I need the silence.

I put on my PJs and lie on top of my bed. After last night's fitful, alcohol-laden sleep and a day filled with running all over the city, I'm exhausted. My back aches and there's a pounding behind one of my eyes.

My phone buzzes. A text from Reiss.

Isla thinks we need to look at Anna Nicholls more closely. Shall I go and meet her tomorrow?

Heat rises within me; I don't want him interviewing people without me. This is my investigation, not his. Part of me thinks he only ever wanted to help me so that he could control the narrative, but no, that can't be true – he didn't know Stella was going to be murdered, did he? Clare asked me to visit her tomorrow afternoon, so perhaps I ought to visit Anna in the morning. She is a good next step, she still has secrets to reveal and she might be able to tell me more about Reiss and Stella's relationship, because I'm certain he isn't telling me the full story. I type my reply.

No, I will speak to her. Alone!

Chapter Eighteen

The Social Sleuth, *extract from most recent post*

Interstellars, I need your help. Find me Anna
Nicholls.

Monday

The Interstellars find Anna Nicholls with a speed
bordering on alarming. If they are to be believed, Anna
Nicholls can be found at a co-working space just around
the corner from Stella Knight's Chelsea house. Their
messages said that Anna works there every day, close
enough to have meetings with her boss in person if
needed, but far enough away to give Stella her own space.
It strikes me as odd that Anna is working today – you'd
think if ever there was a reason not to work, your boss
being dead would be it, but the Interstellars say she is at
the office, and who am I to argue with their network? I
called my boss and told him I was sick. I'm not usually one
to break the rules like this but fortune, as they say, favours
the brave, and I need to continue my investigation.

It's not even nine a.m. and my bedroom is oppressively
hot. I don't know when London started getting summers
like this, but every year it's got harder and harder to bear.

The big old houses of this city are not set up to handle Mediterranean heat. Nothing in England is. The news is filled with reports of chaos at train stations as train after train is cancelled as the steel tracks swell in the heat, losing their shape and making it impossible to travel. There are images of British beaches crammed with sunseekers roasting their flesh, unfazed by the threat of burning, and warnings about not leaving your dogs, children or elderly relatives in airless cars or rooms lest they die from dehydration. You'd think the summer sunshine would bring with it happiness, but it doesn't – the news remains as sombre and doomsaying as ever.

Dressed in a pair of shorts and a loose blouse, I pull my backpack from my wardrobe, fill it with essentials and head out. Until I know more about Reiss Rose and his agenda, I will do this alone. His presence might make Anna less willing to talk; she's wary of him, she suggested as much.

My hands tremble as I gently close my bedroom door and slide the key into the lock. The house is deathly silent, so different to the chaos of last night. As I walk past the living room a quick glance at the state of it causes me to pause. It's a scene that wouldn't look out of place as an image on my true crime blog. There are two half-naked bodies: one on the couch, their arm flopping down over it, the other curled in a ball on the floor. They look like corpses left behind after a massacre, surrounded by debris: paper cups, half-drunk bottles of beer, and there are pizza boxes scattered across the coffee table, lids tilted back to display discarded crusts edged with teeth marks. The air is thick with the stench of cigarette smoke. Further evidence of the party I wasn't a part of.

'What are you staring at?' growls one of the bodies, the tattoo on his arm moving as he tenses. My body jolts and I squeal like a pig caught in a hunter's trap. I'd been so caught up in how still they were, almost corpse-like, that I wasn't expecting them to speak to me; the noise that exits my mouth is humiliating.

'Don't mind her,' says my housemate. 'She lives here, but she's a bit weird.'

I march towards the front door, heat rising in my cheeks. I wrench it open, hoping the loud creak exacerbates their hangovers, and step out into the bright morning sun.

I stand for a moment on the top step, the rays of the sun adding to the warmth of my already flushed cheeks. My housemate said I was weird. I'm weird? I'm not the one sleeping on the living room floor when there's a perfectly acceptable bed that I own two floors up. My hands curl into fists and my fingernails dig into my flesh, the pain getting sharper the harder I squeeze. How am I the weird one just because I don't want to sleep half naked in the communal living room of my shared house?

'Urgh!' I say, shaking my hands out and disturbing a cat who scuttles from the next-door neighbour's hedge. My work as a personal assistant at a law firm isn't worth living in near-squalor with people who behave like hooligans and treat me like a pariah. I wanted to stay here, in London, while I got myself back on my feet and started my blog, but I can't live like this for much longer. I'm not judging my housemates for wanting to party and have a good time, it's more that it's at complete odds with the way I want to live my life. I've worked hard and partied hard before but I'm almost thirty and I'm tired of it.

The street is busy with late commuters; they hurry in lines like ants. The faces around me are flushed and covered in a light sheen of sweat. My phone buzzes in my pocket and I pull it out to see a KnockKnock notification flash up.

Bam! Someone slams into the back of me and my phone flies from my hand, skittering across the pavement. It teeters on the edge of it, in danger of tipping into the road.

'Urgh, you shouldn't just stop like that,' growls a particularly red-faced man as he sweeps past me, not bothering to check I'm all right. Multiple pairs of shoes stomp past, and my phone is kicked this way and that. I dive towards it, ignoring the shocked looks of the people around me. Cars and buses crawl past, overtaken at every point by bikes that whizz by so quickly they whip the air. If my phone tips into their path it will be crushed.

I step forward and bend down to scoop it up in my hands. A crack so straight it might have been made by a knife divides it right down the middle and the edges are scuffed. I wince; a globule of blood, like a tiny cherry, blooms on the tip of my finger where the skin caught on frayed glass.

What did I tell you about getting a phone case? Jessica's voice hisses in my head, and I resist the urge to groan loudly. There is no sentiment in the world more unhelpful and more damaging than *I told you so*, but that's what Jessica would have said if she were here now. Luckily, despite the damage, my phone still works.

I suck my finger, the metallic taste of blood sticking to the roof of my mouth. Commuters continue to hurry past me so, deciding not to risk another incident, I shove my phone into my bag, hurry to the station, tap my Oyster card on the circular pad and rush up the stairs two at a time before squeezing myself onto the packed train.

Rush hour travelling is not a fun experience and something I usually avoid as an early riser. People press their bodies against mine, so close that my nostrils prickle with the musty stench of their sweat. I weave my hand between them in search of a handle as the movement of the train rams me into my fellow passengers. Something digs into my back and I inhale sharply, stiffening as though it's a knife-point. A quick glance around tells me it's nothing more sinister than the buckle of a backpack, and I release the breath. I'm not in danger – why would I be?

–

Forty-five minutes later, I ride up the escalator at the tube station and head through the barriers out to Sloane Square. In the centre of the square, there's a pop-up cafe surrounded by metal chairs and tables. People sit and stand around, chatting. Like the people at the Influencer of the Year awards, they look moneyed. As I walk down the King's Road, well-loved by the Middleton sisters, every woman I pass is wearing the same thing but in different colours. It seems a cotton maxi dress, paired with white trainers, big sunglasses and glossy hair, is the wealthy woman's summer uniform. Are they looking at me, in my shorts and blouse, and recognising that I don't belong here? I'm starting to think that I don't belong anywhere.

After about ten minutes of walking I turn down the street that I'm headed for. It's beautiful; the houses are terraced, their bottom halves painted white, their top halves exposing the brick. Every house looks the same, except for the front doors, which are all painted a different pastel shade. The 4x4s that line the street are almost as big as the houses they belong to.

A little further down, I stop outside the address I'm looking for. It looks just like the other houses, and I feel a flutter of panic. Have the Interstellars sent me to Stella's front door and not the co-working space by accident? The door is wrenched open and man stands before me. My knees knock in the fear that I'm about to come face to face with Christopher Clarke. The man barks in surprise and I scan his face. It isn't Christopher.

'Oh sorry, didn't expect there to be anyone there. Here.' He takes a step back and holds the door open for me. His gesture calms me – surely he wouldn't do that if that was someone's house, especially if it was the house of a dead woman. I slide past him, my legs still strong enough to carry me through.

'Good morning,' says a pretty blonde woman sitting at a reception desk, her tone as bright as her teeth.

'Good morning. I'm looking for Anna Nicholls. Apparently she's working here.'

'One moment,' says the woman and types at her computer. 'Would you like me to tell her you're here?'

'Yes, please.'

'What's your name?' asks the woman, getting to her feet.

'Maggie Shaw,' I reply. The woman nods and heads towards a door at the back of the hallway. She swipes her pass against a reader, pulls the door open and disappears behind it.

There's an oak bench positioned opposite the reception desk and I sit down on it, glancing around. So this is what these houses look like from the inside? It isn't flashy or evidently remarkable, but there is a quiet expense to it all, that combination of polished and rustic. Goodness knows how much Stella paid to let Anna work here.

I stand at the sound of the door being pulled open and the blonde woman returns to her desk. Anna Nicholls walks towards me, her eyes narrowed.

'What are you doing here?' she mutters, glancing at the receptionist, who pretends not to be listening.

'I just want a very quick chat,' I say. Anna purses her lips and I can see her thinking about how best to dismiss me without seeming rude. I've travelled too far to be dismissed, so I add, 'There have been some developments in the case. I know about the girl that Stella killed.'

Anna's forehead creases. 'What the...' She flashes a look at the receptionist, who resumes her typing. 'Follow me. I'm sitting in the back garden.'

Anna leads me through the house, past several people sitting on desk chairs typing away on their laptops. She pushes open a door at the very back of the hall and together we enter the garden. Isn't large, but there's enough space for three tables surrounded by four chairs each. Broad linen umbrellas are open over all of them. Despite the wonderful weather, it seems Anna is the only person working outside apart from one man at the back, pacing and talking jovially on the telephone.

Anna sits down in front of her open laptop and I take the seat next to her.

'What the hell are you talking about? "The girl that Stella killed", what does that mean?'

Anna listens agog as I tell her about Clare Owen and her daughter. 'So that's what the forums were referring to?' she asks.

'Seems so. Clare and Make It, Don't Fake It teamed up to threaten Stella and scare her into coming clean.'

'And you've no idea who Make It, Don't Fake It is?' Anna asks, her eyes studying me as if worried I'll lie.

'No idea,' I say.

Anna takes a deep breath and nods. 'OK, thanks for telling me.'

Up close, I see that she looks awful. It's only been two days since Stella's death, but Anna could have been grieving for a lifetime. Her eyes are bloodshot, the rims of them red and sore-looking. As if reading my mind, she picks up her sunglasses and places them on her face.

'How are you?' I ask as sympathetically as I can.

'I've been better.' Her voice is soft but her jaw tightens. She sighs. 'You're full steam ahead with your investigation then?'

'Yes.'

'I'm sorry, but I don't want to be associated with this. I don't want to be mentioned on your blog or whatever it is you have.'

I nod. 'Yeah, I understand. But since I told you about Clare, could you humour me? Answer a few questions.'

She shrugs. 'Depends what your questions are, but I could do with a break, so ask me and let's see.'

'OK, an easy one,' I say, knowing exactly where to start. 'Why are you working today?'

Anna reaches into her bag and pulls a can of Diet Coke from it. She opens it and takes a sip. 'There's still a lot to be done. Stella might be dead, but that doesn't mean her business doesn't need an assistant. There are meetings to cancel. Contracts to review. Affairs to be handled.'

'Couldn't her husband do that?'

Anna laughs. 'That would require him to work. The very first thing I learnt about Christopher Clarke is that the man doesn't like to work. He's practically allergic to it.'

'Good thing he had a rich wife then.'

'Quite,' says Anna, taking another sip of Coke.

'Can you tell me a little more about Reiss and Stella's friendship?'

'They weren't friends. I've told you that before.' Her white-blonde eyebrow raises, peeking out from beneath her shades.

'Well, he told me they'd been friends since they both started out in the industry, and they've filmed videos together and stuff.'

'That's business. It's different.' I wait for her to continue. She sighs and adds, 'Two narcissistic people spending time together isn't a friendship. Two people only talking about themselves isn't a conversation. The thing about Reiss and Stella is that both of them could only spend time with people who idolised them. People who would sit and listen. Reiss and Stella couldn't stand to be around one another because they were both desperate for the same limelight.'

Anna's words make me uncomfortable. Is that what I am to Reiss? Someone who idolises him, someone happy to sit and listen to him talk about himself? I guess I have been a little in awe, and now Anna's mentioned it, it's true that he hasn't asked me a single thing about myself – it's all been about him or Stella.

'You really didn't like her, did you?'

Anna looks at me, her face set, and I worry that she's going to tell me to get lost. She sighs as if to say, *I don't want to answer but I will.* 'No,' she says. 'I didn't. She was a terrible person to work for. But like I said, I didn't kill her.'

'Tell me what she was like to work for,' I say.

'Is it really that important?' sighs Anna. 'I shouldn't be saying any of these things. I don't want to get myself into any trouble and I would like to be employable in the future. Slagging off my late boss doesn't exactly put me in people's good books. I don't see how what I have to say can help you find out who killed her.'

'It might not be important, but if you felt a certain way about her that wasn't favourable there might be other people who felt that way too. Other people who wanted to hurt her. Former friends, boyfriends, employees. You name it. Also, I remember that when we met on Saturday, you were upset with how mean she'd been to you about the dress that ripped, but you said something about her doing lots of other horrible things. What were they?'

Anna's demeanour of cynicism and careless exhaustion changes now. Her body seems to bristle at the question and she turns her face away from me to look over my shoulder at the man laughing raucously on the telephone. Then she takes a deep breath in through her nose, steeling herself for something.

'I always told myself I'd tell everyone what she was like one day. I've always wanted to get it all off my chest. So I might as well do it now.' I'm not entirely sure that she's still speaking to me, it sounds more like she's pushing herself into being honest. Anna turns to look at me. 'If you must know, I hated her, she was…' Anna's nostrils flare and she bites down hard on her bottom lip as if physically trying to stop herself from saying everything she wants to.

'Go on…'

'She was mean and critical, the type of person who would only point out what you'd done wrong but not tell you when you'd done something right.' Anna is off like a horse from the starting gates – she has started telling her truth and now she's unstoppable. 'I'm not saying I expected daily praise, but when you only get told all the wrong things you've done it starts to make you think that *everything* you do is wrong. But she had this attitude of *I'm paying her well so her happiness doesn't matter.* She also had no respect for boundaries. I was required to keep my phone on me at all times. Holidays, evenings and weekends had no meaning to Stella Knight. The number of times I got indigestion because halfway through lunch she started messaging me frantically about something, or I had to leave parties with friends... I had to cancel my trip to the Vatican last month, something I was bloody excited about, because of some drama that needed handling.' Anna scoffs. 'The pay was good until you divided it by the number of hours I was working.'

'I remember you saying you couldn't quit. That you had responsibilities. What were they?'

'I kept saying I would quit but then...' Anna trails off and gives a loud hiccupping cry. 'Sorry, I haven't talked about this before,' she says, using both hands to wipe the tears that are running down her cheeks. She gives herself a little shake. 'I kept saying I would quit but...' She trails off again.

'But what?' I press.

'But my family needed the income.'

'That badly?' I ask. 'You're clearly talented, Anna. I'm sure you could have got a job anywhere.'

'It's complicated.'

I sensed there was more to this, and now I know I'm right. 'Anna,' I say, gently. 'You can tell me, I want to help.'

She sighs. 'I'm the oldest of four children, and Dad has never been in the picture. I wouldn't recognise him if I walked past him on the street. And... and... about the same time I got the job with Stella, my mum was diagnosed with breast cancer. It meant she couldn't work and the sick leave arrangements at her job weren't good. My younger siblings were at school, in fact two of them are still at school, so I needed to provide for my family.'

'I'm so sorry to hear that, Anna.' I reach out a hand and clasp it around hers.

She pulls her hand away, saying, 'There's no way I would have killed Stella. Even if I wanted to leave, I would need another job.'

'How is your mum now?'

Anna whimpers and the answer hangs in the air before she gives it. 'She died about a month ago.' Anna's nostrils flare again and she pushes her sunglasses up on her head, staring at me with angry, crimson eyes. 'And do you know the worst part?' Anna's body vibrates as she tries to contain the animosity within her.

'What?' I whisper.

'I wasn't there. The doctors had told me it was coming, and I asked Stella if I could leave early to be with her and...' Anna clamps her hand over her mouth to stopper the cry that rises like vomit.

'Stella refused?' I ask.

'She refused,' says Anna through gritted teeth. Anna's chest rises and falls, and her hands grip the wooden table in front of her. Her hyperventilating is contagious. The pain of not being able to be with her mum radiates from her and presses against my body, squeezing my chest. Another story of heartbreak and anguish that has Stella at the centre of it.

'Did you not want revenge?'

'No,' snaps Anna. 'And if I did, I wouldn't have killed her. If I was going to hurt her, and don't mistake me when I say I thought about it, I'd have contacted all her past assistants and built a list of stories and leaked them to the media. I'd want her alive so I could see her expression as the world she built crumbled around her.'

'Do you have any idea who might have killed her?'

Anna takes a deep breath. 'Yes, actually, I do. Mind, it might make you rethink your whole investigation.'

My pulse quickens. 'Tell me,' I whisper, leaning in closer to her.

'Do you know how Reiss Rose became famous?' she asks.

'His make-up tutorials.'

'Partly, but did he tell you about his exposés?'

'Vaguely.'

'Reiss would pick a celebrity who had sworn they'd never had surgery, showed a before and after photograph and recorded himself dissecting the image. The videos went viral. It was a huge deal, and he was celebrated for it. It rocketed him to internet fame because he was saying what nobody else wanted to.'

'What's that got to do with Stella?'

I don't like where this is going. With every word Anna speaks, I can almost feel the rug being tugged from beneath my feet. My muscles tense, preparing themselves for a fall.

'What do you think would happen to Reiss if the world knew that he'd had work done himself?' she asks, her tone challenging. A weight falls heavily into my stomach. 'I overheard Stella and him having a conversation about it. No, not a conversation, an argument. Stella said that if he didn't come clean himself, she would expose him.'

'When did this happen?'

'A week before the Influencer of the Year awards. Stella said he had one week to tell everyone. Why do you think he withdrew his name from the award nominations?'

'Why would Stella do that? I know you keep saying they weren't friends, but exposing a fellow influencer seems a bit off to me.'

'Stella wasn't in the habit of sharing her thoughts and feelings with me,' says Anna, replacing her upset with heavy sarcasm. 'But if I had to hazard a guess, I'd say it was because she was scared about what was being discussed about her. I'm assuming that she thought if she could create a scandal about someone else it might protect her.'

'Why didn't you tell me this before?' I ask. 'When I told you Stella was murdered, why didn't you immediately think of Reiss?'

'It was all happening so quickly. I barely had time to process that Stella was dead, let alone think about who might have killed her.'

My chest tightens. I feel winded. Reiss Rose, the person I've let myself get close to in this investigation, had a motive for murdering Stella – and a bloody big one at that. This changes everything.

'Anna.' A woman's voice makes us both jump. I whirl around to find the receptionist standing behind me, looking down at Anna expectantly. 'The police are here to speak to you.'

'The police?' she asks. Her face clouds.

'Yes. Two of them. I've reserved you one of the meeting rooms.'

'Now?'

'Yes, they're waiting. They asked me to bring you to them.'

'There's one more question I want to ask,' I say, quickly. Anna stops her rise and looks at me, raising an eyebrow. 'Why did Stella give up drinking and drugs?'

Anna's shoulders drop as she exhales loudly and lowers her voice to a whisper. 'She wanted to get pregnant. Thought a baby might save her—'

But before she can finish her sentence the reception interrupts. 'Anna, the police said it was urgent.'

'Urgent?' Anna's face pales and she pushes herself off the chair unsteadily before hurrying away without another backward glance.

I flop back in my chair. Stella wanted to have a baby. She thought a baby might save her what? Her career? Her marriage? Her life?

I need to know the answer to this question. As soon as the door closes behind Anna, I reach forward and drag Anna's laptop towards me, hoping that it hasn't yet logged her out.

It hasn't. What she was working on before I arrived is still visible: the backend of the *Fashionsista* website. I lean in closer.

'Shit,' I whisper under my breath.

On Anna's screen is an article in draft. An article written by Stella, announcing Reiss's surgery. So Anna is telling the truth, Stella was about to expose Reiss's secret. The article is finished and ready to be released, but now it never will be, because Stella is dead. The timing of her death is highly convenient; if Reiss were up in front of a jury, this would surely seal his fate. My spine stiffens. I knew he was hiding something, but I ignored the signs. I can't face any more surprises. I need to know: what other secrets might Stella have been harbouring?

I glance towards the back door of the office and, satisfying myself that Anna isn't about to catch me, close down the article and slide my finger over the trackpad, dragging the cursor to *drafts*.

There are over one hundred articles in draft. If every single one of them is going to reveal some scandal this investigation might go on forever. But to my relief, when the page with the list of draft articles opens, I find that this isn't the case. The headings are mostly innocuous things like 'Things I'm buying this week' or 'My trip to Sorrento'. But there is one that stands out.

'IT IS OVER.'

This is important, I can feel it. I open the article. I don't even give myself time to read it – I copy it quickly, my fingers trembling.

A door nearby opens; Anna is coming back into the garden. I switch the tabs to reopen Anna's email. As quickly as I can I paste the article into an empty email, send it to myself, and delete the sent email before pushing the laptop back to where I got it from. Anna approaches the table. Her eyes dart from me to her laptop and back to me again, her expression darkening as she realises her error at leaving it with me. She slams it shut and shoves it in her bag. But any comment she might have made to censure me is interrupted by two people entering the garden behind her. I feel my expression drop.

'Hello, Maggie,' says Detective Inspector Matthew Alebiosu. He stops in front of me and clasps his hands together. Detective Sergeant Angela Swain positions herself beside him.

'I was just leaving,' I say, jumping to my feet and picking my bag up from the floor. Matthew exchanges a look with his partner. I start to hurry away, not wanting to give them a chance to question me.

'Maggie,' calls Angela. I turn around to face her. 'Be careful. You wouldn't want to get yourself in any trouble now.'

My heart feels as though it's jumped into my mouth but I nod, wrench open the door and rush away from them.

–

I jog down the King's Road, keen to put as much distance as possible between myself and the police officers. The hustle and bustle of the shopping street is disorientating. The pretty colours of the women's dresses seem garish now, clownlike. My head swims, my mind as busy as the street.

Stella was threatening to expose Reiss unless he announced his plastic surgery. Reiss has it all now. He benefited from Stella's death, he had access to the drugs that did it, and the ability to tamper with her drink. Heat courses through my body as anger consumes me. I want to charge up to Reiss and slap him hard across the face. He's made a fool of me. He thought he could cosy up to me to control the narrative.

But it isn't as clear-cut as Anna makes out. It's in her interests to point the finger at Reiss because she has her own reasons for wanting Stella dead. Stella denying Anna time with her mum before she died is so cruel it makes my heart flipflop. It's painfully sad, but it's just as much of a motive as Reiss's. Anna was on the boat too. Anna fits the description of the waitress.

And there's a new piece to this puzzle, the article that I found in drafts. The article that I copied and pasted and emailed it to myself just in time.

Then I remember the message on KnockKnock this morning, the one I got before my phone was bounced out of my hand. I check it now. It's a message from Clare Owen.

> Call me as soon as you can.

'Fuck!' I say to my phone screen. The stupid man who bumped into me flustered and distracted me. Without hesitation, I call Clare Owen through the KnockKnock app. The call rings multiple times before it disconnects because she isn't answering.

But a message comes through from her the second I hang up.

> Come over. Now!

Chapter Nineteen

The Social Sleuth, *extract from blog 20*

> It was a piece of evidence so small that it could have easily been missed, but in the end the tiny scrap of fabric unravelled the whole thing.

I stop outside Clare's house. In the time it has taken for me to travel to her, she hasn't seen my message telling her I'm on my way. The house looks the same as it did before, squashed between two other houses of the same ilk, but something is off. Before my hand even touches the Owens' front gate, Reggie's sharp barks reach my ears, incessant and unbreaking.

The closer I get to the house, the more frantic Reggie's barks become. The noise builds towards a crescendo and my heartbeat matches it. I ball my hand into a fist and I raise it to the door, rapping three times. Reggie's paws scuffle against the wooden floor inside the house and he whines and scratches at the door. Bees hover around the lavender plant blooming in the little patch of soil that runs parallel to the path, their gentle buzzing in complete contrast to the frustrated moans of the dog behind the door. There's no shuffling of human feet behind Reggie. Surely if Clare was in, she'd have heard the dog? The whole street has probably heard the dog.

Something is wrong. I crouch down and lift the letterbox an inch.

'Ouch,' I yelp, pulling my hand away and sucking on the finger that Reggie nipped. I proceed again, this time being careful to keep my fingers out of Reggie's reach. The second the letterbox fans open his little white teeth nip upwards, trying to get at me. The effect is part horror, part comedy. My heart pumps hard as I lean towards the gap in the door.

'Clare!' I call over Reggie's growls. No reply comes. I call her via KnockKnock again, but there's no answer. I move round to the front window. Reggie follows me, reappearing in the living room. Through the window, I watch him leap up to the top of the sofa, wobbling there on his short legs, barking and barking and barking. The simplest explanation is that Clare has gone out, popped to the shops or something. But that doesn't stop the clenching in my stomach. Clare's message told me to come over now. I press my face against the glass, cupping my hands around my eyes to look in. I stand on my tiptoes to avoid my sightline being blocked by Reggie, his slobbery mouth streaking the window as he knocks against it in his bid to get out. The glass is warm against my forehead. The sun beams directly onto it, darkening the inside. I have to strain my eyes to make everything out.

'Shit,' I say aloud. My hands drop to my sides and I rush back to the front door.

I pull off my blouse without even stopping to think that I'm standing in the front garden of a woman I barely know in just my bra. I wrap my fist in the blouse and force it through the top pane of glass in the front door. It shatters easily and I push my arm through the gap, the jagged edges of what remains catching on the fabric. I wince as a shard slices against the fleshy skin of my arm, blood pooling around the wound, but it doesn't stop me. My fingers shake as I reach for the catch of the door and flick it downwards. Carefully, I extricate my arm and push the door open.

The door swings inward and Reggie launches himself at me like a grenade. I expect him to start nipping at my ankles but he doesn't, he runs from me to the living room and back again. He's begging me for help.

I enter the living room.

'Oh my God, oh my God, oh my God,' I cry.

Clare is on the couch. Her bum is planted on the seat, but her upper body has slipped sideways, so she's twisted into an awkward position. Her whole body is leaning forward as if she's about to fall off the couch, her arms drooping by her sides. The cushions are dark with the dampness of vomit and drool.

Shit, shit, shit, shit.

'Clare,' I shout, my knees crashing against the carpeted floor. My phone is stuffed roughly into the back pocket of my shorts and I pull it out. Nine, nine, nine. I punch in the number and press it to my ear. 'Ambulance,' I say in answer to the operator's question. 'Woman. Late forties. Collapsed. Unconscious.' I'm unable to speak in full sentences and just manage to give Clare's address.

'An ambulance will be with you shortly,' says the operator. 'Would you like me to stay on the line until they come?'

'What the fuck is going on?' I hang up the phone in a panic at John's shouts. 'Clare, oh my God!' The rush of blood pounding in my ears is so loud that I didn't hear him enter the house. He looks at Clare's collapsed body, his cheeks quivering in panic and fury. 'What have you done?'

'I've called the ambulance,' I say. 'I broke in because I saw her and thought she was in danger.'

John isn't listening to me, though. His hands grip his wife's shoulders, and he is shaking her, calling out her name frantically, in time with Reggie's barks.

The sirens pip outside and I remember that I'm not wearing my blouse. I pull it roughly over my head, displacing fragments of glass. John rushes to the front door.

'Hurry,' he shouts, 'she's in here.' Feet pound along the hallway and two men in green uniforms barrel into the room. One of them starts CPR while the other starts asking questions, but his words can hardly be heard over Reggie. John bundles the little dog up and takes him away before coming back and pacing the room, answering the questions fired at him.

Her full name is Clare Elizabeth Owen.

She is forty-four years old.

She has no allergies that I'm aware of.

She takes statins every day because of her high cholesterol.

No, I can't think of what would have caused this apart from her.

John points at me, and my knees wobble at the accusation. I perch on the arm of the couch, my hands gripping my bare knees, waiting for Clare to give a sudden and gulping gasp of breath like they do in films. But she doesn't. The paramedic pulls his hands away from her chest.

'Why are you stopping?' shouts John. 'No. No! Don't stop! Please don't stop. Clare.' He goes to dive towards Clare but one of the paramedics holds him back. John points at me; his lips are moving but I can't hear what he's saying, it's like my head has been plunged under water. More sirens, more people in uniform, more conversations that I can't understand.

The room is spinning, and I can't focus on anything. I find strength in my legs to walk towards the couch, the one that hasn't become a crime scene. I sit, my bum sinking into its fleshy cushion. The officers are talking to John, they're both in uniform, sent no doubt to make an initial assessment of the situation.

John agrees to them having a look around but he insists that she wasn't depressed, so this couldn't be suicide. It's only when he says this that it hits me: Clare is dead.

John keeps pointing the officers in my direction, telling them I was here when he got home from work and that I had been harassing his wife. Heat rises in my cheeks and my vision blurs. I run my fingers along the seat of the couch, focusing on the roughness of the fabric against my fingertips, trying to ground myself. I've found two bodies in three days. This is bad for me; this is very bad for me. I force myself to stay calm and continue to run my hand up and down the length of the couch; the texture bristles against my skin and I channel all my energy into the movement as my chest rises and falls violently. Oxygen seems to flood my brain and I sway. Then my fingers brush against something smooth and round, different to the couch. I collect it into my palm and bring it towards my eyes. A gold band sits in my cupped palm. Without thought, I slip it into my handbag.

–

The room is dimly lit and cold. The walls are padded with a purple-blue felt, like someone deconstructed a sofa and positioned its cushions from floor to ceiling. Goosebumps tug the skin on my bare legs, but I resist rubbing them; instead I keep my hands on the scuffed table. Splinters of MDF fray outwards from the corners. Two police officers sit opposite me, their faces so blank they could almost be dead. They give me their names and they ask me to confirm mine. For the tape, they say.

My hands are clasped together, and I squeeze my fingers against my knuckles to stop myself wringing them. My skin is ice and yet damp clings to my palms. This is serious, very serious, and it has all escalated very quickly. Two women are dead, one of whom wouldn't be if I hadn't dug when I was warned not to. Will the police think this is my fault? *Is* it my fault?

Clare's body was left prostate on the floor next to the couch where I found her and exactly where the paramedic stopped resuscitation. The paramedic told John it was so the crime scene investigators could come and do their work. Her body will eventually be taken away to wherever bodies get taken when a death is sudden and unexplained. There will probably be a post-mortem, perhaps in the same place where Stella was post-mortemed. Is that the word to use when someone has a post-mortem done to them? The police arrived and I was escorted into the back of a police car. John, Clare's husband, was put in another, shouting and protesting that he needed to be with his wife, not treated like a suspect. I didn't argue, I was too shocked, I'm still too shocked.

My arm aches from where I cut it on the glass of the front door. There's a tight cream bandage wrapped around it now, thanks to the paramedic. The police officers don't ask if I'd like a solicitor, which must mean I'm not under arrest, but I'd decline the offer anyway, I didn't hurt Clare.

I would say that she hurt herself, but the memory of the round, golden band makes me think there is more to this than meets the eye.

'Maggie,' asks the officer, making me jump. My mind had wandered off, picturing the golden band. I've seen it before, but where?

'Yes, sorry. What was the question?'

'We'd like you to tell us what happened, from the very beginning.'

The very beginning. I don't think they're ready for the very beginning, but I decide to do my best whilst framing my side investigation as casually as possible.

I tell them that I met Clare at the Influencer of the Year awards, that I found out she was threatening Stella on the internet and that we talked about it. Then today, I tell them Clare had something she wanted to tell me, so I went to visit her. When I arrived there was no answer from the door, but Reggie was barking. This was strange, because Clare had told me she'd be around, she'd asked me to come over. I looked through the window and saw her slumped on the sofa. I broke in because I was worried, saw she was unconscious and called the ambulance.

The officers don't interrupt me as I speak but occasionally, they write something in their notebooks. Once I finish my story, one of the officers uses her pen to point to a particular note she has made on her paper.

'You met Clare at the Influencer of the Year awards where Stella Knight was murdered?'

'Yes,' I say, simply.

'Did you know her before then?'

'No.'

'How did you meet?' asks the officer, tilting her head ever so slightly to the side.

'We bumped into each other and got chatting,' I lie.

'And she invited you over today to discuss something? Even though you'd only just met?'

'Yes,' I reply, I could elaborate but I'm concerned where this might be going so I don't.

'What did Clare want to tell you that she couldn't simply write in a message? You've said you were communicating on KnockKnock?'

'I don't know because she wasn't able to tell me.'.

'Why didn't she want to write her message?' asks the second officer, finally breaking his silence.

I shrug and shake my head. I can't answer his question because I don't know why she wouldn't put the name of Make It, Don't Fake It in writing. Maybe it was so that Make It's unmasking couldn't be tied to her. So, she wouldn't look like the snitch. Maybe she was concerned about her safety. This could be something to do with her death. My skin crawls. The feeling spreads from my chest and along my arms until my fingers tingle from it. My investigation got Clare Owen killed. I'm guilty by proxy.

'I don't know that either. I'm sorry,' I reply.

'Right,' says the first officer with a sigh. She looks to her colleague and they exchange the briefest of looks. I can almost hear their brains whirring. Clare Owen was at the Influencer of the Year awards where Stella Knight was murdered, and now Clare is dead too. The two are linked, how can they not be? I wait as patiently as I can for them to speak, hoping that they will let me go while they make the necessary connections with the team dealing with Stella's murder. Matthew and Angela aren't going to be happy when they find out I called it in.

'Is there anything else you can think of that would be helpful for our investigation?' the officer asks.

I force myself to not sigh loudly in relief.

'I don't think so,' I reply.

'OK, if we have any more questions we will be in touch. This is an open investigation, so we expect you to stay in the area.'

I nod to show my acknowledgement. I don't need to tell them that I have neither the means nor the inclination to flee the country, especially not now. Not now that I have two deaths to investigate.

Chapter Twenty

The Social Sleuth, *extract from most recent post*

Did Clare Owen kill Stella and then take her own life, unable to live with the guilt? Clare made no bones about her dislike for Stella, or about the fact that she was at the event where Stella died. Or was she killed by whoever is hiding behind the pseudonym of Make It, Don't Fake It — and did this person also kill Stella?

It's late by the time I get back home, and I'm so exhausted I can barely raise my hand to slot my key into the front door. The door swings open to reveal the hallway, looking as dark and bleak as ever.

I trudge to my bedroom on tired, slow legs and, sitting on my bed with my back rested against two pillows, I heave my ancient laptop off the floor. Fighting back tears for Clare Owen, I write a post on my theories surrounding her death. Posting it will be crossing a huge line in the eyes of the police, but I promised to document my findings for Stella's fans, and this is a major development. I'm too tired to debate it any further so without care for the implications, I upload the article to my blog and as a post on KnockKnock. If Make It, Don't Fake It was angry before, this might send them apoplectic.

There's a loud knock on my bedroom door and I jump so violently that my laptop loses its balance on my knees and topples on the floor with a crash.

'Who is it?' I call, sliding off the bed and scanning my room for something I could use as a weapon. A solid-looking hardback book on female serial killers is the best I can find and I hold it in my hands, ready to throw it if confronted.

'It's me.' My whole body slumps forward in relief at a voice as familiar to me as breathing. 'I'm coming in whether you're decent or not.' The door opens and in walks my sister, Jessica. She closes the door behind her but doesn't proceed any further into my bedroom. Her dark-haired head tips sideways as she looks at me, her hands resting on her full hips.

'What are you doing, M?' she asks, frowning. I'm suddenly aware how ridiculous I must look, holding a book about female serial killers above my head.

'Nothing, and don't call me that,' I reply, as curtly as I can muster, dropping the book onto my bed. 'What are you doing here? It's almost midnight.'

'I came as soon as I finished work, I was on a late shift. But that doesn't matter,' she says, waving her explanation away and proceeding deeper into my room. 'As I've said several times already over the last few days, I'm worried about you. You're not responding to my messages as usual, you hung up on me earlier and...' Jessica trails off and perches herself on the end of my bed. She smooths down her cotton skirt and clasps her hands tightly in her lap. Conversations with Jessica make me feel like a child at the best of times, but having her sit on the edge of my bed while I hover in front of her awkwardly is particularly humiliating. I stand and fold my arms over my chest, my feet wide in a stance that hopes to take back some control.

'And what?' I challenge.

'And I've seen your posts.' My hands fall at my side limply. Trust her to make something I'm excited about sound like something I've done wrong.

'You shouldn't be involved in this.'

'I don't want to hear it, Jessica,' I say, my voice involuntarily rising. Jessica's brown, mascara-laden eyes widen at the volume of my voice. Jessica is a softly spoken woman, she never shouts. She never has to – one look at you with her perfected expression of disappointment and you know your place.

'Why do you have to do this? Why can't you just—'

I cut her off. I'm not Jessica, I never have been, and I *do* shout. 'I don't want to hear you criticising me all the time. For the first time in a long time, I have a purpose, and it's working for me. People want me to solve this.'

'I really—' Jessica tries to say.

'No,' I bark back. 'No, no, no. I'm not listening to you. I don't want to be lectured.' I rip my phone from where it's charging, grab my backpack from the floor and storm out. Jessica calls after me but only once – she won't want the other housemates to think she's the type of woman who shouts. Jessica doesn't like causing a scene. Her call doesn't stop me; I'm not listening to another word from her. My feet slap against the outside steps, disturbing the silence of the night, and I leave under cover of darkness, hurrying along the street unclear of my direction. My face is hot from anger and exertion which protects me from cool night air. There's a tiny park not too far from my house and I hurry towards it, throwing myself through the gate and moving towards one of the benches.

It's more of a square of grass than a park and, at midnight, it's completely deserted. The lamps which line the perimeter illuminate it in a toxic orange glow, making monsters out of shadows on the ground. I slam myself down on the bench; it wobbles. It's quite literally on its last legs, but it holds. I'm shaking. Just because her life is perfect, it doesn't give her the right to tell me how to live mine.

Two women are dead, one of them because of my meddling. I have to put that right, and if that means Jessica is annoyed with me, see if I care. With trembling hands, I pull my phone out of my pocket and open my email, where the article from Stella's website is waiting. There is only one thing that can distract me from my anger, and that is this case.

IT IS OVER. I read the words again and my heart hammers against my chest. The enormity of this article is only now starting to dawn on me. I don't know what Stella is talking about, what is over, but I get the strong suspicion that whatever it is will take this case in a direction I couldn't have predicted.

> Hello to all my lovely followers: to those who have been with me for ages; to those who have just discovered my channel; and especially to those of you who call yourselves the Interstellars. It is with the heaviest of hearts that I write this post, but write it I must, because one chapter of my life is closing.

My heart thumps against my chest. The wind whistles softly through the trees around me, ignorant to the bombshell that my senses tell me is about to be dropped.

After three amazing years, my marriage is over.

My breath catches in my throat.

> Why? I hear you asking. The answer is a simple one, but many of you will be surprised at my candour for giving it. The answer is one that many people will understand. I'm not the first to have had a marriage end for this reason.

My stomach twists; there is something grotesque about reading the words of a dead person, especially a message as shocking and poignant as this. I push aside the feeling of disgust that seeps through me and steel myself to read on. At this point, the article becomes a series of hastily written, bullet-pointed notes.

- Mention affair… what it showed me.

- Was only a fling but showed me something was FUNDAMENTALLY missing between me and husband.

- Fans will want to know who other party was… if I do name, what would be impact on Adam's family?

Affair. Stella Knight was having an affair, and she was going to publicly announce the end of her marriage. This upends everything.

Suddenly there's a thunk next to me and the bench shakes on its weak legs. I yelp, nearly jumping out of my skin. To my right a man has sat himself down next to me.

He's in his mid-fifties, his face pockmarked with scars. My breathing quickens as I glance down at his gold-ringed, heavily tattooed hands; he looks like he's stepped straight out of a nineties gangster movie. Around his fingers he's twisting a rope. I want to stand and run away as fast as my legs will carry me, but I can't – my legs are like lead, weighing me down. I'm frozen, unable to run.

The man narrows his eyes. 'Don't look at me like that,' he says, displaying a front tooth plated in metal. I want to respond but my throat has closed around my words, stopping me. 'This bench is made for two people, so if I want to sit on it while my dog takes a shit, I will.'

A crazed laugh of relief bubbles out of me. Then there's a crunch of splintering wood and the bench tips sideways, causing my body to slide towards the man. I jump up and without giving him a backward glance, I sprint away from him, back home. It wasn't a narrow escape, but it felt like one.

–

Jessica is gone when I get back to my room, but on my bed there's a note written on a page torn from the notebook she carries with her everywhere. She's written something on it for me but I crunch it between my fingers before I can read whatever patronising words she's decided to leave me and I throw it straight in the bin. A spot above my left eye is throbbing and I massage the skin on my forehead, willing the pain to subside. There are so many more people involved in this that I thought there would be. The pain behind my eyes intensifies, like someone is hitting them with a tiny hammer, and I squeeze them shut.

The list of suspects is only getting longer, not shorter. If Stella was having an affair that she was about to announce on the internet and she was worried about the impact on Adam's family, then that gives him a motive, whoever he is. Another player with another motive. Who knew one woman could have so many enemies?

Reiss Rose, friend. Motive: silencing Stella to protect his career.

Anna Nicholls, assistant. Motive: revenge for how she was treated.

Clare and John Owen, parents of Abbie (deceased). Motive: revenge for Abbie's death.

Christopher, husband. Motive: knew about the affair.

Adam, lover. Motive: to stop Stella announcing their affair.

I need to find out who Adam is. I search my room for my laptop, but I can't find it anywhere.

'Jessica,' I say aloud, and sprint to the bin, pulling out her note. My fingers tingle as I unfurl it.

> *You need to stop this. I will keep your laptop until you do.*

'No!' I shout, slamming my hand against the wall. My laptop is what I use to write my blogs, it's how I access my website, where I store all my Social Sleuth files. I grab my phone and call her, pressing the screen hard against my cheek.

'It's for the best,' she says as soon as she answers.

'You had no right,' I say through gritted teeth.

'I had every right. This needs to stop, M. It's not good for you. Now, get some rest.'

With that she hangs up and I stand, frozen, the phone still to my ear, my chest rising and falling. I'm about to throw my phone on the bed but I stop. There are about twenty messages in my house WhatsApp group.

> OMG, did you hear the argument between Mad Mags and her sister?

> Yup, what is Mags up to?

> Dunno, but her sister was pissed.

> Yeah, but TBF her sister looked like a bitch.

> True. I don't know about you but I think it's time Mad Mags found somewhere else to live. She is such a buzzkill.

> Agreed. I'll check the rent agreement, see what we can do.

Evidently they've forgotten I'm still in the group – or maybe they just don't care. I knew they didn't like me, but Mad Mags, really? I wasn't aware it was particularly out of the ordinary to not want to participate in their raucous house parties. A knot of tension tightens in my shoulders when I read the line about them wanting to get rid of me. It's not that I don't want to leave, I do, but I don't like that the choice is being taken out of my hands. There is nothing I hate more than feeling powerless.

This time, I do throw my phone on the bed. I will *not* let them affect me. I'm not powerless, not any more.

Chapter Twenty-One

The Social Sleuth, *extract from blog 16*

Not only was he defrauding his company of hundreds of thousands of pounds, he was also sleeping with the CEO's wife. He is the poster boy for gross misconduct.

Tuesday

When I wake, my eyes are thick with sleep. I glance at the time. *Shit*, I've slept through my alarm, any other day and I'd be sitting at my desk by now. I push myself into a seated position and try to decide whether to go to work or not. The whole day stretches in front of me. If I wasn't confined to an office, I could use it to find Adam and crack this case. No, I decide, going to work isn't an option. I'm already late so what does it matter?

There's a knock at my bedroom door and my heart sinks. I want to pull the duvet back over my head and pretend not to be here. *Please don't be Jessica.* I couldn't face it.

'Who is it?' I call, my voice pitching. There's no answer and I flip the covers back, ready to call again, when an envelope slides under the door.

Maggie is written in scrawling letters across the front of it. My heart quickens. I wrench the door open. The straw-coloured head of my housemate, Josie, bobs down the stairs, but she doesn't look up at me. Retreating back into the safety of my bedroom and closing the door behind me, I flip the envelope over and slide the note out.

Maggie, it reads, in the same scruffy handwriting:

> *We're very sorry to have to tell you this, but we are handing you your notice to leave. The terms of the lease say that we are able to do this as long as we give you one month from notifying you. That month starts today. You're not the right fit for the house and we don't think we're the right fit for you either. Happy to discuss the practicalities with you if you'd like, and even help you to find somewhere new and more appropriate.*
> *Best wishes, Josie, Carl, Mark and Lucy.*

I grip the letter tighter and tighter until the paper crinkles at the edges. I can't believe they're kicking me out, that *they're* evicting *me*. I rip the letter in half, and in half again, and again, and again, until the floor around my bare feet is littered with fragments of paper. I was planning to move out anyway, but it still stings. They hate me. Everyone hates me. My cheeks flush and tears prick my eyes. Warm, angry tears that now they've started won't stop. My shoulders shake and I clamp a hand over my mouth to try to stop the wail that is rising. A wail because I've spent months living with these horrible people who've never included me, a wail at my sister's disrespect and lack of understanding, a wail for Clare who did nothing wrong but has ended up in the crossfire of my shoddy investigation. *Breathe in for seven, out for eleven, in for seven, out for eleven*, I try to instruct myself, but it's like a bomb has gone off inside me. It's too much to deal with, it's too much to handle. My emotions are more powerful than my brain and I curl up in a ball and let myself be taken away with them.

My phone screen lights up with an incoming call from my boss. He's the managing director of the law firm and I'm his assistant. I forcefully wipe away my tears and sit up.

'Hello.' My voice is croaky, I've been curled up in my protective ball for an hour. This isn't going to be good; he's going to be pissed.

'It's eleven thirty,' he snaps. 'Where are you?'

'I'm sorry, but I'm still not well.' I can barely speak without gasping for air.

'That is disappointing to hear,' he replies, his displeasure clear. I shake my head, trying not to let his words and his judgement get to me. In his opinion, the only reason someone shouldn't make it to work is if they're in labour or dead. Anna Nicholls springs to mind, and my upset hardens into anger at the people who think it is fine to be so unreasonable. It gives me the burst of courage I need to reply.

'I'm sorry that me being unwell is disappointing to you.'

'No,' he snaps. 'You misunderstand me, I am disappointed to hear you're still unwell. I wish you a speedy recovery, and a quick return to the office.' He remembers to say all the things he ought to, but there is nothing genuine in his words. 'Should this go on any longer, I will expect a doctor's note.' The steel is back in his voice and before I can say anything else he has mumbled his goodbyes and hung up. My jaw tenses. He's no Stella Knight, but he can't hide how little he cares for me. His call is the kick up the bum I need to get over myself. No one will look out for me except for myself, and I have work to do.

—

It's past one o'clock by the time I make it to Reiss's. The letter from my housemates lost me several hours but I can still do this. Reiss opens the door for me and lets me into the flat with a smile, evidently assuming I've got over the shock of learning about the GHB connection. He offers me a seat and a drink, but I can't sit down, not until I've got it all out.

'What's happened?' he asks, frowning. I don't answer him; my mouth is dry. 'What's happened?' he asks again, and when I don't answer for a second time, he adds, 'You look like you've seen a ghost.'

'You lied to me,' is all I can manage to reply. The gall of him, thinking he could come to me and ask for my help while hiding such a major secret. The normal thing to do would have been to go straight to the police and tell them, but for some reason, even after everything I've learned, I still trust him.

'I've what?'

'You had plastic surgery, and Stella was threatening to expose you. And now Stella is dead.' Spit flies from my mouth along with my furious words. I've been betrayed before, I'm familiar with the way it feels. My heart pounds, my breath is too fast, my stomach twists and makes me want to vomit. Of all the things a person can do to another, there is nothing like the breaking of trust.

I watch him as the truth is exposed, observing every minute movement he makes, trying to discover what is going on behind the tilt of his eyebrow, the crease of his forehead, the twitch of his lips. Reiss's expression keeps changing, like he's about to do some sort of acting performance where he needs to display his full range.

'How did you find out?'

'Anna told me. She overheard you and Stella arguing.'

Reiss runs his hands through his hair and walks away from me. He whips open the doors to his balcony and strides towards the edge. I follow him, and for a heart-stopping second an image flashes in my mind of him, wrapping his fingers around the bar, swinging his legs one after the other over it and tipping himself forward to tumble to his death. I start towards him, ready to reach out my hand and grab the flowing fabric of his shirt. He reaches the balcony but does nothing more than lean his elbows against it.

'Anna's right, Stella did threaten to expose me. When I found out she was dead the only thing I could think about was how it was going to look. I was terrified that I was going to be blamed.' Reiss is trembling and holding onto the railing of his balcony for support. 'Shit, shit, shit. I need to call my lawyer. This looks bad.'

'Yes, it bloody well does,' I say. 'You used me.'

'Only because I'm innocent.'

'For an innocent man, you keep a lot of secrets.'

'If I was guilty, would I have asked you to investigate? Surely I would have kept things quiet. I would have said it must have been an accident, I would have agreed with Isla.'

'Why didn't you just tell me about the surgery?'

'I didn't want anyone to know. All my success is founded on promoting natural beauty and calling out celebrities who hide having plastic surgery. Isn't it obvious why I didn't tell anyone? I'm a big, fat hypocrite. Except less fat now, because of the surgery.' Reiss pushes himself away from the railing and storms inside. I follow him as he tears around the flat looking for something. 'Where is my phone?' he shouts at the room. I watch him, wondering what I should do. 'Maggie, honestly. I didn't kill her. Part of me always knew I'd have to talk about it one day. I was preparing myself for it, I just wanted to do it when I was ready. I knew there'd be backlash given how critical I've been of others in the past and I was preparing myself for that, but I wouldn't have killed her for it. Help me find the real killer – it's the only way I can exonerate myself. It's what I've wanted all along.'

Heat rushes through my body.

'I wanted to support the police in finding Stella's killer and support her fans getting justice,' I say. 'My followers were trusting me to do that. I thought you wanted the same thing, but if this comes out I'll look like a complete idiot. And yet you're still asking for my help.'

Reiss gives a bark of shock. 'Is that all you care about? Your image? I could go to prison for a crime I didn't commit and you can only think about yourself and how you look online. You didn't have any followers before I got you involved in this, so you can fuck right off passing any blame to me.'

'I...' There are no words to reply to him because he's right. His liberty might be in jeopardy, and without him I wouldn't have the traction I've gained. Reiss stands and runs his fingers against his forehead.

'You haven't even ruled out all the other people on the suspect list. Anna. Christopher. Clare.'

'Clare Owen is dead.'

Reiss's mouth falls open. 'Sorry. What did you just say?'

'She's dead.'

'What happened?' he asks. I look at him with a dawning realisation that makes me want to throw up. He knew where Clare lived. He knew that Clare was invited to the event by someone who hated Stella Knight. He knew that I was going there that afternoon.

'I need to go,' I say. But Reiss blocks my way.

'Did someone kill her? Maggie, if she was murdered I need to know. We could both be in danger.'

'I don't know what happened. I went to see her yesterday. And...' The tears come unbidden.

'Oh honey.' Reiss approaches me, his arms outstretched. I don't step away like I should. I let him fold me into his chest. His body is warm and the perfume he wears smells woody and floral. It reminds me of an expensive scented candle my ex-boyfriend gave me for one of my birthdays. Back when I was loved and desired; when I was loveable and desirable. My limbs are heavy, and I slump against Reiss, needing him to help me carry the weight. The sadness inside my heart pushes upwards, threatening to spill out of me, but I suppress the tears, feeling a lump in my throat where the emotion gets stuck. The hug is too comforting, and I'm danger of letting my sorrow get the better of me. I break away from him. Tears are bubbling in my throat like a saucepan of boiling water. Reiss reaches out his hand and wraps it around mine.

He sits on the couch and signals for me to do the same. Sweat clings to my back from the heat of the day but, through the window, grey clouds gather in the sky; a storm is coming. I feel the spectre of its presence, dominant and threatening, lurking like an assassin in the shadows.

'Tell me everything that I've missed,' he says, and, shrugging off my suspicion, I do. I talk about Anna, and Clare my voice wobbling slightly as I recount her last moments.

'It's not your fault,' he says once I've finished.

'Isn't it?' I ask, not convinced.

He shakes his head. 'Of course it isn't sweetie. Do you think we should tell the police about the affair?' he asks, changing the subject.

I bite my lip. He wants to tell the police because it takes the focus away from himself. I understand this, but I don't think the detective inspector will take too kindly to knowing that I stole information from Stella's website.

'Not yet. We need to find out more before we speak to them. We don't have enough information. We need to find this Adam.'

'How?' asks Reiss. I shrug.

'Google seems like a good place to start.'

Reiss dutifully fetches his laptop. 'What should I search?'

'Try Adam and Stella Knight,' I say.

A quick Google search for 'Adam and Stella Knight' produces several responses from the same website. The website for the Influencer of the Year awards.

'Click on that first link,' I say to Reiss, pointing to one. He does so, and the page loads to display all the award nominees and categories. I shuffle in closer.

'Do you think Stella was having an affair with another influencer?'

Before Reiss can scroll down to inspect the page further, a pop-up appears with a message of regret and sadness for the death of Stella Knight. Reiss hastily closes it and skims his fingers over the trackpad, moving us down the page. He stops on a shiny image of Stella; her shoulders are tilted away from the camera and she's twisting her head to look into the lens; her head is tipped slightly backward and her mouth smiles widely, as if the picture was taken at the exact moment she threw her head back and laughed. Her cheeks shimmer lightly, and her hair looks thick and glossy. She is perfect.

Reiss bows his head and sniffs. I shake my head – it really is amazing how deceiving appearances can be. She looks like a happy, charming woman, and yet Stella's path is littered with enemies of her own making. I push Reiss's fingers off the trackpad impatiently and use my own to continue further down the page.

'No way,' I say. I've found what I'm looking for. Exactly what I'm looking for. I point my finger at the screen.

> The nominations for the award for best blogging duo are:
>
> G&T – Gill and Tim are two best friends in search of the best gin, the best tonic and the best combination.
>
> By Hook or by Crook – Meera and Pasha are two motivational powerhouses helping thousands of people achieve their goals.
>
> BeauTEAs – Sandra and Karen are sexy septuagenarians serving the perfect cup of tea with a slice of cake and a wee bit of scandal.

The Adams Family – Noel and Kate are a husband-and-wife duo who document the ups, downs, rights and lefts of family life.

'Do you think this is him? Do you think this is the man that Stella was having an affair with?' asks Reiss.

'Think about what her article said, about the impact on Adam's family. Maybe she mistakenly used an apostrophe, and the impact she was referring to was as much to do with the brand of the family as it was to do with the real-life family itself.'

Reiss's eyes widen. 'Could be!'

'Go to their website.'

Reiss nods vigorously and navigates us to *The Adams Family* website, selecting the 'about us' page following further instruction from me.

'Shit!' I cry, slapping my hand against my head. I should have remembered the name.

'What?'

'I know him.'

Chapter Twenty-Two

The Social Sleuth, extract from blog 32

The woman had been trying and failing for years to have a child, so when she saw a baby screaming blue murder in a pram while its mother chatted to her friend, she decided to take it.

'It's the man who spilled his drink, the one with the controlling wife.' I'm saying the words more to myself than to Reiss. 'My God, he was so... nervous.'

'Nervous?'

'Yeah, he was standing alone, and I wanted someone to talk to so I approached him. He nearly leapt out of his skin when I said hello, most of his beer jumped out of his glass. Then his wife, this Kate, came over and sort of flashed her engagement ring at me and then quickly steered him away.'

In the photograph he is stood next his wife, his bearded face pulled into a smile that looks as genuine as they come. He has his arm around her and she is leaning towards him, her head resting on his broad chest. Next to her husband, Kate looks positively miniature. She's slim-hipped and athletic – the only big thing about her is her hair, which falls around her face in tight auburn curls. If anyone asked me what I saw, I'd say a happy, loving couple.

A sour taste forms in my mouth as Reiss and I travel around their website, viewing article after article about family or marriage or parenting or keeping your identity as a mother. Kate and Noel Adams have carefully crafted their online presence. The personas they've created are perfectly imperfect; they're the type of couple that say they're happy to openly discuss their challenges but then only share details of problems that are palatable. She claims to show her life warts and all, but the warts she's sharing aren't all that ugly. Maybe I'm being sceptical, but it's hard to sympathise with a woman who has written numerous articles on making peace with your postpartum body when her postpartum body is so enviable to those with or without babies. The sour taste travels south, making me a little nauseous.

'The Adams Family brand is their livelihood. How much of a stretch is it to suggest that one of them might kill to protect it?' I ask, leaning in to stare into Kate Adams's eyes. The eyes that had scrutinised me as a potential threat on the yacht.

'An affair could ruin everything, but also it might not. There's no such thing as bad publicity, remember,' says Reiss.

'So you wouldn't mind the truth of your plastic surgery coming out?'

'Don't joke,' replies Reiss, looking scandalised.

'I know what you're saying, but you should have seen the way her hand gripped Noel's arm and the way he recoiled at her touch.' I get to my feet and head inside, hunting around for the whiteboard pen. I pull off the lid and point it like a dagger, ready to write. 'Do you think she knew about the affair? And if she did, what would she be willing to do?'

Reiss, who's followed me inside carrying the laptop, makes a noise that suggests he isn't convinced.

'Come on,' I say. 'Years of work and dedication – would this woman really let it be ripped from her because of her husband's wandering eye?' I pace up and down; I'm on a roll now. 'Or maybe Noel didn't want Stella to go public, maybe he was happy for a shag on the side and didn't want to risk his reputation. How reasonable is it to suggest he killed her to protect himself? And then there's Christopher. Did he know about the affair? Did he kill her out of jealousy?'

'Maggie. Slow down,' says Reiss, prising the pen out of my grasp. 'Adam is such a common name. Stella could be talking about anyone.'

'But…' I say, pointing towards the laptop where the smiling faces of Kate and Noel look out at us. My hand drops to my side. I hate to admit it, but he's right. 'Fine, it's a leap, but my gut tells me I'm on the right track. I need to speak to Noel Adams.' Reiss, who had just taken a large sip of water, chokes and splutters. 'What?' I ask.

'Don't you think if you speak to Noel Adams you could be putting him in danger?' he asks.

'Why? Because of what happened to Clare? That wasn't my fault.' My tone is more forceful than I intended, but his words were accusatory; they hurt despite his protestations that it wasn't my fault.

'Maggie, someone is watching our investigation, and it seems like they don't want us to uncover the truth.'

'But if we don't speak to Noel, we might never know the truth. And if Noel Adams *was* having an affair with Stella, he could already be in danger.' The realisation is like a slap to the face. He could already be in danger. I need to speak to Noel Adams. I need to make sense of everything that is going on, and as much as I want to believe Reiss, as much as I wanted to have an ally during this investigation, I can't take the risk of having him anywhere near it any more.

'I'm sorry,' I say, 'but I have to go.' And with that I fly from his house as if on wings, ignoring Reiss's shouts and questions, on a mission to find Noel Adams.

—

With the same precision that the Interstellars found Anna Nicholls, I'm able to pinpoint Noel Adams's location in a matter of seconds. His KnockKnock profile was last updated at 14.57, barely minutes ago. He posted a video of his hand pushing the front bar of a swing in which a girl dressed up like Belle from *Beauty and the Beast* sits shrieking with laughter. At the top, his location is marked. He's in a playground about a half an hour cycle from here and, if memory serves, there's a bike rank not too far away. This could be my only chance to speak to him – he might not be nearby for long, and if I miss him I'll have to wait until he posts again. That could be ages.

My feet pound the pavement as I run and I'm grateful I've chosen to wear my trainers. I reach the end of the road; the bike rank should be just around this corner.

Please let there be bikes, please.

The blue posts of the rank stand ahead of me in a row. My heart sinks; every rack is empty except for one, and that one is about to be snatched away by another woman. The customer taps her card against the reader. She's going to take the bike, the bike that I need if I'm going to successfully meet Noel Adams.

The woman is young, probably only just out of her teens. She's petite. I could take her in a tussle, if it comes to that.

I'm level with the base of the bike rack now. The woman walks towards the bike she has paid for. She types in the code and, wrapping her fingers around the handlebars, yanks it from its holster. She rests it against her hip as she places her bag in the basket at the front. If I'm going to do it, it's now or never. I lunge forward and, knocking her sideways, grab the handlebars. The woman instinctively seizes her bag, thinking that's my intended target.

'Hey!' she calls when she realises I want the bike and not her bag. I swing my leg over the saddle and push off the ground. She starts to approach me. 'Hey,' she says again, louder and more aggressive this time. She's striding towards me. I place my feet on the pedals and start cycling. She's running now. She draws level with me and her hands reach out to grab my arm. I twist away from her, bumping the bike down onto the road in front of incoming traffic.

A car honks its horn as it swerves to avoid colliding with me. The driver leans out the window to swear at me but I don't give him a second thought. I circle my feet round and round, putting distance between me and the woman I stole from.

The wind blows my hair out behind me and I relax, knowing I'm out of reach. I shouldn't have done that, the poor woman, but I'm sure she'll get a refund and maybe it will give her something interesting to talk about at home this evening. Exhilaration burns through me, I'm like James Bond or Jason Bourne, commandeering vehicles in the pursuit of justice, except instead of driving at full pelt in an Aston Martin or a Maserati, my legs are going like the clappers on a bike that seems to have been designed by someone who has never actually ridden one. The pedals are stiff and the handlebars heavy, and the burn of exhilaration quickly becomes a literal burning in my thighs. But I can't stop or slow my progress. I have to meet Noel. He might be in danger, he might be dangerous.

The buses lining the street crawl forward, stopping every fifty metres, forcing me to pull out. I make slow progress along the road as I try my best to not be knocked down. People throng the pavement, queuing for the restaurants and bars or walking with crates of beer in their arms. It might only be mid-afternoon on a Tuesday, but in summer every day feels like a weekend.

I press on, turning right onto a quieter road, then left and cutting through a housing estate. The green leaves of the trees of the park where Noel is peek around the buildings of the estate. I whizz through the park gates, ignoring the sign asking cyclists to dismount, and follow the signs to the children's playground. My heart is hammering in my chest and my thighs are screaming at me to stop, but I grit my teeth. I'm almost there. The red, blue and pink of the pyramid climbing frame is visible, growing larger with every passing second. I squeeze the brakes and stop the bike, placing my feet flat on the ground.

The playground is full of parents, guardians, grandparents and the like. None quite so organised or disinterested in the kids as the group of women in their thirties who are sitting on one of the benches in the corner, passing around a flask of what is very unlikely to be tea. A short, foldable table sits in front of them covered in an assortment of Tupperware and plastic cups into which some of the women pour the contents of their flask. One of the women is talking animatedly while the others listen aghast. Children flock to all the playground's attractions:

the pyramid is crawling with little bodies, and there's a queue for the slide and the merry-go-round. I move towards the swings; this is where Noel Adams recorded his last post, but none of the three people pushing tots in the swings is him. Panic squeezes at me. I've missed him, he's already left.

'Oh,' I whisper under my breath. He hasn't left. He's in the corner near the picnicking mothers. He's kneeling on a blanket packing up the Tupperware that he too has brought to the park. His daughter runs around him in circles, stopping in front of him every turn and pressing her hands together in a begging motion. She clearly isn't ready to go home yet.

My hands are shaking as I let myself through the gate. This could be a very stupid thing to do, but what have I got to lose? I've come too far to give up now.

I walk past the group of mothers. Once it's clear I'm heading towards Noel, they watch me. One of them narrows her eyes. I'm almost at the picnic blanket. Noel Adams still sits cross-legged on the floor and a tired but warm smile spreads across his face as he places his hands around his daughter's, whispering softly to her. Catching this private moment between him and his little girl floods my heart with warmth. My eyes linger over his big hands enclosing hers, moving from them to his mouth and his soft, thick beard.

Noel doesn't register me as I approach, he only has eyes for his daughter, but I can feel the stares of the women. Maybe his affair with Stella Knight is common knowledge and he's got a reputation locally as a serial philanderer. I can see why women are drawn to him.

He's a suspect, I remind myself, and then clear my throat to get his attention.

Noel Adams looks up with surprised eyes, letting go of his daughter's hands. The little girl twirls around, then scuttles away to hide behind her dad's broad shoulders.

'Oh, hello,' he says, his voice unsure. Suddenly I too am unsure. Being so focused on getting to Noel meant I neglected to prepare what I would say to him. I can hardly blurt *'Stella Knight is dead and you were having an affair with her, so either you're the killer or you're in danger. Which one is it?'*

He doesn't look like a killer, he looks kind and gentle and loving. But if my blog has taught me anything, it's that the ability to commit murder comes from the inside – it isn't defined or predetermined by a person's hairstyle or eye colour or height.

I clear my throat again and tip my chin down towards him. I want to sound confident, but not announce my words to the entire park. 'Noel, I'm investigating the murder of Stella Knight, and I was hoping to chat with you about it.'

The sight of such a big man sitting cross-legged on a picnic blanket pulling an expression of wide-eyed surprise is both comical and heartbreaking at the same time, and I suddenly wish I could wrap my arms around him and tell him I'm only joking, that none of this is true. Noel gets to his feet and shakes his chinos so they're straight.

'You're what?' he says to me. He has a light Scottish accent that I missed when we first met on the boat.

'I'm investigating the murder of Stella Knight, and I'd like to chat to you about it. We met at the awards ceremony. I'm a true crime blogger, do you remember?'

His daughter, now standing behind his legs, pops her head around them to look at him.

'Daddy, who is the lady?' Noel looks from her to me and then to the women on the bench.

'No one, sweetheart,' he says to her before addressing me. 'I had nothing to do with Stella's death, so I can't help you, I'm afraid.' He speaks as though he is genuinely sorry he can't help me; he doesn't have the frantic energy of Reiss or the dismissive tone of Anna. But he's wrong, he can help me, and I want him to.

'I know about the affair,' I say, and he twitches at the word.

'I'd appreciate it if you stopped talking about this in front of my daughter. We have to be going.' He lifts his bag over his shoulder and reaches out a hand for his little girl. 'Come on, sweetheart.'

'She was going to go public with it. I have a copy of the article she drafted, and there's nothing stopping me from posting it.'

'She was… public… sh…' he stammers. 'Ow, Daddy,' squeals his daughter, squirming to release her hand from his tightening grip.

'Sorry, darling, sorry.' He crouches down and kisses her hand with a loud smack. 'Daddy got distracted.' He stands back up and glances quickly over my shoulder. 'We can't talk here,' he says, keeping his voice low. 'My wife is away tonight, and Lily is staying with her grandparents. Can you come over tonight at, say, seven? We can talk then.'

He doesn't question my involvement in the case. Clearly his infidelity has him on the ropes. I'm probably taking advantage, but I don't care.

'OK,' I say, suppressing my smile. 'I'll come over later.'

He gives me his address and then moves on, leaving me standing in the park, the women's stares keeping me company. I smile at them and make my own exit. Something tells me that this evening's interview is going to be very, very interesting.

Chapter Twenty-Three

The Social Sleuth, *extract from blog 40*

The four victims were strangers to one another. On paper, they had nothing in common. It took the police months to realise they all knew someone who worked at same nursery. Four colleagues conspired to help one another eradicate their problems, resulting in four very different and seemingly unrelated murders.

There isn't anything for me to do while I wait for my conversation with Noel Adams. I could go home, but I'd have to leave as soon as I arrived, so that seems a bit pointless. Instead I find a spot in the middle of the park and lie down, enjoying the warmth of the sun caressing my legs and arms.

The park shows no sign of quietening down. The children and their parents are trickling away, but they've been replaced by adults keen to enjoy an afternoon drink or a picnic, having snuck away from work early. I listen to their chatter about how annoying their boss is and who's sleeping with who.

I close my eyes. Unbidden, Christopher Clarke's face stares back at me. There's been something about him that's been niggling at me since the start, ever since he told Anna to 'deal with her'. The discovery that Stella was having an affair is just another tick in the column that says I should be looking into him. If Christopher knew about the affair then he has motive, and Anna didn't exactly paint a flattering picture of him.

I reach for my bag and sit up, wincing at the stiffness developing in my thighs. Riding that awful bike is already making movement difficult.

Retrieving my phone, I type in *Christopher Clarke* into Google. Hundreds of results come up, although not all of them are related to Stella's husband, unless he is a realtor in Southern California, a tour guide in Western Australia, or a long-dead film star from the 1950s. Christopher Clarke is a very generic name. When I type 'Christopher Clarke Stella Knight' into the search bar the results are significantly more relevant. Article after article about Stella's death now appears.

> 'Stella Knight's husband confirms police are treating her death as suspicious'

> 'Fundraiser page for Christopher Clarke and family after death of Stella'

> 'Husband of Stella Knight says he'll miss her "drive and determination"'

Drive and determination? It might just be me, but that strikes me as an odd thing for a husband to say after his wife's death. Unless what he really means is that he'll miss the money her hard work was bringing in. That would make quite a different headline. I continue scrolling until I find one that catches my eye.

'The aftermath of Stella Knight's death: what happens now?'

It's another article from the infamous *hashtagnofilter*, and it was posted this morning. I click open the article and start reading.

> Hashtagnofilter – you're thinking it, we're saying it
>
> The aftermath of Stella Knight's death: what happens now?
>
> It's safe to say that social media has changed the way we look at death. Sure, before social media you could look at photographs of your dearly departed loved one. You might even have videos of them recorded on an old camcorder, but social media has completely changed the game.
>
> Several days ago, Stella Knight was found dead at the Influencer of the Year awards. The police are treating her death as suspicious (see previous article about that here).
>
> Despite her death, Stella's online profile remains very much alive and, in fact, has seen an uptick in the number of followers, an additional 30,000 to be exact.
>
> If you're reading this thinking, God that's creepy, that's because it is. But it got me thinking – what happens to her online life now that she's dead?
>
> Most of the social media platforms I looked into appear to have the same policy: the

immediate family get to decide what happens to it, assuming they can prove to these platforms that said person is dead, and that they weren't responsible for the person's death. So, in regard to Stella's own profiles, it seems likely that her husband, Christopher, will get to decide. Given how lucrative her accounts are, and the fact that they've only been gaining followers since her death, he might choose to keep them, and keep posting. Though one can hardly imagine that being a successful long-term strategy.

Hashtagnofilter were able to find out that Stella Knight and Christopher Clarke had a prenuptial agreement. We can't help but wonder: did Stella protect her social media presence in that agreement? Did she have a plan for what would happen to virtual her in the event of her death?

Whatever happens, Christopher Clarke is likely to inherit everything, and we can only speculate what that will mean for the Stella Knight brand.

I lock my phone and flop back down onto the grass, the blades tickling my skin beneath my blouse, trying to process what I've just read. Stella Knight is even more famous in death than in life, with her follower count growing by the day. *Hashtagnofilter* is right about one thing, it is creepy that people have flocked to their channel upon news of their death. But then, as humans, we are oddly obsessed with tragedy. I run a true crime channel, so I can hardly talk. But it's the information about the prenup that draws my attention. Stella and Christopher had a prenup. Surely there would have been a clause about adultery in the agreement? But if Christopher wanted Stella's money, then divorce would be a better option than murder. She was at fault, not him.

I push down the desire to let out a loud groan. When I started this, I thought it would be easy. I thought that my conversations would lead me to the obvious culprit, I'd point the police in their direction and I'd be lauded as a heroine. But the dirty secrets my suspects have been harbouring have muddied the water. However, the police are yet to make an arrest, so the complicated landscape must be confusing them too.

The sun warms my skin and I close my eyes, letting the heat wash over me, comforting and relaxing. It has been a while since I've been on holiday, since I've lain on the beach and swum in the sea, tanned my pale flesh in the sunlight. Mum sometimes took us on day trips to the seaside when we were children. It was for her own pleasure, not ours, but we had fun regardless. Jessica and I would take our towels and set up camp for the day while Mum went to bars. We'd make sandcastles, and eat ice cream, and drop two pence into the slot machines. Those trips to the sea are my fondest memories from childhood. They burn so brightly, they even eclipse the horror of travelling home again with a very drunk Mum.

I should take another holiday.

I don't notice myself drifting off to sleep, but the next thing I know the alarm I'd set starts buzzing aggressively. Sitting up, my neck twinges and I roll my head around a few times to loosen it. I stand, brushing off bits of grass that have imprinted themselves onto my legs, and then leave the park, heading in the direction of Noel Adams's house.

The houses here are much more residential-looking than those around Reiss's flat, and there's nothing taller than a few storeys. They're made of red brick, with wide bay windows on each floor. The front gardens are lusciously green, even though there hasn't been any rain for at least two weeks. The set-up isn't dissimilar to Clare Owen's street, but it's distinctly more expensive. The cars are newer and shinier, more luxury brands. There isn't a single house that looks rundown or unkempt.

I stop outside Noel Adams's house, staring at the forest green front door with an ancient-looking knocker shaped like a lion. My heart beats loudly in my chest, but unlike during my visit to Clare's, there's a flutter in my stomach and a tingle in my fingers, neither of which have anything to do with the fact that he might be guilty or dangerous and everything to do with the fact that I can't stop thinking about his chocolate brown eyes and gentle smile. I give myself a shake. I have a job to do, and Noel Adams is married *and* was having an affair.

The door gives off a deep boom as I pound the handle against the wood. It swings open and Noel stands in front of me wearing an apron with the slogan *I kiss better than I cook*. Reading it makes my cheeks flush and I hope that he won't notice. He waves me inside and the smell of whatever he's cooking hits me, making my stomach growl. I want to slap my hand against my forehead. I need to get it together, for God's sake. This is a murder inquiry, not a date.

The entrance hall has a high ceiling and black and white mosaic floor. Pictures of Noel, Kate and Lily adorn the walls, their smiling faces beaming down at me like angels on high, watching me as I proceed deeper into their home.

I follow Noel into the kitchen, where he points to one of the stools placed around the island. The kitchen matches the hallway in style, tasteful and timeless. The cabinets are wooden and sage green in colour. It's classic, like it belongs in a big old country house, but there are modern touches throughout: the handles are small and gold, shining under the spotlights, and there are gadgets of all sizes positioned along the countertop. The space is immaculate despite the fact that Noel is midway through cooking a meal. Looking at it now, it's almost hard to imagine anyone lives here, especially not a child under the age of five. I sit as instructed and Noel stands opposite me.

'Would you like a glass of wine?' he asks, nodding to a broad crystal decanter on one of the work surfaces. I shouldn't accept but the beautiful kitchen, the steaming Le Creuset pot of ragu, the fact that he decants his wine, is an image of domestic bliss too perfect for me to resist.

'That would be nice,' I reply, deciding that whatever happens later, whatever Noel tells me, I can let myself imagine for one short moment that this could be my life. Noel opens one of the sage-green cupboards and pulls from it a glass so large it looks like it could hold a whole bottle of wine. The glass tinkles as he places it in front of me and I look up at him.

'Everything OK?' he asks with a raised eyebrow.

'Fine,' I say breathlessly. He swirls the decanter and tips it towards my glass. The wine is a deep crimson and it pours like a waterfall. I decide I need to get to the point of why I came here in the first place.

'As I mentioned in the park, I'm investigating the death of Stella Knight, but I'm not with the police. I'm doing my own investigation on behalf of Stella's fans, and...' I pause, unsure if I should mention Clare. 'And I'm hoping you can help.'

Noel nods and comes to sit down on a stool facing me.

'I know you're not with the police. I can't imagine the police threatening to expose an affair on social media.' He speaks now with a wry smile that seems good-natured rather than sarcastic; his initial shock at me springing this on him in the park seems to have passed.

'I guess not.' I take a sip of wine to cover the fact that he has disarmed me. The wine, in an unsurprising turn of events, is delicious. 'I want to ask you about Stella and the affair, but first, could you tell me a bit about your blog and how it all got started?'

'Sure,' says Noel, draining his own wine glass and refilling it. Something tells me this isn't his first drink of the night and that his slight inebriation is making him more amenable. 'Are you hungry, by the way? I was planning on eating a bit later on but I'm actually quite peckish.' He gives me a weak smile as we both acknowledge that drinking on an empty stomach can do that. 'I've purposefully made lots of ragu so I can freeze some,' he adds. 'I can put on some extra spaghetti if you'd like to join me.' As if deciding to answer his question for me, my stomach rumbles loudly. 'I'll take that as a yes,' he says.

'Thank you, that would be lovely. Since starting this investigation food hasn't been my top priority.'

Noel gets up and turns away from me. He takes a clear glass jar filled with dried spaghetti from the shelf, fills a cauldron-sized metal pot with water and places it on the hob. He brings the hob up to its highest temperature and re-joins me.

'What was your question again?' he asks.

'How you got started as a blogging couple.'

'Oh yes. The blog was Kate's idea. She already had a blog, one that she started when she went backpacking around Asia. She's a fantastic photographer and thought that if she was going to be updating family and friends anyway, why not spend her time updating others. She also thought about sharing the dos and don'ts of travelling around the region: which hostels to avoid; which activities to do if you wanted to go a bit off the beaten track; which foods to try, that sort of thing. She built up a fairly good following during her year, and then she moved on to Australia for another year.'

I nod and smile as he talks, as though I understand what it means to travel the world and have the burden of keeping my family in the loop.

Noel doesn't notice the stiffness in my features and continues, 'Kate loved Australia: the heat, the laidback attitude, the outdoor activities. She decided there wasn't nearly as much for her in the UK so applied to extend her Australian student visa and stay longer. Forgive me if I'm telling you something you already know, but to extend your visa, you have to do three months of farm work, it's the Australian government's way of supporting their farmers and forcing rowdy British backpackers to do their bit. That's where Kate and I met. We both reached for the same broccoli.'

Noel smiles at this, but it isn't the same smile he gave earlier, it's different, more practised. He has told this story many times before, and I wonder whether what he's saying is true, or if he's just been down this path so many times now that even he doesn't remember the original.

He takes another slug of wine. 'We had a whirlwind romance and ended up getting married out there after only ten months of dating. Our families weren't happy, thought we were throwing our lives away, said we were too young to know what we really want.' Noel's nostrils flare almost imperceptibly, the timbre of his voice harder now, he's going off-piste from the agreed lines. 'But Kate's followers were obsessed, it was a great story. They wanted to know everything. They were desperate to know how we were getting on, they wanted clues as to whether I was the one, whether it would last. They wanted to see how their beloved, wild adventuress Kate was adapting to life as a married woman.' Noel narrows his eyes. 'My wife has a skill for knowing how to please an audience. She satisfied the curiosity about our private life by starting the Adams Family.'

He drains his glass for a second time and gives us both a top-up.

'Could I have a glass of water?' I ask, suddenly aware that I'm drinking on a very empty stomach.

'Still or sparkling?'

'Tap is fine.' The answer I give on the rare occasions I visit restaurants. He fills a tumbler for me and sets it down next to my wine glass. 'What happened next?' I ask. 'What took you from being two backpackers working on a broccoli farm to this?'

He raises his eyebrow at me.

'You mean to being the type of person who decants his wine and offers his guests still or sparkling water.' He gives me another easy smile and I laugh, partly out of relief that the seriousness of his earlier tone has lifted.

'Well, yes, that's exactly what I mean.'

'I honestly, honestly, don't know. It just became huge. There are so many blogs out there covering what we cover, and we weren't the first by any stretch, so our success came as a shock. Maybe the fact that we're a couple and we *both* blog about marriage and parenting, that sets us apart, but there's also the legacy of Kate's success and the excitement she garnered around our marriage. Kate was also savvy enough to make sure we had a good presence on all channels. We don't just write about our experiences, we talk about them too, and do Q&As and lots of different things.'

'Do you like what you do?' I'm not sure why I ask this, but there is something in his demeanour that makes me want to know.

Noel scrunches his face up. The lid on top of the metal saucepan starts rattling and he gets up and turns the heat off. Steam rises as he drains the spaghetti over the sink. 'Between us,' he says, speaking more to the window above the sink that overlooks a beautiful garden than to me. 'It's a love/hate relationship.' He places two bowls onto the kitchen island and fills them liberally with pasta and sauce before topping up my glass. 'In the beginning, I really hated it. I had fallen in love with Kate and wanted to marry her, but I'm a shy person and by extension a private one, so it never sat that comfortably with me. Then our brand became so successful that I had to give up my job. Not that Kate forced me, before you go thinking that. She didn't, but it became unmanageable doing both, and we didn't need my salary. That's also not to say I absolutely loved my job in IT – I didn't. It was fine and it paid the bills, but I was quite reticent to become a full-time blogger, I didn't like that that defined me. Again, not that being an IT guy is a much more attractive definition. Sorry, I'm not explaining myself very well here.'

'I understand what you mean.'

'Yeah? OK, good. Well, I didn't really want to give up my job, and my God, did my friends make fun of me for it, but it made Kate happy, and I was happy to make that sacrifice for her. Eat,' he adds, prodding his fork in my direction.

I don't wait to be told twice. I plunge my fork into the spaghetti and wheel it round until my fork looks more like a spaghetti lollipop. It's so good, if my mouth weren't so full, I'd groan with delight. Chunks of beef so tender they melt before I have the chance to chew; rich, sweet, earthy tomato sauce full of flavour. I can't remember the last time I ate proper home-cooked food like this. Jessica invites me round for dinner all the time and I go sometimes, but sitting here with Noel is different. With him, I'm not the poor relation, we're just two adults having dinner.

'I think we should talk about it,' I say, placing my fork down. Noel nods and tops up our glasses again. He doesn't show any signs of the nerves you might expect from a man about to be questioned about his affair, and I feel no awkwardness in asking the question. It must be the wine – how much have I had?

'Go on,' he says, intertwining his fingers and looking at me through his long eyelashes. Steady, I think to myself. If he was having an affair with Stella and she wanted to go public and he didn't, that is motive.

'When did the affair start?' I ask.

'A year ago,' he says without a hint of shame. 'But I'm not a hundred per cent sure. Not that it really matters.'

I furrow my brow. 'What do you mean?'

'I don't think it was her first.'

'Oh,' I say, 'you think she had affairs before you?'

Noel face clouds with confusion. His forehead creases with deep lines, his thick, bushy eyebrows knitting together. 'Before we were married, you mean?'

'No.' I shake my head, wondering whether it was a bad idea to interview someone who has been drinking red wine for at least the last hour. 'Are you saying Stella had affairs with other men before she had the affair with you?'

Noel, who has just taken a drink from his wine glass, splutters. 'What? I didn't have an affair with Stella Knight!'

'But you just said—'

Noel wipes away the drops of wine that are dribbling down his chin. 'No, no, no. You've completely misunderstood. I didn't have an affair with Stella. Kate, my wife, had, or is having, an affair with Christopher. Stella's husband.'

Chapter Twenty-Four

The Social Sleuth, *extract from blog 44*

Every single one of her husbands served a purpose: elevating her social status, providing her with a luxurious lifestyle, helping her flee the country. She was known as the Black Widow, for reasons that you will soon find out.

Noel's words hit me like a ton of bricks.

'You thought it was me?' asks Noel, his voice suddenly pleading. 'I have, never, ever cheated on my wife. Despite how many times she has done it to me, and despite how many times I've had the opportunity.'

His voice breaks as he says this, and I think of the women in the park eyeing him up. How many of them have propositioned him before? Without warning, jealously stabs at my stomach. He sniffs and grabs a tissue from the counter, blowing into it loudly. 'Sorry,' he says. 'The wine is making me emotional. I always drink too much when she's away.' His large frame crumples in on itself, making him seem smaller and more fragile than he would otherwise. Cheaters, I've always hated cheaters.

'No, I'm sorry.' I reach my hand out and take his in mine. The hairs on my arms stand up as our skin makes contact. His hands are soft, apart from rough calluses that run along his palms, perhaps a product of rowing, or long stretches working in the garden. My breath quickens.

What the hell is Kate playing at? She has a handsome, loving husband, a great career, a beautiful daughter, a gorgeous house. Why would she throw it all away for an affair? Outrage raises its fiery head and I release my hand from Noel's, quickly finishing my wine as a distraction. I'm getting too involved, too invested. It's dangerous.

I stand to top up my own wine glass, but instead of sitting back down in the same seat, I walk around the island. Noel's eyes are red, and his face is damp with tears. Standing near him, I envelop him in a big hug and pull him tighter as his shoulders shake. Behind the lens, the snapshots of perfect lives, there are many imperfect people.

'You deserve so much more than her,' I say to him. Noel looks up at me and whispers a word of thanks and, in that moment, I feel a kinship with him. I understand the shame and sadness that comes with abandonment. I deserved better too. We're leaning in closer to one another now, so close that our noses are almost touching, and without thinking about the consequences, I press my lips against his. He recoils, pulling back from me and jumping to his feet. He steps away, huffing like a startled horse. His behaviour makes me want to curl up in a ball and die from embarrassment. 'Oh my God, I'm so sorry. I shouldn't have done that. The wine,' I say, mirroring his earlier words.

But Noel doesn't reply. He looks at me with wet eyes and a serious look. Then, as suddenly as he moved away from me, he takes one of his hands and places it on the nape of my neck and pulls me into him. He kisses me intensely, like he's channelling all his emotions through me. I step forward, placing my hands on his broad hips. We pull apart and I stare deep into his kind eyes. I'm sure he isn't Stella's killer, but Kate could conceivably be: she was having an affair with Stella's husband, an affair that Stella was about to expose, potentially threatening her whole career. Kate could even be Make It, Don't Fake It – she saw Stella as a threat and was working with Clare to bring Stella down. When she found out Clare was going to expose her, Kate might have killed her too. None of these are unreasonable or far-fetched assumptions.

'Could Kate have hurt Stella to protect her career?' Noel is silent; he just looks down at me, his eyes wide, as if wrapping his brain around what his wife might and might not be capable of.

'Kate has some issues,' he says. 'Issues that she's seeing a therapist about. She didn't have the most stable of child-hoods, and it's given her a lot of anger.' He bites his lip. 'She's done a lot of things in anger,' he adds, his voice even lower than before.

I look at him. The expression on his face, his rounded shoulders, his lowered voice. He's scared of her. If Kate did kill Stella, then as terrible as it would be for Noel and Lily, at least they'd be free from her tyranny. From what I've heard I think she's capable of it, but does he?

'So, could Kate have done it?' I ask him again, urgently this time.

'Could Kate have done what?' The sound of a woman's voice coming from behind Noel makes us both lurch. Kate Adams is standing in the doorway to the kitchen with a raised eyebrow and a look of complete disgust on her face.

'Kate!' says Noel, his voice strangled. 'You said you'd be out all evening.' He turns to face her, clutching the rim of the island for support. I can almost hear the pounding of his heartbeat. A memory flickers in my mind; I've been here before. In a past life, I've been where Noel stood while the person who controls you and your life bears down on you, angry and ready to explode. The way the stress and panic wrap themselves around you is a feeling you can't easily forget. The need to fling myself in front of him and protect him from her fury rises inside me.

'Maybe if you weren't so busy drinking wine and entertaining another woman, you'd have noticed that I texted to say that I wasn't well and was coming home.'

Noel starts at her words and scrambles around for his phone. 'Shit,' he mutters under his breath. 'Kate, I'm—'

'Who are you?' asks Kate, ignoring her jittery husband and glaring at me. She doesn't remember me. I'm not important enough for her to remember.

I take her in, all five foot nothing of her. Her hair is scraped back in a low bun; her eye make-up is simple and severe, two clean lines of black liner slicked over both lids. She's wearing a thigh-skimming halter-neck white dress that's been designed to look like a double-breasted suit jacket, with two pairs of round white buttons stuck on the front.

'Maggie Shaw,' I say assertively, ignoring the trembling of my insides. 'I'm here because I'm investigating the murder of Stella Knight.'

She frowns at this and looks ever so slightly wrong-footed; I resist the urge to laugh aloud. 'Are you with the police? I don't remember seeing you before, though I do recognise you.'

'I'm working with the police, yes.' It isn't a complete lie. 'You probably recognise me from the event, though you were far too busy flashing me your engagement ring to actually remember me. I know about your affair with Christopher. Did you know Stella was about to out the affair on her blog?'

Kate's nostrils flare at my words. 'I think it's time you left, don't you?'

'And I think stopping Stella from posting that article is a bloody big motive for murder, don't you?'

Noel plonks himself down on a bar stool, dropping his head into his hands. Kate puts her hands on her hips and widens her stance, flashing her whimpering husband a look before turning back to me.

'People have affairs,' she snarls.

'Yes, but most people's livelihoods aren't built on their rock-solid marriage, perfect parenting and enviable but accessible lifestyle. An affair would shatter all that, wouldn't it?'

Kate's jaw is now clenched so tightly I'm worried she might break a tooth. 'Get out of my house,' she growls.

'Did you kill Stella Knight because she found out about your affair and was threatening to go public?' Kate storms towards me and wraps her tiny fingers around my bare arm. The skin pinches, making me wince. She jerks me from the kitchen. I lock eyes with Noel but he looks away, retreating into himself; he isn't going to get involved. Kate drags me in front of her and shoves me into the hallway. She is stronger and more powerful than she looks.

'Is this what you did to Stella?' I ask, goading her. 'She threatened you, so you killed her.'

Kate's eyes are wild now, and she pushes me again in the direction of the doorway. 'I'd advise you to stop meddling.' Kate pulls the door open and a cold breeze whips into the house, making the hairs on my arm stand on end.

'Or what?' I ask. Her eyes spark, she's barely able to contain her venom as I prod the beast within her.

'You don't want to know what.' With that, Kate elbows me over the threshold and slams the door in my face. The ornate door knocker shakes on its hinges, the handle thrashing about as if trying to escape from the lion's razor-sharp teeth. From inside, the shouting begins, reminding me that it is not always apparent from the outside who is the predator and who is the prey.

—

It's still light as I walk down Kate and Noel Adams's street. Adrenaline courses through me but it is unable to drown out the distress that plucks at my heart. I can't ignore the rollicking Noel will be taking on my account. I stop and reach out a hand to steady myself on a stranger's gate; people keep getting hurt around me. My pity for Noel crystallises into something different, something directed at his wife. Kate Adams is cruel. She doesn't deserve to have the life she does. But I know the truth about her, and I intend to expose her before she hurts anyone else.

As I walk towards the tube station, I decide to call Reiss.

'Maggie?' He sounds confused that after my swift exit I've decided to call him.

'I need to tell you what just happened,' I snap.

'Let me just...' he murmurs. There's a rustling in the background and the sound of a door closing. 'Go on.'

Reiss is beside himself when I tell him about my evening with the Adamses.

'Good God, do you think they were both in on it – Kate and Christopher, I mean?' he asks.

'Well, the fact that Stella knew about their affair puts them both high on the list of suspects. If their prenuptial agreement said that the cheating party would get nothing, then Christopher was set to lose everything. Anna Nicholls did say he didn't like working, so money would be important to him.'

'He didn't seem that upset about Stella's death either, when I spoke to him on the yacht. Maybe that's because he wasn't surprised.'

'And then there's Kate,' I say, wondering if, as awful as it would be for her husband and daughter if it were her, would it also be a blessing in disguise?

'You need to tell the police. They need to know all of this, Maggie.'

'I don't know. I still don't have any actual proof.'

'You can't keep this from them. It could get you in serious trouble.'

'Fine, fine. I'll call them tomorrow.'

–

Back in the comfort of my own bedroom, if I can really call anything to do with my house a comfort, I sit on the edge of my bed and stare down at my phone, wondering whether I should make a call to Detective Inspector Alebiosu.

I turn towards the window, gazing out into the empty garden. The debris from the weekend's shenanigans still covering the grass. The sky is a dark pinky orange, ablaze from the tail end of the sunset. It's late on a Tuesday evening. He might not even be working; perhaps it's best not to disturb him off duty. But the affair is huge news; not having this information could slow their progress, it could be a huge gap in their investigation. Retrieving the piece of paper from my handbag where it has sat since Matthew gave it to me, I punch his number into my phone.

'Detective Inspector Matthew Alebiosu,' comes his voice, curt but professional, picking up after only three rings. There's a lot of background noise coming from wherever he is; it sounds as if he's stood in the middle of a motorway. He must still be at work.

'Detective Inspector, it's Maggie Shaw. I have some information that might be useful for the case.'

There's a pause, but the background noise continues to crackle on, so he hasn't hung up on me. Matthew sighs, sounding ever-so-slightly exasperated at being disturbed by me, but says, 'I'm listening.'

'Stella's husband was having an affair with Kate Adams – she's another social media person who was on the yacht. Stella was about to announce their affair online. It could have ruined Kate's reputation as the doting wife and mother. And when I was at Kate's house, she practically threatened to kill me if I told anyone about the affair. I also read online that Stella and Christopher, her husband, had a prenuptial agreement. Maybe Stella told Christopher she knew about the affair and said she was going to divorce him? He was at risk of losing everything, so he killed her?'

There's silence at the other end of the phone for a moment. 'What were you doing at Kate Adams's house?' asks the detective inspector when he eventually gains his voice.

'Does your question imply you already know about the affair and the prenup?' I ask.

'I cannot discuss an ongoing investigation with you. And while the police are always happy to receive information from the public, it's not appropriate that you are speaking to witnesses or potential suspects in this case.'

'So Kate and Christopher are potential suspects?'

'That isn't what I said. I've warned you before, but clearly that message didn't go through, so let me put it to you more strongly. If you continue to involve yourself in this investigation and potentially hinder it, you will be arrested for obstruction of justice.'

With those words the background noise is cut. The detective inspector has hung up on me.

Arrested? Maybe they already looked into Kate and Christopher and ruled them out. But maybe they haven't. What if they didn't know about the affair and they've decided not to take me seriously?

I splash my face with water from the sink in my bedroom and look at my reflection in the mirror. 'If the police don't believe me,' I say aloud to myself, 'then I'm going to have to prove it to them.'

My face is set in a picture of determination, my eyes are hard, my jaw clenched. My fingers grip the edge of the sink. I'm a woman with a plan.

I turn my phone face down on the duvet, smothering its glow. The only light in the room comes from the orange-tinged streetlight positioned on the opposite side of the pavement. I undress, not bothering to roll down the window blinds, and pull on my PJs.

Moving my pillow out of the way, I lie straight as a board on my bed. My back sighs in relief as the pressure it has carried all day is lifted. My arm throbs from where Kate grabbed me. It's going to bruise.

The effects of the wine are wearing off and the boldness that had let me stand up to Kate is replaced by doubt. Pointing the finger at her and Christopher could have put a target on my back in more ways than one. And that's to say nothing of how I might have annoyed the police.

I can't help wondering what Christopher Clarke is doing now. Is he sitting alone crying into one of Stella's cashmere jumpers, ashamed at how he mistreated her? Or has Kate Adams snuck away from Noel and climbed into his bed; are they snuggled up together? Are they planning how best to eliminate the complication that I've created in the same way they eliminated Stella and Clare?

Tomorrow, I'm going to turn my attention to him. I'm finally going to look into the person I've avoided looking at because I wanted to explore other suspects. Tomorrow, I'm going to investigate Christopher Clarke, whether the police want me to or not.

Chapter Twenty-Five

The Social Sleuth, *extract from most recent post*

Where are the police? Why don't they know about the affair? Why aren't they interrogating Kate and Christopher? Kate was out for the evening all dressed up and fancy free while two women are dead! And what about Christopher Clarke? From the very beginning I had said I didn't want to start with him, I didn't want to be so cliché or to fall back on so obvious a stereotype, but maybe it's a stereotype for a reason. From where I'm standing, there are gaps in this police investigation that could potentially result in a miscarriage of justice. I cannot let this happen.

Wednesday

The vibrations of my phone against the windowsill wakes me up and I open my eyes to find I've fallen asleep on top of my duvet.

'Hello?' I croak, my throat parched after the wine I consumed with Noel.

'Maggie! What's happened to your channel?' It's Reiss; his voice is sharp and alert, a world away from me and my punch-drunk state.

'What do you mean?' I try to sit up but the intense cycle from yesterday makes my muscles ping in pain like the tight strings of a harpsichord being plucked. Whoever said exercise was good for you was lying.

'Your KnockKnock channel. It's gone.'

'What?'

'Gone. Maggie, it's all gone.'

Pain forgotten, I hang up on him and open the Knock-Knock app and go to my profile. The latest post isn't there, and neither is the one before that, or the one before that. Panic grips me as I visit my website, where for the last year I've been posting blog after blog, but they've all gone, all of them, and in their place two words that make me light-headed. Content removed. I scroll down my page, my eyes scanning each line: *content removed, content removed, content removed*.

My heart is pounding in my chest. Surely this is a mistake. There's no reason for these channels to have removed my content, not unless someone asked them to.

My hand squeezes around my phone as I try to stop myself from crying, but tears cloud my vision. Everything I've worked for, gone. My security blanket, my insurance for the future, gone. Without the legacy of this invest-igation or the followers that I've gained, my chances of turning this channel into a career are basically zero.

There's only one person that could have done this: Detective Inspector Matthew Alebiosu. I regret telling the police about my channel, and I seriously regret giving them information. My relationship with them, if you can call it that, hasn't helped me a jot.

There's a knock on the door. My head snaps up and my heart begins to thump loudly. Nowhere is safe any more.

'Maggie,' calls my housemate Josie. My lips curl at the sound of her voice. What can she possibly want this time? 'I just wanted to check that you got our message. About moving out.' I ignore her; I have more important things to deal with. I scramble to open my photos to see if I screenshotted any of my posts there. But I haven't. Jessica has taken my laptop and the police have erased me from the internet. Sweat pools in my palms as my mind scrambles for solutions.

In my camera roll, there's the only piece of evidence that I was ever involved in any of this: the photo I took as soon as I got on the boat. My smiling face shines up at me, my poor attempt to capture a picture of myself on the yacht, and all I caught was a reflection. My breath catches in my throat and I frantically zoom in closer. The image captured more than just me. In the background, there are two people deep in conversation. Here in my sweaty, trembling hand, in the photograph I dismissed as useless, is a vital piece of this puzzle. I can't believe I almost missed it. In the picture, one of the people is short and round in a crimson chiffon dress, her hair hanging in dank curls around her shoulders; the other is the owner of the golden band.

Clare Owen, deep in conversation with her killer.

My chest rises and falls, rises and falls, getting quicker with each breath. Not only does this picture point to Clare's killer, but it also points to it being my fault. Probing into Clare's history with Stella was tantamount to signing her death warrant. Bringing her killer to justice won't bring her back to life, but it's something. I try to stand, but I sway on my feet. I feel myself hyperventilating, but I'm powerless to stop it. My thoughts and heart are running haywire. Clare's killer knows who I am and they know that I'm investigating. I perch on the edge of my bed, clutching my chest and willing myself to calm down. A panic attack will help no one, least of all myself.

Give the police Clare's killer, it's the only thing you can do for her now.

But it isn't as simple as it sounds. I'd have to take them the picture and the gold band. The police would have nothing but my word and knowledge that I stole a vital piece of evidence from the crime scene. Detective Inspector Matthew Alebiosu made his feelings clear as day: *If you continue to involve yourself in this investigation and potentially hinder it, you will be arrested for obstruction of justice.*

But if I can get a confession, then maybe they don't need to know about the band at all. They don't need to know that I stole it. If I can lure Clare's murderer to me and get them to admit it, then the police will have their culprit. I won't be arrested, and maybe I'll get my channels back.

There is one thing I need to check before I set my plan in motion. I call Reiss and ask him one vital question. When he answers, my suspicions are confirmed. Who, why, how: it all fits.

Then I ask him to do something for me.

'Why?' he asks.

'I'll tell you when I see you. I'm coming to yours, now.' I hang up, only just managing to keep the wobble from my voice. This is risky. Reiss can't know what's about to happen, I don't want to scare him off.

—

My palm is sweaty as I press the buzzer of Reiss's building. Its sound drones low and sinister, signalling ominously for me to enter. My arms are shaking so much I struggle to muster the strength to push open the door. It feels heavier than it did on my previous visits. I'm the only person in the lift as it takes me up to the penthouse, passing floor after floor. The building is silent save for the gentle whirr of the lift.

Ding.

The lift announces its arrival at Reiss's floor with a bright, cheerful sound and my heart thumps against my chest in response. Part of me feels like I'm handling this the wrong way, but what choice do I have? I knock on the door and prepare myself to confront a killer – Clare Owen's killer.

The door opens a fraction.

Isla James stands before me, her hair threaded with the golden beads and rings that I recognised as soon as I first held one in my hand. The photograph I took the morning of the Influencer of the Year awards captured Clare and Isla deep in conversation. They knew each other. That confirmed for me that it was Isla who invited Clare on board the yacht, and Isla who was trolling Stella from behind the username Make It, Don't Fake It. When Reiss told me that the vial containing his recreational GHB was missing it was checkmate. That morning in Reiss's kitchen, Isla saw the message Clare sent me and she knew that the mask was about to be ripped off. She made a decision; she chose herself and her career over Clare Owen's life.

'Come in. I'm sorry about how snappy I was with you last time we met,' she says, mistaking my hovering on the threshold for awkwardness rather than repugnance. 'I've had a lot going on. Come, sit. I want to hear everything about your investigation.'

Isla's smile, though fake, is broad, displaying a set of perfectly white teeth. Her incisors are fang-like, wolf-like. I fight the urge to launch at her and pull more of the gold beads from her hair; instead, I drag my mouth into as believable a smile I can muster.

Of course she wants to know, she wants to know how safe she is. I head to the sofa but don't sit. I stand in between Isla and the intercom, ready to let the police in when they arrive. I've called them, they're on their way, but can I get her talking before they get here?

Isla perches delicately on the couch while Reiss clatters about in the kitchen. He's put two and two together and his nerves make him noisy.

'You don't want to sit?' Isla's forehead creases and she gives me a look of concern. 'Is everything OK?'

'Why?' I ask. She tilts her head to one side and narrows her eyebrows.

'Why what? Why do I ask?' She gives a little trill of a laugh that cuts through me like shards of glass. 'Because you look as pale as a ghost.'

'No,' I say, my own mouth drying up with every word. 'Why did you kill Clare Owen?'

CRASH. Reiss drops the tray he's busy loading with teacups and a full pot of tea.

He cries out, leaping backward to avoid being burnt by the boiling hot tea as it splashes across the floor. But Isla doesn't flinch, she only has eyes for me. Her mouth falls open in a small, round O.

'What?' She gives herself a shake and regains her composure.

'You heard me. Why did you kill Clare Owen?'

'I don't know anyone called Clare Owen,' scoffs Isla. 'Reiss, your friend has officially lost it.'

'Clare found your channel after her daughter died. You have a class called yoga for grief and anger – I think she did that class, and it gave her comfort. Yoga was important to her, that much was obvious from the items in her house. I think she reached out to you, you got chatting. I think you cultivated a friendship with her, but instead of following your own advice about letting go of anger and grieving peacefully, you saw her story as fuel.'

'I… I don't know what you're talking about.'

'You're Make It, Don't Fake It. You've been threatening Stella online for months, maybe years. You never liked Stella because of how she gamed the system and profited from having family members in the right places. You convinced Clare to join your crusade. But she thought you had something to do with Stella's death. She was about to come clean about your trolling. She had nothing left to lose, but you did.'

The sound of the intercom reverberates in the silence hanging between us. Reiss scurries towards it, jabbing his finger against the button.

'Police,' says Detective Inspector Matthew Alebiosu, his voice booming through the speakers.

'Hurry!' Reiss's shout is almost drowned out by Isla's shriek.

'You bitch!' She launches herself at me and, before I can move or react, her fingers are in my hair, tugging my head backward. The pain in my scalp makes my eyes water and my hand curls around hers, trying to prise her off me, but years of yoga have made her strong. She throws my head backward and forward, shaking me violently.

'Isla!' shouts Reiss. 'Get off her.'

'I've got about one minute until they get here. Enough time to throw you off the balcony,' she snarls in my ear. All trace of the woman she purports to be is gone. All that's left is the reality: a woman who spends all her free time trying to destroy another from behind the shield of a computer screen. She pulls in the direction she wants to take me, and I cry out as strands of hair part ways with my flesh.

'No,' I say through gritted teeth. My arm jabs out and makes contact with her rock-hard stomach. She grunts and tips forward, but she doesn't release me, the movement only makes her grip more tightly. My scalp sears as she tugs harder, the agony of it sending tears streaming down my cheeks. I fight to breathe and remind myself the police should be here soon, they'll get her off me, she's given herself away.

My feet move where she pulls me, step by step towards the balcony. The tip of my trainer catches the leg of a side table; it topples sideways, sending a vase tumbling to the floor. The dried flowers it contained fan out among the broken china.

There's a banging on the door.

'Police!' booms the voice of the detective inspector. Isla's fingers release me, and I fall to the floor, rubbing my scalp.

'Reiss, please,' she whimpers. 'Don't do this. I'm a good person. You know I'm a good person.'

Reiss's eyes are filled with tears as he looks at her. Then he jumps as there is another bang on the door. 'Sorry,' he mouths, and hurries towards it. It swings open and the detective inspector bounds in, accompanied by his sergeant.

'Isla James,' shouts the detective inspector, storming towards Isla, who has backed herself into a corner. 'I'm arresting—'

'No!' shouts Isla as he draws closer. She kicks out at him, her foot colliding with his crotch. He barks in agony and doubles over. I scramble to my feet and press my back against the wall, trying to keep myself out of harm's way. The detective sergeant hurries towards her. Isla swings her arm round, her hand colliding hard with Angela's face.

Matthew stands up straight, grimacing as he walks towards Isla, handcuffs drawn.

'Isla James, I am arresting you on suspicion of the murders of Clare Owen and Stella Knight.'

My head snaps up. Stella Knight? They're arresting her for the murder of Stella Knight too?

'No!' shouts Isla again. She ducks out of the way of the two officers, her lithe body moving nimbly through the flat. She manages to pass them and make a break for it through the front door which remains wide open. Her footsteps echo as she sprints down the hallway. The detectives groan.

'Stay here,' they order Reiss and me, and hurtle from the flat after her.

Reiss leans against the kitchen island, his hands pressed against his lips, looking in danger of collapse.

'Isla killed Stella too?' he garbles. 'Where are you—'

But I don't wait around to hear the end of his question. The police will want me to go to the station and give a statement, but I can't do that. They've got it wrong. They've got it all wrong. Isla might be a murderer, but she's not the one who needs to be punished. Out in the hallway, the two officers are preoccupied by wrestling with

Isla, who continues to fight furiously against their binds. Their focus is on her, they're not watching me. So silently, I slip behind them and down the stairs.

Chapter Twenty-Six

The Social Sleuth, *most recent post*

If you're reading this then there's a chance I'm dead, and that my investigation into the murder of world-famous influencer Stella Knight has been cut short.

I know who killed her and why, but at the time of writing I lack the evidence to prove it, and without it the police will never believe me. My goal is to expose the truth, for Stella, regardless of how dangerous it might be. I write to you, my loyal followers, hoping that if I fail, you can finish what I've started and bring the killer to justice.

This case had everything: secrets, lies, money, sex. Stella Knight – beautiful, rich and loved by millions – was surrounded by a group of people all of whom had motives to make her disappear...

Could it be Reiss Rose? Stella was threatening to expose him and he regularly took the drugs used to kill her.

Or Anna Nicholls? Stella's bullied and downtrodden assistant, a woman who was furious at Stella for her lack of compassion and her cruelty.

Or perhaps Clare and John Owen? The parents who held Stella responsible for the death of their daughter? Clare was on the boat and was even seen arguing with Stella at the event.

What about Kate Adams, the so-called mumfluencer? She was having an affair with Stella's husband, an affair that Stella was about to out. Kate has a violent personality and has proven herself ruthless at getting what she wants.

And finally, there's Christopher Clarke, Stella's husband. His wife knew about his affair, an affair that could have left him with nothing. Did Christopher Clarke find a way to end things for her before she ended things with him?

I stand at the end of the road, my body pointed in the direction of the house Stella Knight shared with Christopher Clarke. Its columned front is like central London's answer to a stately home. It's early in the evening and the sun is nowhere near set. There's the same fizzle in the air that accompanies all summer evenings, the hum of possibility. I lean against a high wall to relieve the aching in the balls of my feet. I've been here, watching and waiting, for an hour at least. I didn't come here with a plan. How stupid that was.

I know who killed Stella Knight.

The article sits in the drafts folder, scheduled to be published this evening. They've removed all my content, but they haven't shut me down. Not yet. So now, if anything happens to me, the world will know who did it and why, my post left for all to see even if he catches me.

A door opens and my head jerks up. I inhale sharply, my backpack crumpling as I press myself tighter against the brick wall, willing him not to see me.

Christopher Clarke has exited the house.

He glances up and down the street as if checking there is no one around. That's normal enough, I guess, the press have been hounding him since Stella died. He's dressed in his gym kit with a baseball cap pulled low over his forehead. He turns and locks the front door and heads off down the street, slinging a bag over his shoulder.

The houses on this street, though slim, are grand and imposing, white-stuccoed terraces, constituting multi-million pounds' worth of real estate. Security will be tight.

Christopher gets to the end of the street and turns left. I give it another minute, allowing him to put more footsteps between us, and then peel myself from my lookout post. As my legs carry me tentatively towards his front door, my heart hammers in my chest. Am I really going to break in? I'm almost level with the black and white tiled steps that lead up to his front door. I glance at the facade of the house, take a deep breath and continue walking, not stopping outside it, not doing anything yet. I will, I just need to figure out how.

I pace slowly along the street, my eyes scanning each house I pass. They're all the same. Black, chest-height spiked railings run parallel to the pavement; three steps up from the street to the front door; white columns, one detailed with the house number in shiny black paint; a broad bay window to the left or right of the stairs; and a set of stairs that lead down to the basement. If there is going to be any way in, it will be there.

I reach the end of the street and turn left, following the direction that Christopher went. My knees quiver as I turn left again, now walking down a street parallel to Christopher's. I've gone around the block, not wanting to simply stop at the top of their road and just turn around. I don't want to draw attention to myself.

By the time I reach the end of Christopher's street again, my whole body is trembling. Of all the risks I've taken during this investigation, this is the biggest. I look up and down, my eyes scanning the pavement, but it's empty. I peer into the windows of the neighbouring houses but there's no one looking out, it doesn't even look like there's anyone home. It's typical, the nicest areas of London are owned by people who are rarely there. It's the height of summer, and the neighbourhood will have vacated London in favour of beach houses and villas and yachts. My breathing slows a little at this thought; maybe I will be able to break in, look around and get out without anyone noticing me.

For the second time, I'm level with the house. Discreetly checking my surroundings once more, I bow my head low and descend the stairs.

My muscles tense with every step, prepared for a shout from someone wanting to know who I am or what I'm doing, but nothing comes. I slip away down the stairs as if I were invisible.

Though it's only about two metres down the difference in temperature is noticeable. The sun that bounced off the road can't reach here. I press my hand against the cold underbelly of the stairs and recentre myself.

There are three sash windows and, unlike some of the other houses on the street, they're not covered in steel bars. Perhaps this added layer of protection was on Christopher's to-do list. Perhaps if he'd done it earlier I wouldn't be here, about to break in and reveal to the world that he is a killer. The windows all have latches, and the mechanism is swivelled round in a locked position. I sigh. It would have been a stroke of luck if he'd forgotten.

I bite my lip and look around. A broom has been shoved beneath the stairs, its frayed bristles sticking at odd angles like a hedgehog. The wooden handle is rough and splintered. The windows, wide and tall, are delicate and single-glazed. This will do it. I lift the brush and turn the hard, jagged end to face the window. I pull my arm back, tensing it like a coiled spring, then fling it forward with force. The handle goes straight through the window, creating a perfectly formed round hole. The glass tinkles as it shatters and I clamp my mouth shut, straining my ears to listen for any shouting coming from above me, but it's silent.

I jiggle the handle around until the hole is large enough for me to push my hand through. Unlocked, the window slides open easily now, and I bundle myself into the room. I pause, waiting for the wailing of an alarm that will send me scarpering. My muscles jitter in anticipation and I take a deep breath, but the house stays quiet.

I stalk several paces into what looks like a home office, and still there's no alarm. The air leaves my lungs and the quaking in my limbs dials down a fraction. I'm inside the home where Christopher Clarke and Stella Knight spent their final days as a couple, where Stella walked out on

Saturday morning to the Influencer of the Year awards and never returned.

I don't bother to close the window. In its current position, slid upwards, it isn't obvious that it's been smashed. Should a passer-by glance down all they will think is someone wanted some fresh air.

I go deeper into the room, my footsteps soundless as my shoes sink into the oatmeal-coloured carpet. A slim rose gold MacBook sits atop a sleek white marble-effect desk, beneath which is nestled one of those kneeling chairs. In the far corner of the room there's a mini studio set-up where Stella must have recorded her videos. This doesn't look like a room Christopher would inhabit, so I doubt this is where he would hide evidence.

Exiting the office, I find myself in a short hallway with stairs leading up to my left. There are no other rooms on this level, so I creep upstairs into a living room that leads to a long, narrow kitchen. There are a set of French doors which open onto a garden abloom in more shades of pink than I knew existed. It's tiny. It seems that you buy a house in this part of London for the social status, not the square footage. But if I've learnt anything about Stella Knight since starting this investigation it's that it didn't matter to her how things *were*, only how things *looked*. My mum was the same. I didn't like that about her.

A blur at the edge of my vision makes my heart leap into my mouth and my body whirl around. A fat ginger cat saunters across the lawn. Pushing aside my reflections on Stella and my mother, I force myself to focus. I don't have time to get distracted, Christopher could be home any minute.

The cat pounces onto the garden wall, sending petals into the air like blushing snow, and disappears with a swish of his orange tail. I stand in the hallway and close my eyes. I imagine I am Christopher Clarke, and I used drugs to kill my wife at the awards ceremony. I took a vial of GHB on board and put a fatal dose in a bottle of lime green food colouring. I gave that bottle to a waitress, who gave it to Joe, the bartender. I come home with the vial; it's covered in fingerprints and, as her husband, the police are watching me.

Surely, he would have destroyed it – why would anyone keep the murder weapon, unless they were planning on using it again? He didn't kill Clare, Isla did. But he might have kept the drugs to use on someone else – the waitress who could incriminate him, or maybe he was worried about my investigation.

I climb the stairs to the top floor of the house, which is entirely taken over by the master bedroom. My chest tightens as I enter; it's the most private of rooms. My armpits are damp with sweat, and not only because the windows in this room are tightly shut and the sun is streaming in. When Stella was alive this bedroom was surely social media ready. The pale grey carpet is even thicker than the one in the office; there's a wide king size bed with a high grey button-studded headboard; white antique-effect fitted wardrobes span the length of the room. It's a beautiful room, but it's a mess. The bed is unmade, and clothes lie scattered over the floor and the chair of the dressing table. My heart is beating so fast now that I can't hear anything but the sound of it. I take a deep, calming breath, willing it to quieten. If Christopher returns I need to be able to hear him.

I open the drawers beside the bed. There's nothing out of the ordinary: lip balm, moisturiser, phone chargers, books worthy enough to be posted about. This doesn't seem like the place Christopher would hide drugs. I close the drawers and get to my feet. I open one of the wardrobe doors. Shoes stand to attention on three rows of shelves and above hang clothes of all sorts: dresses, tops, trousers, all united by their obvious quality and expense. I close the door; it wouldn't be in here. I take a couple of steps to the right and open what I hope is Christopher's section of the wardrobe. It's the same set-up as Stella's. I thrust my hand to the back of the wardrobe, the bottoms of the hanging clothes brushing against my skin. I tap my hand around, trying to feel for something that might constitute a good hiding place, whatever that feels like. My fingers pat along the back of the wardrobe. Nothing.

I pull my arm away and tilt my head upwards, looking at the ceiling, trying to calm my panic and frustration. Maybe this doesn't make as much sense as I thought it did. Coming here I was so certain it would be obvious, but it isn't.

Then I spot it. A square cut out of the ceiling, wide enough for a person to fit through. I grab the chair from the dressing table and drag it along the carpet so it's underneath the space. Standing on the chair, I strain my arm upwards and dislodge the trapdoor. This is it. If Christopher was going to hide anything, it would be here.

With the lid moved away I run my hand along the rim of the loft space. My fingers hit something. The long, pointed cardboard edge of a box. A shoebox, perhaps. My body is trembling now. Oh my God, this is it. I use my fingers to wiggle the box towards the edge and pull it out. Grasping it with my fingers I lift it down.

The shoebox is old but not dusty, like it's been opened recently. Carefully I flip open the lid. *Dun dun, dun dun, dun dun* goes my heart as it rattles against my ribcage.

This is what I was looking for, and more. I slide my phone from my backpack, open the KnockKnock app and starting streaming, live.

'This is Maggie Shaw,' I say, my voice barely able to contain my emotions. The number at the bottom left corner goes up as people start watching. 'I am in Christopher Clarke and Stella Knight's house.'

> STELLAISMYSTAR: Hi Maggie.
>
> STELLAGAZER97: Any news on Stella?
>
> GABIWOOP: What you in their house for?
>
> INTERSTELLARFELLA: R u OK? Y r u whispering?

Questions float on the screen as I speak; the viewer count increasing with every second that ticks by.

'In their bedroom I found a trapdoor in the ceiling that was hiding this box.' I push my phone closer to the contents of the box. 'As you can see...' I pause and swallow, my mouth dry.

> STELLAISMYSTAR: What should I be seeing? What's going on Maggie?
>
> SMooTHCRIMINAL: Can't see.
>
> AMSLEUTHS: OMGGGG

'As you can see, there is a small clear vial of what looks like GHB, the drug used to kill Stella. Christopher Clarke is in possession of the drugs used to kill Stella Knight. Christopher Clarke murdered his wife.'

The sound of a door opening downstairs makes my stomach drop like I've fallen off a cliff. I lock my phone and shove it back in my pocket.

'What the fuck?' shouts Christopher. His voice is loud enough to reach me on the floor above. I'm frozen, unable to decide what to do. Footsteps pound against the floor, but they seem to move further away rather than closer. He's seen the open window; he's going downstairs to inspect. I want to put things back to the way they looked before, but I don't have time. The shoebox is open on the bed and, leaving it there, I creep down the stairs.

'Hello,' says Christopher from the basement. I clamp my hand over my mouth to stop myself from screaming. 'I'd like to report a break-in.' My shoes tap lightly against the wooden floor in the hallway and I tiptoe towards the front door. 'I haven't checked if anything has been taken, I called you as soon as I saw the smashed window. Does it matter if anything's been taken?' My hand is on the handle of the front door. 'Oh well, let me just bloody check if anything's been taken and then maybe you'll take me seriously.' Christopher's feet drum against the stairs again. I don't have the choice to wait any longer – I wrench the door open and throw myself through it. My backpack jolts from side to side as I run, my arms pumping by my sides, urging my legs to go faster.

'Hey!' shouts Christopher from behind me. My chest screams from the effort, my cheeks burn, and my ankles ache, but I don't stop, I can't stop. 'Hey!' shouts Christopher again.

Don't look back, don't let him see your face, I tell myself, and focus my eyes on the road ahead. *He can't hurt you in broad daylight*. I keep running, but Christopher's shouts get louder. Not louder, closer.

Up ahead there is a busy road. Cars moving at a glacial pace line both sides of the street. If I can get across it maybe I can slip into one of the shops and lose myself among the throngs of people. I run towards the road. Christopher's angry energy swells behind me. The adrenaline coursing through my body makes me light-headed but I press on, I'm almost at the road.

Then suddenly, I jerk backward. He's grabbed my backpack. I slip my shoulders out of it but as I try to keep running my hand gets caught in the strap and I stumble.

Pain shoots through my shoulder and I squeeze my eyes shut as the road comes up to meet me. My head bangs against the pavement and there's a pain so strong that it drowns out anything else. I feel fingers wrap around my arm as I'm pulled roughly to a standing position.

'I'll get her home. Call the doctor from there. It's my girlfriend. She tripped.'

Christopher's voice is gentle as he speaks to passers-by, trying to assuage their concerns as he drags me away from the road. I want to cry out and call for help, but the ringing in my ears is so loud I can't seem to remember how to speak. My legs are jelly as I stumble in the direction he pulls me. Back along the street, up the stairs towards his front door and through it. It slams shut behind us, closing off any hope I have of getting out of this. Hidden from the outside world, he scoops me up and carries me to the living room before throwing me onto the couch.

'You little bitch.' He paces in front of me. My body is screaming for me to stand up and run from him, out of the house and away from the danger, but I can't. The room is spinning, and I squeeze my eyes shut, desperate for it to stop. I pull my knees up to my chest, curling myself up into a tight ball. My instincts shout at me to make myself as small as possible.

'Chris—'

'Don't speak to me. What the fuck am I going to do with you?'

He is close to me now, I can feel the anger radiating from him. My heart is racing. The adrenaline shoots through me. I must get away from him. It's my only hope. I plant my feet on the cream carpeted floor, noticing the dark splashes of blood. My blood. My hands are covered in it. Sticky red syrup mixed with flecks of gravel and dirt from the ground. I try to stand but Christopher's face contorts and his broad hands push me backward. The jerking movement sends my vision scattering. I'm desperately trying to cling on to consciousness, but the darkness creeping at the edge of my vision gets stronger and stronger. Christopher walks towards me. Light bounces off the silver surface of the item he holds in his hand. I know what he's going to do, and I know that it's over for me.

Chapter Twenty-Seven

The Social Sleuth, *extract from blog 11*

It is common knowledge that woman are most likely to be killed by someone they know. More often than not, a husband or male relative.

Thursday

Detective Inspector Matthew Alebiosu and Detective Sergeant Angela Swain sit side by side, their faces expressionless. Matthew's deep brown eyes are trained on me, unblinking and unwavering. My body aches from the altercation with Christopher. My wrists are purple with the imprints made by his fingers, my lip is swollen from the fall, and it sticks out from my bottom teeth – it needed stitches. Someone we passed as Christopher manhandled me along the road felt uncomfortable with what they were seeing. They followed us and called the ambulance themselves. The flashing lights arrived before Christopher could do his worst. Now I'm alone with the two officers and I must tell them everything, my life depends on it.

'I avoided looking into him because I thought it was too obvious.' My voice is even and calm despite the turbulence buffeting my insides. 'People always think it's the husband, so I told myself I wouldn't start there, with him. I told myself that Stella's killer was cunning to have done it so brazenly. There were so many other people it could have been. It could have—'

'Before you roll into a Shakespearean monologue, can I stop you right there?' says DI Alebiosu, holding up a hand. I sigh; it's a bit annoying being interrupted just as I'm about to reveal how I uncovered it all, but I don't want to appear rude, so I nod.

'Sure,' I say. 'It's your interview.'

'How did you discover his motive? Christopher Clarke's, I mean.'

'Oh,' I say with a smile, pleased that the question allows me to continue to unravel the mystery. 'Well, at first I thought it was Stella that was having an affair, but I was wrong. If she had been having an affair, then I thought to myself that jealousy is an excellent motive. But when I found out it was Christopher having the affair, I thought that there had to be some other reason. A little bit of digging and I discovered it. If Christopher was having an affair, then that was a direct violation of the terms of their prenup. That's what got me to look at him. Then I found the drugs.'

'You broke into his house.'

I shrug. 'It's disappointing, really. Obviously it's great he's been caught, but it's rather unoriginal. Not a crime of passion but a crime of greed.'

'It's funny that you say that, though. The money motive always made more sense to me than the revenge one,' says Matthew. His words are unexpected, and I frown at him.

'What do you mean?'

He intertwines his slender fingers and places them atop the manila file sitting closed on the desk in front of him. 'Money, you get something from it, but revenge, the risk is much higher than the reward.' He exhales loudly and stares me dead in the eyes. 'But then I wouldn't know. I've never had my life ruined by two generally quite awful people.'

I draw back, my cheeks flushing. 'I don't understand.'

'It's like you said: appearances can be deceiving,' says Detective Sergeant Angela Swain, reading from her notebook.

'Indeed,' says the inspector, giving his sergeant a grateful nod. 'But the person hiding the most is you. Isn't that right, M?'

I bristle. 'Don't call me that.'

'I don't like my name being abbreviated either. I was called Angie at school, absolutely hated it. How about we call you by your proper name then? Emma.' My nostrils flare. My hands clench into fists. Angela flicks her eyes up to a point above my head, probably towards a camera, a nod to say things might get heated.

Matthew unwinds his fingers and jabs his index finger towards me.

'You attended the Influencer of the Year awards with the intention of killing Stella Knight and eventually framing her husband for the crime.'

'I thought you just said revenge didn't make sense to you as a motive,' I snap. He can't have it both ways.

'That's true, but this wasn't only about revenge, was it, Emma? If you'd pulled off murdering Stella and framing Christopher, all the while gaining followers and building a career for yourself in the true crime space, then you didn't have just one motive – you had three. Revenge, money and power.'

'No,' I say. Disappointment rages inside me. The organisation this took, the sacrifices I made, the time I dedicated. I built my plan like a house of cards, layering one on top of the other, delicately balanced, finely tuned. Now it's all come crashing down. I shake my head. He's got it wrong, he's got me wrong. 'Not power, *influence.*'

Epilogue

~~Dear Jessica,~~

~~I know you will never forgive me but let me at least try to explain.~~

~~Dear Reiss,~~

~~Thank you for protesting my innocence as vocally as you did. It was nice to have someone on my side. But you'll know now that I'm not innocent. I'm as guilty as they come.~~

Dear Anna,

I didn't know who else to write this to so I settled on you because I thought you of all people would understand. And though I don't expect you to agree with me or condone my actions, I need to believe that someone understands. So here it is, here is my story:

My real name, which you probably already know by now, is Emma Edwards. EE, that was the thing Chris and I clicked over when we first met. He was CC, I was EE. It isn't very funny or even interesting when you think about it, but there you are. Chris – he didn't mind being called Chris then. I don't know when that changed.

Chris and I had been dating for about a month when I saw that Stella Knight was looking for an assistant. I can remember the day like it was yesterday. I was perusing her website at the time, reading her latest blog, about the perfect date night outfit or something like that, when a pop-up interrupted my reading.

I'm hiring.

I nearly jumped out of my chair. I don't know what your motivation for applying to work with her was or what you knew about her before you did, but I was obsessed with Stella Knight. She was the same age as me, but I looked up to her immensely. She wasn't anywhere near as famous as she is now, this was before her huge success on Knock-Knock, but she was doing well and I loved everything about her: her style, her fashion, her life. All the tips she had on how to look good, feel good and be good were my manifesto. I sent her my CV that week. I'd been working as a receptionist-slash-administration assistant at a doctor's surgery for about three years. I studied marketing and media at university and was planning one day to put that to good use, but I hadn't been able to decide what that use should be yet. The job with Stella seemed like the perfect opportunity for me. I could use my experience, both academic and professional, all the while learning more about what it took to be an influencer.

I know now that most people who are internet famous get their start by simply setting up a channel and doing their thing, but I foolishly thought there was some big mystery to all. Maybe if I'd done my own thing from the beginning this wouldn't have happened.

Anyway, I sent off my CV, and you wouldn't believe my surprise when I was invited to interview. Chris was so pleased for me, he gave me loads of encouragement, told me I'd be streets ahead than everyone else who interviewed. At the time, I believed that to be true, especially when I was offered the job. What I know now is that Stella was looking for an assistant slightly older than her normal work placement girls, someone with more experience than the one she'd had before – but also that, crucially, she was looking for someone so desperate for the job they wouldn't care how she treated them. That said person would be her dogsbody, no questions asked. Enter me, from stage right.

Maybe you remember the exact moment, but I couldn't tell you when I discovered it wasn't going to be the job I'd dreamt about. It was very early on. It was just small things at first. She'd get annoyed if I didn't answer the phone immediately and roll her eyes when I'd explain that I had just popped to the toilet, as if having bodily functions were beneath her. But after several months, she really showed me her fangs. What she said to me is still crystal clear in my mind, and from that day onwards my job was nothing more than something that set my heart racing and my stomach churning.

Stella had asked me to help her with putting *Fashionsista* forward for an award. It was a business award and it required lots of research and so on. I was happy to help, I thought the business deserved to win and was worthy of the recognition. I was delighted when we were selected and invited to an awards ceremony in Paris. I'd never been to Paris before, and Stella had indicated that I'd get to come to the ceremony with her. I had the date saved in my diary, my trains booked to Paris, a hotel for the night. As the date grew closer Stella hadn't mentioned anything to me about the event and I felt uncomfortable broaching it with her. On the Monday of the awards week and I told her which train I was getting to Paris and where I was staying. She laughed, and then told me I wasn't coming to the awards ceremony; it wasn't my business, it was hers. I voiced my surprise and reminded her she'd mentioned it when she asked me to do all the work of nominating *Fashionsista* and then promoting us winning the award. She'd even told me to go ahead and book my travel to be reimbursed later. She told me I was wrong. I asked for the time off to at least go and see Paris. She said no. All that money for the trains and the hotel down the drain. It was then I knew I was worthless to her.

I worked for her for about a year after that, and it was the worst year of my life. I didn't sleep properly, I survived on coffee and cigarettes and little else, I was paranoid and detached from my friends and my family and flew off the handle at any tiny piece of criticism that might be levelled at me by anyone. I remember somebody in a coffee shop once told me that I'd stood on their foot, and I burst into tears. The barista was alarmed and gave me my coffee on the house. And yet, despite all of it, I strived to be the best I could be, I strived to make her happy, I strived to get a single 'well done' that I knew would never come.

I don't know when she and Chris started sleeping together. I first introduced them at a social media Christmas party Stella was invited to. She'd invited me and told me to bring Chris. At the time I thought it was all very exciting, but I recognise now that she only did that to cover the fact that she was trying to get me to work out of hours. I could tell she was impressed with him and possibly surprised that I'd managed to bag myself such an attractive boyfriend. He was tall, in great shape, with thick chestnut brown hair. Whereas I was as nondescript as they come. Average height, average build – although working around Stella made me absolutely convinced I was on the podgier side. I had limp, mousy brown hair, and a face that wasn't striking or memorable. When I worked for Stella, I tried to make my appearance more impactful by copying her – I bleached my hair blonde (that's the colour she was at the time), regularly wore fake tan, put on loads of make-up every morning and worst of all, I was always on some unsustainable diet in an effort to be slimmer. Being constantly hungry and constantly belittled does no favours for one's stability.

It all came to a head after about eighteen months of working for Stella. I was a complete mess. I wasn't eating because of my diet, I wasn't sleeping because of the stress of working for her. I was at rock bottom. Then, one day, Stella called me and asked if I could come round to her house. I remember how much I trembled as I waited for the lift up to her flat. I had no idea what she wanted, but given that most of our encounters involved her huffing or complaining or shouting at me, my body had learnt to react with fear whenever we met. I don't know why I stayed so long, but I think I was addicted to proving I could do it, that I could achieve what she thought I wasn't capable of.

The lift came and I stepped into it, my heart beating harder and harder with every floor the lift passed. When the doors slid open, there was so much adrenaline coursing through my body I thought I was going to faint.

You're probably wondering why I'm telling you all of this. You might already know this feeling, but you need to understand the state I was in. How she had made me feel for almost a year, and what effect that has on a person. I became a completely different person, I was no longer confident and outgoing, I was jumpy and paranoid. She was in my mind at every moment of every day, and I was always on edge waiting for the next criticism to sting me or steeling myself for the next issue that would arise. I was at breaking point.

Stella opened the door and gave me a tight smile.

'Come in,' she said, as if I was a disobedient student, and she was the head teacher. The power dynamic was off from the start, but I kowtowed to it and let myself be trampled, be patronised. I walked into her living room, which was beautifully designed. All neutral colours and cashmere throws, you can imagine. I remember stopping dead. Chris was standing at the far end of the room, on the other side of a square kitchen island which divided the room between living space and kitchen. My brain went into overdrive wondering who had died.

The next ten minutes are almost a complete blur. Stella and Chris told me how they had met and how something had 'just clicked' between them, and how they didn't want to carry on in secret any more. Then Stella dealt the final blow by saying this obviously would make it difficult for us to work together, so she was letting me go.

I don't think I even said anything in my own defence. I just said that I understood, got up and left.

I went home to the flat that I was one day hoping to share with Chris and sat for a bit, my heart rate and breathing not slowing. I was numb. It was only when I went into the bedroom and saw that Chris had already emptied his drawer that I felt anything. And it was then that the rage that had been burning inside me since I started working for Stella came out. I completely trashed the apartment. I tore apart the one shirt that Chris had left behind. One of my neighbours called the police. When they came to check everything was OK, they found me. I was bleeding because I'd slashed my finger on a piece of glass from one of the photographs. They helped me call my sister.

Jessica came round, packed me a bag and I moved in with her. I was there for far too long, but eventually she helped me leave my lease and moved me out of the apartment. She helped me get the job at the legal firm and, when I was ready, helped me move into a house share. It was during this time, my darkest time, that Stella's career soared. She married Chris and she was famous enough by this point to get a big splashy magazine deal attached to it. It felt like our fortunes were intrinsically linked. She was spiralling upwards while I was spiralling down.

I started *The Social Sleuth* as something to channel my energy into. I'd always been interested in true crime, I loved listening to the podcasts, watching the shows on TV, the usual fare. I'm not sure when I decided to kill Stella, frame Chris and build my own career as a true crime blogger. Researching the crimes I wrote about showed me that people killed for all manner of reasons, but also taught me what they did wrong.

I was consumed with a deep and dark desire to get revenge on the woman who had ruined my life. Part of me was still convinced we were linked: if she fell, I'd rise. I wanted to frame Chris, but I knew that if she was still the woman who I'd worked for then she would likely have people around her that could be considered suspects, and that would keep things interesting. I'm sorry that you were collateral in that.

Stella wasn't the best when it came to choosing pass-words. During the time I worked for her she only asked me to change them twice and were always variations on the same theme: where she had gone on holiday, the year and an exclamation mark. Tulum2017! Crete2019!

And so on. Luckily for me, this was still the case and she meticulously documented her trips on her channels. It was easy for me to work out the right combination, log in as her and send an email to the Influencer of the Year awards instructing them to invite me. I deleted it from the sent box immediately so you wouldn't notice anything. I arrived at the awards with the drugs and a disguise. I asked the bartender to make Stella a drink, telling him that her husband had asked me to get the drink made. It was a blow when the bartender didn't remember that part, but then I didn't expect it to all go perfectly.

There were things I knew heading into it. Clare and John Owen and the death of their daughter, for example.

Clare and Isla's relationship was a shock. I wish I'd picked up on it earlier – the signs were there. Clare's healing tree and yoga paraphernalia. Isla's references to Stella's impact on young girls. The online trolling brought an interesting dynamic to the case, but Isla killing Clare was unfortunate and forced me to take poorly calculated risks.

Reiss was another spanner in the works. When we started, I was delighted he wanted to help because his fame brought me followers, but his plastic surgery secret and drug usage ended up making him seem far more suspicious than Chris. I had intended to expose Stella's bullying behaviour and paint a picture of a man who couldn't take it any more. His affair with Kate gave me a bit more ammunition against him. I took a risk breaking into Chris's and planting the evidence. When he caught me, he recognised me and my fate was sealed.

I started this with three goals:

Kill Stella.

Frame Chris.

Gain influence.

I mostly got what I wanted in the end. My lawyer keeps me in the loop about what the papers are saying about me. My story will be known by millions of people from all over the world, and I will be influencing the way people look at true crime bloggers for years to come.

I am being genuine when I say I was very sorry to hear about your mum, but I hope Stella's death is some comfort to you. I know how damaging she was, how many lives she ruined.

It was nice to meet a kindred spirit, albeit briefly.

Look after yourself.

Love, Emma x

Acknowledgements

It feels slightly surreal to be sitting down to write the acknowledgements for my second book but it is also an honour to be able to thank everyone who has helped me get to this point.

A big thank you to my agent, Emily, who is always there to answer my questions however small or silly and knows exactly how to give me a confidence boost when I have a wobble. Thank you to my editor, Siân, who helped me shape this book into what you have just read. She worked extremely hard with me on it and my writing is so much better for it. Thank you to everyone at DHH Literary and Canelo who have continued to support me and my books, I'm very grateful.

A big thank you to Martin at the Port of London Authority for answering all my questions about boats in the Thames, to Simone for her advice on what a doctor would do, and to Jamie for always being on hand to provide police procedural guidance. I'm very grateful to you all for being so generous with your time.

A huge thank you to my sister, Robyn, who read the earliest version of *The Influencers* and cheered me on every step of the way. Her stream of texts as she was reading was both heartening and entertaining. Thank you to Krzysztof, my parents, my Uncle Ian, wider family and all my friends who told me how much they loved my first book and how much they couldn't wait for my second, this gave me the drive to keep going. I feel very lucky to have such amazing support.

A new set of thank yous to the author community that has grown around me since starting on this journey. Their warmth and friendliness constantly makes me smile and I cannot wait to meet them in person when the world allows.

And finally, to you, my reader. Thank you choosing my book out of all of the millions of books you could have chosen. It is a great honour to know that you could be anyone, reading this anywhere, at any time.

Love, Sarah x

CANELOCRIME

Do you love crime fiction and are always on the lookout for brilliant authors?

Canelo Crime is home to some of the most exciting novels around. Thousands of readers are already enjoying our compulsive stories. Are you ready to find your new favourite writer?

Find out more and sign up to our newsletter at canelocrime.com